*the*

# PERFECT

# GAME

## J. STERLING

## DEDICATION

This book is for every guy who has
ever loved a sport...

and for each girl who has
ever loved that guy.

## CHAPTERS  PG #

# ONE

"Cassie, are you almost ready?" my roommate, Melissa, yelled down the hall.

"Just give me one sec! I'm almost done," I shouted.

I ran my fingers one last time through my stick-straight blonde hair, trying in vain to give it the appearance of volume or thickness. One final coat of mascara on my eyelashes and I'd be all set. The purple strappy top I was wearing really brought out the green in my eyes.

"Perfect," I muttered to my reflection, admiring the way my low-cut jeans hugged the curves of my butt.

"If you're so perfect, then let's go!"

"Good God, woman. It's not like we're heading to the prom." I walked out of the bedroom and down the hall toward my stressed-out best friend. "It's just a party. There is no *late* at a frat party, you know?" I leaned into the door frame, determined not to hurry.

"All the good guys will be taken." Melissa stuck her bottom lip out in the pout that she had perfected, and I couldn't help but laugh.

"This is a frat party, Meli. There are no good guys."

"I hate you." She frowned, twirling her shoulder-length wavy brown hair around her finger.

I smiled. "Good. Let's go."

I tossed my arm around my pint-sized friend and headed out the front door, locking it behind us. I'd known Melissa since high school. She moved here right after we graduated, while I was forced to attend community college. "You have to take the same courses the first two years anyway. It's much cheaper," my mom had insisted. So I stayed close to home, while Melissa's parents happily paid for all her expenses at Fullton State.

After two years of general education, I applied to three universities in Southern California and was accepted at all of them. I knew immediately which one I wanted to transfer to. Not only was my best friend at Fullton, but it also had one of the best photo communications programs in the state, with an award-winning student magazine and newspaper. And since my major was photography, the choice was easy.

Melissa's parents insisted on getting an apartment for us to share and refused to let my parents pay for any of it. We weren't poor, but we didn't have an overabundance of cash the way Meli's parents did. They told my folks that college tuition was expensive enough without all the extras and then they paid our rent a year in advance, including the summer. I remember my dad *promising* to pay them back during one of the many pre-moving discussions, and my eyes met Melissa's with an all-knowing glance that the repayment would never really come to fruition.

Her parents had always been overly generous when it came to me. But then again, they were privy to the many times my dad had promised me something and then not delivered. On more than one occasion, Melissa's mom's was the shoulder I cried on and whose ears I vented my disappointment and frustrations to. I intended to start paying them back as soon as I graduated and opened my own photography business.

The night air was warm on my exposed skin as we walked the five blocks toward the fraternity house. "That top looks fierce on you," Melissa complimented me with a slight smile.

"It's cute, right?" I smiled, looking down at the formfitting top hugging my curves and accentuating my tiny waist. "You look as hot as ever." I winked before slapping her black-skirt-covered ass.

Melissa was truly beautiful. Her dark brown hair contrasted with the blue of her eyes, making it hard to look away from her at times. She honestly looked like she belonged on the cover of a magazine, with her stunning figure and flawless features. We were total opposites, what with my five-foot-eight-inch frame and disproportionate body shape. I used to joke and say that God put me together like a Mr. Potato Head toy. One piece for my butt, one for my waist, one for my boobs…all a mismatch of sizes.

But it worked on me.

And I worked it.

The sound of hip-hop music filled the air. "Ooooh, I love this song! Let's dance!" I grabbed Melissa's hand and dragged her along, jogging closer to the source of the music.

"You always want to dance." Melissa rolled her eyes. I'd smack those perfect blue eyes right off her face if I didn't love her so damn much.

"Well, I'm a good dancer. And this butt of mine—oh, you know what it does." I started shaking my hips in the crowded driveway of the fraternity house.

"Oh, no. Please stop."

I laughed and slowed down my booty-shaking when I noticed the number of eyes ogling me. I hated being gawked at. *I know, I know. I'm a fucking hypocrite.* I scanned the crowd before suddenly stopping on the most delicious pair of chocolate-brown eyes watching me. The fact that the eyes belonged to one of the hottest faces I'd ever seen was merely a bonus. He ran his fingers through his black hair before resting them against his tanned, scruffy face. He smiled lazily at me and I felt my stomach flip.

*Stupid stomach.*

"No. Tell me you are not looking at him, Cassie." Melissa stepped in front of me, breaking the eye contact.

"Hey, move." But every direction I craned my neck, she blocked me with her annoying face.

"No freaking way. Don't you know who that is?" She threw her hand in front of my eyes before I swatted it away.

"Obviously not, or we'd be dating." I hopped up to steal a peek over her head.

"Jack Carter doesn't *date*. He sleeps with girls and all their friends." Melissa's mouth curled with disgust.

"So that's the infamous Jack Carter, huh?" I was intrigued. This guy's name was all over the school papers and online.

Melissa threw an arm over my shoulder. "The one and only."

"Is he really as good as they say?" Jack would

be eligible for the Major League Baseball draft after the season ended. Everyone said he'd get drafted within the first five rounds. And apparently that's a pretty big deal.

"His ego certainly thinks so."

"Typical." If there's one thing I know, it's athletes. They're all the same. Superstitious, cocky, insecure egomaniacs. Yes, I realize the words are contradictory, but most are somewhat normal guys. They just hide behind a hundred-foot-tall brick wall, built entirely on ego. Plus, they don't know any better. They've been baseball players their whole lives; they don't know how to be anything else.

"What is it with you and assholes, Cass? Jack Carter's a world class jerk and you need to stay away from him."

"Hey!" I stomped my foot and firmly placed my hand against my hip. "The question isn't, 'What is it with *me* and assholes.' It's more like, "What is it with most guys *being* assholes?'"

"Valid point. But still. You already know up front this guy's a player, so why bother? You'll only end up hurt."

"Not if I hurt him first," I mumbled under my breath.

"Trust me, you won't. Jack Carter doesn't get hurt by girls. Promise me you'll stay away from him." Melissa pinned me with a glare to let me know she was serious.

"I promise I'll stay away from him." I batted my eyelashes, my tone of voice insincere.

"Ugh! Don't say I didn't warn you." Melissa pushed her way through the crowd and I watched as

Jack stopped her before she passed him. He reached an arm out for her and she moved it away, her foot tapping against the ground the way she always did when she was irritated. He turned to eye me and she matched his gaze before gesturing wildly and shaking her head no. A wide smile crossed his face as Melissa threw her arms up in the air before storming inside the front door.

Jack walked, no, make that *sauntered*, over to where I stood. His black cargo shorts and tight-fitting gray baseball t-shirt did a number on his body. The definition of his arm muscles rippled against the fabric, accentuating his well-defined shoulders on his six-foot frame as his arms swayed. He tilted his head and narrowed his eyes at me like I was some tiny, helpless creature who didn't have a clue it was about to get eaten alive by the most beautiful, albeit dangerous, creature in the jungle.

I almost felt violated.

Dirty.

Like I needed a shower to scrub that look off my body.

It wasn't until he got close enough that I could read the writing on his shirt. It said, "No Glove No Love" with a picture of a catcher's mitt in the middle.

*What a Pig. Yes, with a capital P.*

Two can play this game.

*Defenses up.*

"So you're Melissa's roommate?" The words came out smooth like butter, his voice deep and sexy.

"You're a genius," I said, going for my most

uninterested tone.

"Hey now, don't be mean. I just wanted to meet you." He looked me in the eyes with a focused, unbreakable stare. "You have beautiful eyes."

"Nice shirt." I gave him a disgusted once-over, trying to cover the fact that I wanted to laugh. It was clever, but I'd be dammed if I would admit that to a guy like him.

He looked down and smirked. "Ah, you like that? I think it's a pretty responsible message I'm sending out, don't you?"

I said nothing, questioning whether anything that came out of this guy's mouth was genuine or not.

"What? Cat got your tongue? You don't believe in safe sex?"

Was this guy for real? "What do you want?" My lips pursed together, making my tone harsher than I had intended.

"I told you, I wanted to meet you. I'm Jack Carter." He reached out his hand and I looked at it, my arms firmly crossed against my stomach.

"I know who you are." I pretended not to care. He was beautiful. And he was charming. And a man-whoring pig. *God, what is wrong with me?*

"So you've heard of me, huh, Kitten?"

My lips suddenly felt like they were filled with lead as they turned downward in disgust. "You did *not* just call me 'Kitten.' Do I look like a stripper to you?"

He looked me up and down and then did it again. "Well, now that you mention it."

"You're an asshole." I pushed past him to walk

away, but he grabbed me.

I tore my arm from his grip. "It costs fifty cents every time you touch me. Don't do it again."

"Oh, so you're not a stripper, you're a whore?"

"Oh, so you're not only an asshole, you're a piece of shit," I responded as I stomped away.

"I like you," he shouted at my back.

"So you're dumb, too," I tossed over my shoulder with a glare. "I'll add it to the list of your many redeeming qualities."

I heard him laugh before I entered the house to search for Melissa. I finally found her in the backyard, drinking something out of a red plastic cup and talking to a group of people I didn't recognize. I appeared at her side before she realized I was there.

"Oh my God, Cass, what did he say to you?" She ushered me toward an empty clearing in the yard.

I grabbed a drink for myself off a nearby table and rolled my eyes. "Nothing. He's a jackass."

"I told you." She smirked and shrugged her shoulders. "Well, he's clearly gotten over you already. Look."

She pointed toward an open window where Jack was attached at the lips to a scantily clad blonde. One of his hands gripped her backside, while the other pulled at the back of her head. I shook my head in disgust at his public display of man whoredom.

"And then what? He'll just never talk to her again?" I asked, trying to figure him out.

Melissa turned to eye me, curiosity lurking

behind those baby blues. "No. They'll talk. I mean, unless she gets all pissed off at him for…being him. But he won't ever hook up with her again. He never hooks up with the same girl twice."

"And the girls…they know this?" I was shocked. *Seriously, do these girls have no self-esteem?*

"They know."

"Pathetic." I frowned and looked back at Jack just in time to see him leading the girl away by the hand, a smile plastered all over her perfect little face.

*****

And that was my first introduction to Jack Carter.

Jack fucking Carter.

The next big thing in the world of baseball. Word has it he throws somewhere between ninety-three and ninety-four miles per hour when he's on the mound. That's fast. *Real fast.* Especially for a lefty. And you can't teach speed. You either have the ability to throw that fast or you don't.

And apparently he had it.

On and off the baseball field.

*****

Two days later I walked into the student union, scanning the area between the bowling lanes and the bar for Melissa. Everyone on campus seemed to congregate there since it's where the lone pizza restaurant was located. When it came to college and college students, pizza seemed to be on everyone's diet menu.

She spotted me and waved her tanned arms frantically above her head. Melissa looked like a lunatic and it made me laugh out loud. I waved back, then grabbed a tray and bought my lunch before weaving my way through a crowd of other students toward her table.

"Kitten."

The deep, sultry voice stopped me in my tracks as my smile faded. I turned toward the source of the voice with revulsion. "You know, I don't even like cats." I lifted one brow and fixed Jack with a fierce stare.

He fiddled with his baseball cap before putting it back on his head and tucking his dark hair underneath. I felt almost mesmerized as he ran his fingers absentmindedly across the white stitching of our school's initials. I found myself noticing the way his dark blue shirt fit snugly against the muscles in his arms and shoulders. I hated how good-looking he was.

"Actually, I didn't know. But I'm glad I do." He smiled and I swear part of my heart melted right then and there at the sight of his dimples.

*I totally suck.*

I tried to walk toward Melissa, who eyed me with piqued curiosity, but he stood his stupid gorgeous body in my path. I quickly moved to the right, but he hopped to his left to block me. I took another step to the left and he quickly moved too.

"What do you want, Jack?" I said, the anger in my voice taking us both by surprise.

"Are you always this hostile?" His smile told me he was teasing, before forcing his dimples to reappear and my body to flush with heat.

"Only to guys like you."

"So tell me, Kitten, what's *a guy like me*?"

"Not worth my time." I shoved my tray into his gut and when he let out an *ooof*, I scurried past him, trying not to spill my soda.

"You'll come around," he shouted.

"Don't hold your breath."

I rushed to our table, throwing down my tray of food.

"Nice scene." Melissa's eyes were huge as she fought a grin.

"Huh?"

"Look around." She waved an arm, gesturing toward the crowd.

I glanced around the bar and the other tables. All eyes were either on me or Jack. *Great.* The last thing I wanted was the entire school thinking I was Jack Carter's latest conquest.

"Is he always that obnoxious?" I ripped the top off my raspberry yogurt.

"I don't know, Cass. I've never seen him act that way before if that's what you're asking."

"I don't know what I'm asking." Irritated and annoyed, I scanned the room for Jack's face. He sat at a table surrounded by giddy girls, tossing their hair, pawing his muscles, and laughing obnoxiously at whatever he said. His eyes briefly met mine before I turned away, and I felt my heart beat a little faster.

"Jesus. How have I never noticed this spectacle before?" I wondered out loud.

Melissa chuckled. "I honestly don't know. Happens every day."

"Those girls have no shame. I'm almost

embarrassed for them."

"You know they all want to be the one he actually falls for." Melissa sounded sympathetic as she removed the crust from her slice of cheese pizza.

"Good luck with that, ladies!" I gave the gawking girls a fake salute, then turned my attention to attacking my yogurt.

Curiosity got the best of me when I heard shouts and the sound of slapping high-fives. I looked back to Jack's table to see a boy about Jack's height and build sitting down next to him. "Who's that?" I asked Melissa, nosy in spite of myself.

"The one who just sat down? That's Dean…Jack's little brother. He's a freshman." "How the hell do you know that? You're like a freaking college directory," I teased.

"He's in one of my classes."

"Wait," I said, putting one hand up in the air. "How do you have a class with a freshman?"

"I still have a couple of lower-level classes to take and he's in one of them. He's really sweet. Not like Jack at all," Melissa added with a smile and a faraway look in her eyes.

"Oh my God, you like him!"

"I do not!" Melissa whispered defensively. "I barely even know him! I'm just saying he's nothing like his brother, is all."

"Okay, calm down. Jeez. It's okay to like Jack Carter's little brother." I glanced back at Dean, admiring his smile, but noting the lack of dimples his brother wore so well. "He is cute." I poked her shoulder.

"He is, right?" She eyed him from a distance.

"At least you like the good one." I smiled, turning back to see the brothers throwing their arms around each other's necks.

"As if I'd like the other one! Jack's disgusting." She pretended to stick a finger down her throat and made gagging noises.

"So you keep saying," I said, taking another spoonful of yogurt.

"I swear to God, Cassie. If you end up falling for his shit, I don't want to hear it. I've watched him the last two years before you got here. I'm telling you, he's the ultimate playboy." She silenced her rant with a quick chomp at her banana.

"I hear you. Okay? Steer clear of Jack Carter. It shouldn't be that hard, considering I don't want to go anywhere near him."

We both smiled, momentarily satisfied with my promise.

# TWO

The sun warmed my body the moment I stepped out of the three-story Communications & Arts Building. A gentle breeze swept across my face as I observed my fellow students. Some rushed to get to class, while others fought for sunny areas on the lawn. I smiled as I passed a long-haired kid playing the guitar. He played under the same tree every day, and I started to wonder if he was a student at all or if he just liked being on the large, sprawling campus.

I passed by the university bookstore and shops, making a mental note to pick up two scantrons for my upcoming tests. Herds of people milled in and out of the student union entrance as I walked in. My eyes immediately fell on Jack and his harem of fans. I couldn't get over how I'd never noticed it before, but now it was all I saw. He flexed his muscles for a couple of girls who screamed when they grabbed on to his bicep. I heard him say, "Hold on," as he lifted them into the air. I frowned with disgust as he demonstrated his pitching motion in slow speed, much to the delight of the squealing girls.

"He is such an attention whore." I slammed my body down in the seat across from Melissa.

"Then stop paying attention to him."

"It's sort of hard not to when he's always creating a spectacle." I waved my arms toward the gaggle of girls following his every move.

"Hi, Melissa." A deep voice interrupted my Jack-bashing.

"Oh…hi, Dean," Melissa responded, her voice all soft and sweet. I shot a quick glance at her under my eyelashes, and smiled to myself.

"Would you mind if I sat with you?" Dean smiled when he asked and kept his hazel eyes locked on Melissa's.

"No. We're much better company than your brother's table anyway," she teased, poking him in the ribs.

He glanced in Jack's direction, shaking his head. "It just gets old sometimes, you know?" He placed a slice of pizza on the table and sat down.

"Hi, I'm Dean." He stretched his hand across the table.

"I'm Cassie. I'm Melissa's roommate." I grabbed his hand and squeezed.

"It's nice to—"

"Dean! What are you doing over here?" Jack's sultry voice echoed throughout the student union, and I felt my stomach lurch. I lifted my gaze to find him staring at me, so I pinched my lips together, hoping my annoyance would be loud and clear.

"Oh, Kitten. I see you've met my little brother." Jack winked before placing his hand on Dean's shoulder and squeezing.

"Thank God he seems nothing like you. I might

actually be able to tolerate him." I tilted my head and smiled sharply before taking a bite of my turkey sandwich. I noticed Melissa and Jack sharing an amused glance, and I wanted to kick Melissa under the table. The last time I did that it left an ugly bruise on her shin and she didn't speak to me for days, so I restrained myself.

"You need me to work some of that aggression out of you?" Jack offered with a sexy smile.

My mouth was full, but I didn't let that stop me. "I'd rather eat dirt."

"I almost want to see that." Jack chuckled and one dimple appeared on his cheek.

"You would. Go torture someone else," I begged, nibbling at my sandwich before looking away.

"But I like torturing you." He grinned and moved to sit next to me.

"Uh, no!" I shouted before throwing my bag right where he was about to plop his perfect little ass. He stopped short and stood back up.

"Why so angry, Kitten?"

"Why so annoying, jackass?" I mimicked his tone.

I had just taken a bite of my pickle when Jack's warm breath in my ear stopped my chewing. "You'll come around. You'll see. You can't resist me forever."

I suddenly had the urge to spit my half-chewed

food all over his arrogant face. The thought of doing it made me laugh, and I accidentally inhaled a little of what I was chewing. As I choked and struggled to swallow, he walked away smiling.

"Sorry about my brother. He isn't really a jerk." Dean smiled as he defended his brother, his head cocked to one side with sincerity.

I coughed to clear my throat and picked up a napkin. "He just plays one on TV?"

"Something like that. Don't take him too seriously. He's just having fun with you."

I half smiled. "But I'm not having fun."

"But you are. And he knows it," Dean added, his expression a mixture of confidence and knowing.

I didn't respond to Dean's accusation, not wanting to prove him right...or wrong. I took a healthy bite of my sandwich when Jack walked back over to our table. Caught with a mouth full of food again, I couldn't speak, so I simply narrowed my eyes and glared at him.

He shoved a napkin into my hand and walked away without saying a word. I started to unfold it before reading *#23 on the field, #1 in your heart*, followed by some numbers written in black ink. I quickly crumpled it up and threw it in my bag.

"What was that?" Melissa interrupted the thoughts swirling around in my head.

I swallowed. "His phone number, I think. I

didn't really look at it."

"He gave you his number?" Dean's face appeared puzzled.

"I think. Maybe I'm wrong. I'll look at it later." I was suddenly embarrassed at the assumption that Jack had given me his number, when maybe it wasn't Jack's number at all.

Melissa turned toward Dean. "What's with the face?"

"He doesn't give out his phone number. There's no point with him." Dean's gaze darted from my face to Jack's, turning his head to scrutinize his brother, now sitting several tables away.

"He has a cell phone, right?" Melissa asked, her head bobbing.

"Yeah…?" Dean responded, dragging out the word like a question.

"I'm just saying, caller ID!" She rolled her eyes.

"His number is private. It doesn't show up."

"Really? Who does that?" Melissa's face crinkled.

"Someone who had to change his phone number fifteen times in high school because it never stopped ringing, or pinging with text messages."

"*Fifteen times?*" I asked, far louder than I intended. I ducked my head as several people sitting nearby stared at me with curiosity.

"It might have been more, but it was insane. The girls would post his number online and then his voice mail would fill up within a day. And then they'd all start calling my phone looking for him when he didn't answer."

"Holy shit, that's bananas!" Melissa laughed at the insanity.

"That's why it's weird that he'd give you his number. He doesn't give anyone his number." Dean shook his head.

"Well, like I said, I could be wrong," I quickly recanted.

Melissa gestured toward my bag. "Then get it out and read it now."

Heat spread throughout my cheeks and down my neck to my chest. "No. Not in the freaking student union while he's right over there, thanks. Later."

I rose from the table, grabbed my bag and my trash, and walked nonchalantly past Jack and his pack of groupies. I heard the sound of female voices whining when Jack pulled himself away to jog over and catch up with me.

"I expect you to call me, Kitten."

"I'm sure you expect a lot of things," I said rudely, refusing to look at him as his stride slowed and he let me walk away.

"Come to my game tonight!" he shouted when I opened the glass doors.

I turned toward him before walking out. "I don't think so."

"Don't you want to see me pitch?" He raised an eyebrow, his voice cocky.

I tilted my head, holding the door open with one arm. "I saw you pitching earlier. In slow motion, remember? I think I got the gist."

The glass door closed behind me with a loud bang and I walked to my next class, wondering how long I'd be able to resist him.

*****

I opened the door to our two-bedroom apartment, the smell of this morning's bacon still lingering in the air. Mail and schoolwork were strewn across the top of our table, and I added my backpack to the mess.

Melissa sat watching TV on our L-shaped couch while eating a bowl full of cottage cheese and green grapes. I smiled at her odd food combination and headed straight into the kitchen, grabbing a bottle of water from the fridge and some chips from the cupboard.

I took a sip of the water, letting the cool moisture replenish my dehydrated body.

"So, we're going to the baseball game tonight," she informed me, and the water in my mouth sprayed out all over the carpet.

"Shit." I laughed and grabbed a towel before bending down to soak up the mess. "*You* might be, but I'm staying here."

"Cassie, the whole school goes to the baseball

games. It's like the state of Texas and high school football." Her head tilted as I looked up from my carpet cleaning, my eyes clearly confused. "*Friday Night Lights*, hello? Ugh, don't you watch *any* TV?"

I chuckled at her frustration with me as she continued. "Anyway, everyone goes. Especially when Jack's pitching. It's sort of a spectacle, really."

"How so?" I asked, tossing the wet towel into the sink before leaning my shoulder against the wall.

She glanced up toward the ceiling and pursed her lips together. Then she looked back at me, draping her body over the side of the couch. "Well, a ton of scouts are there for starters. And reporters from all the local newspapers and TV stations. You just have to see it. Even if you only go to one game, Cassie, it has to be one when Jack's pitching. Plus, you can take some really cool pictures for that *Tuck* magazine, or whatever it's called."

My eyebrows lifted at the thought of photographing the school's new stadium and fans. "It's called *Trunk*," I corrected, referring to the university's student-run magazine. "And someone is already assigned to the baseball team. But I do need to work on my night photography." I pulled away from the wall and glanced at my camera bag, mulling the idea over.

"And you can work on your action shots too," she added with a sly smirk.

I rolled my eyes. "Three hours ago you hated this guy, and now you're like his biggest fan. What gives?"

"*Excuse* me!" Her voice was animated as she held up one finger. "Jack Carter the guy sucks and should be avoided at all costs. Jack Carter the baseball player is totally amazeballs and should be observed whenever possible. You see the difference?"

I laughed at her insane logic. "They're both the same guy. Just want to put that out there before I agree to go."

Her eyes lit up as a grin spread across her face. "You'll see. So you'll go with me then?"

I released a breath and closed my eyes. "Yes. I'll go with you," I promised, doing my best to sound disappointed.

Her squeals of delight filled the air and I couldn't shake the feeling of anticipation welling within me. I didn't want to be excited to see Jack in his element…but I was. But I'd be damned if I was going to admit it.

# THREE

Our apartment was only a few blocks from campus, so we walked everywhere we could. In the grand scheme of things, it was much easier than dealing with the parking situation. There were too many cars and never enough spaces. Not to mention the fact that the price of a semester parking pass cost more than my first camera. This is partly why my parents refused to let me bring my car to school. So I sit at school, car-less. And my car sits at home, driver-less.

The lights of the stadium caught my eye before anything else did. The tall fixtures beamed in every direction, giving the school the appearance that it was lit up from the inside out. I stopped quickly and dropped to my knees, unwinding the camera's thick black strap from around my wrist. I removed the lens cap and tucked it into the back pocket of my jeans. Melissa, used to my photographing ways, had already noticed my absence and silently waited for me.

I brought the viewfinder to my right eye and closed the left, as strands of my hair dangled in my line of vision. I let out an aggravated breath before gently placing my camera on the ground between my feet and twirling my long blonde mane into a knot at the back of my head. With my hair firmly out of my eyes, I angled the lens to show only the top of the baseball stadium, with the lights and the illuminated sky as the focal point. I manually adjusted the focus and the shutter speed before pressing the shutter release button and hearing the familiar *click* sound I'd grown to love. Satisfied with the preview on the screen, I stood up and walked over to Melissa.

"Good shot?"

I shrugged my shoulders. "We'll see," I said, reaching in my back pocket to fish out the lens cap.

I was still learning how to use my new digital camera. I'd saved for two full years to buy it, hoarding every bit of Christmas and birthday money from relatives and doing small photography jobs for local businesses and high school seniors. Oftentimes I thought the picture on the camera's small preview screen looked gorgeous, only to find out it was blurry or nowhere near as pretty once it was full-sized on my computer monitor. But I was learning.

We walked side by side toward the stadium's entrance. Melissa wasn't joking when she said it was a spectacle. The line to get in exceeded the length of the field and spilled out into the parking lot. We took our place at the end and I removed my lens cap once again, mesmerized by the sea of orange and dark blue that engulfed us. Everyone was decked out in our school colors, some wearing mock baseball jerseys with players' names on the back. I laughed to myself at the sheer number of "Carter, 23" shirts I saw and couldn't resist photographing a few.

"Cassie, come on! You can do that once we sit!" Melissa urged, scanning the seat numbers on our tickets.

I followed obediently behind her. "Don't most of the students sit in the bleachers?" I pointed toward left field.

"Depends on what you're trying to see." Melissa batted her long black eyelashes.

"Oh no. What have you done?" My legs began to tremble as I watched Melissa lead me all the way down the stairs to the front row, closest to the field.

She turned around, grinning from ear to ear. "Here we are," she announced before plopping down and looking left into the team's dugout.

I turned my head as well and realized we were practically in the freaking dugout. I leaned toward Melissa, almost knocking some poor guy's drink in his lap. "Sorry," I said quickly before squatting next to her. "I am *not* sitting here!"

"Yes, you are. These are our seats and the game's sold out." She smiled innocently and patted the empty seat next to her.

I scowled. "At least switch seats with me then. I don't want to be the one closest to their dugout."

"Fine," she said before hopping up and flipping her hair.

I begrudgingly sat and slinked down into my seat, trying to conceal myself behind Melissa's tiny frame. "I didn't want Jack to know I was here. Now there's no way he won't see me."

"This isn't about you. You're thinking too much." She sloughed me off with a wave of her hand.

"You better be right." I sighed, wondering how long I had to stay. I avoided looking anywhere near the team's dugout, afraid of who might be looking back at me, when Melissa called me on it.

"He won't see you, Cass. You can look in there. Hell, you can even photograph the dugout. He won't know," she informed me, her face serious.

"How is that even possible?" I gave Melissa my best *duh* look.

"Because Jack's all business out here. He doesn't look in the stands. Ever. And I mean, ever. Last year this girl took her freaking top off and screamed Jack's name like a lunatic the entire time he was up to bat. He didn't move a muscle to look in her direction. I could light your ass on fire and he wouldn't even know."

I laughed super loud. "Please don't test that theory."

"Look around, Cassie. I'm pretty sure this is the one thing in life he takes seriously." Melissa leaned back into her seat, taking a sip of the soda she'd just bought from a roaming vendor.

I scanned the crowd and noticed that we were surrounded by what appeared to be major league scouts. Each carried their own radar gun to measure the speed of Jack's pitches, and notepads to write everything down. There was a forest of television and press cameras lined up on tripods behind home plate. It was the closest thing to a media circus I'd ever seen. And I currently held my own professional-sized camera, which definitely helped us fit in with all the madness.

"Ladies and gentlemen, welcome to Fullton Field!" The announcer's voice filled the air, as the cheers slowly died down in volume.

"Here to sing the national anthem is our very own Fullton State student, Laura Malloy!" Cheers reenergized the atmosphere as Laura smiled nervously before closing her eyes tightly and singing the opening words in perfect pitch.

I instinctively grabbed my camera and adjusted the lens, focusing on the emotions of her face, and snapped multiple pictures. When she finished, I watched as she walked toward the players lined up along the third base line and smiled hopefully at Jack. I secretly loved it when he didn't acknowledge her.

"We have a sold-out crowd tonight, folks, and we all know why! Taking the mound against our rivals from Florida is the one and only Jack Carter!" The announcer enunciated Jack's name like he was the savior of the free world, like he'd cured cancer, or delivered rainbows to colorless skies everywhere.

No, I take it back.

He said Jack's name like Jack was a *hero*.

And I guess in a way he was. He brought media attention to the school and recognition to the baseball program. That attention translated into revenue for the school and top baseball prospects all wanted to play here. Jack was this university's very own marketing machine.

The school worshipped him. It wasn't just the girls on campus who wanted to be around him, it was *everyone*. I never realized the extent of his popularity before tonight.

"Now taking the field, *your* Fullton State Outlaws!" The announcer's voice paused before continuing. "And now taking the mound, Jack Car-terrrrr!" He dragged out Jack's last name, just like the wrestling announcers on TV.

The stadium erupted with ear-piercing shouts, howls, cheers, and screams. I looked at Melissa, shock clearly written all over my face, and she laughed, having witnessed this all before.

Jack walked confidently toward the dirt mound, his white-and-blue pinstriped sliding pants hugging his body in all the right places. I watched as his thigh muscles contracted against his pants with each step he took, and admired how good his butt looked in his uniform. His upper body was unfortunately hidden underneath a loose-fitting dark blue jersey with orange and white lettering.

His face looked different, more focused. This wasn't the playful guy from the student union anymore. This was the confident, serious baseball player.

"What'cha smiling at?" Melissa's voice cut through my inner dialogue.

I quickly dropped the smile I didn't know I was wearing. "Nothing," I snapped, and looked away, embarrassed.

"It's irritating how good he looks in his uniform, right?"

I jerked my head back toward her. "Seriously. Why does he have to be so hot?"

"'Cause he's a jerk. Jerks are always hot," Melissa reminded me with a nod.

Jack stood on top of the pitcher's mound, his left cleat kicking at the dirt in front of him. He placed his toes on the white rubber, dropped his glove hand to his knee, and gripped the ball with his left. His eyes focused solely on his catcher squatting sixty feet away. With a brief nod he leaned back, his body performing a motion so fluid and smooth it looked like it was made for him.

When his left hand released the ball, it flew by at a speed so quick I could barely make out anything but a white blur. The sound of the ball impacting against the catcher's mitt was so loud it echoed against the backstop. The batter stepped out from the batter's box and looked nervously at his coach before stepping back in. Two more pitches screamed by and that was out number one of the night.

"Strike three! You're out!" the umpire shouted enthusiastically and the crowd cheered wildly.

The scouts in the stands huddled together, comparing the red "97" digital readout on their radar gun screens.

"Holy shit, that was ninety-seven miles an hour," I said out loud, my mouth slightly open.

"I told you he's good."

I focused my camera on the pitching mound, with Jack's feet and the bottom of his glove dangling in the viewfinder. *Click.* Then I moved the lens up to view his bare left hand, gripping the baseball between three fingers, the red-stitched seam barely visible. *Click.* He brought his glove up to his face and all features except his brown eyes disappeared behind it. *Click.* His face twisted as he released the powerful pitch, his eyes never leaving their target. *Click.* Sweaty dark hair briefly saw light as Jack removed his cap and wiped the sweat from his brow with his sleeve. *Click.*

When the inning ended, I watched Jack jog off the field and into the dugout, never once looking into the stands. He instantly reappeared, a dark blue helmet on his head, two bats in hand. He swung the bats around like a windmill, stretching his shoulders. And when he bent over to stretch his hamstrings, girlish screams filled the air, along with flashes of light.

"You've got to be kidding me." I shook my head, looking around at the people taking pictures.

"Spectacle," was all Melissa said with a laugh.

Jack stepped around home plate and into the batter's box, his demeanor completely relaxed. Since he was left-handed, the front of him was in full view, as opposed to the back of all the right-handed hitters. I started to grab my camera, but then shoved it back on my lap instead. I had enough pictures of Jack for one night.

The opposing pitcher went through his motion and as he released the ball, Jack took a small step forward before his hips twisted with his swing. The ping of the ball against the metal bat quickly disappeared amidst all the cheering. Jack easily rounded first base and picked up speed as he raced toward second. The outfielder fired the ball at the shortstop as Jack slid headfirst into the bag, a cloud of dust encircling him.

"Safe!" The umpire shouted his call, his arms outstretched on either side of his body.

Jack planted both feet on top of the dusty base and brushed the dirt off his chest before dipping down the belt of his pants and allowing clumps of dirt to fall out. I was completely turned on.

*I suck, I suck, I suck.*

I overheard one scout ask another, "What did you clock him to first?" Referring to Jack's base running speed from home plate to first base.

The other scout glanced at his stopwatch. "Four point one." The first scout nodded his head in agreement and scribbled down more notes.

The photographer in me couldn't hold out any longer. I zoomed in on Jack's hands, now covered in batting gloves as he stepped away from second base with three long strides. *Click.* The dark of his eyes, now shadowed from his helmet, gave him an almost ominous appearance. *Click.*

"Gonna make a Jack photo album for yourself later?" Melissa flicked a finger at my shoulder as she teased me.

"You're the one who said I needed to work on my action shots!" I whisper-shouted.

"I didn't say they all had to be of Jack."

"Shit." I snapped the lens cap on and quickly flipped the power button into the Off position, where it stayed for the remainder of the game.

When it finally ended, Jack had pitched all nine innings and only gave up one run and three hits. The final score was eight to one, us. I grabbed my camera and shoved it into my purse before looking back at the team celebrating on the field. The coach pulled Jack aside and escorted him over to the press area where he was besieged by reporters, scouts, and fans.

Jack glanced up from the field and directly into my eyes. That single look stopped me in my tracks, and I was slammed into by the man walking behind me. Jack smiled and turned his attention back toward the cameras and journalists.

# FOUR

I strolled through the tree-lined campus, following the cement pathway that would eventually lead me to the *Trunk* offices. I'd joined the award-winning student-run magazine at the insistence of my visual communications professor. Even though I was required to take writing classes with my major, my focus was on the visual reporting side of things. I yearned to improve my craft, bringing life-changing visuals to accompanying articles.

I spotted the one-story brick building up ahead. All the newer buildings on campus were constructed with red and white brick, while the original buildings were large white stucco structures. It never made sense to me why they wouldn't at least attempt to match the newer buildings with the older ones.

I pulled the tinted glass door open and a gush of air conditioning greeted my face. I moved my sunglasses on top of my head, pulling my long hair back with them as I rounded the corner.

"Hey, Dani," I said as I entered, not wanting to startle Danielle, who squinted at the computer before she looked up.

"Hey, Cassie, come look at this." She waved me over, her expression still tight. I peered around her puffy brown ponytail and over her shoulder at the photograph on the screen. "I need this picture to have more expression. It's not giving me what I want. What am I missing?"

I looked at the eight-year-old boy standing in front of spilled water buckets, his expression sorrowful. "First of all, I don't think it should be in black and white. The details get lost in this photo. May I?" I pointed at the seat she occupied.

"Please." She jumped up from the seat as we switched positions.

I reopened the original picture in the photo editing software and manipulated the colors before pointing to the screen. "Look at the dirty rug hanging behind him. I barely noticed it in black and white. The cracks in the buckets, and the rubble at his feet," I paused, "were all lost before. This picture needs to be in color. This picture *deserves* to be in color."

Her hands clapped together behind my head before she squeezed my shoulders. "You're such a fucking genius. I love you."

I smiled, my eyes glued to the screen. "Thanks."

"So what's up?" Dani smiled, the tension creases between her eyes easing up as she relaxed.

"I just stopped by to work on some photos I took of last night's game. I thought you might want to use them for the feature you're running on Jack Carter."

"Tell me you're not one of…" she hesitated, "*them*."

"One of…*what*?" I asked, my eyebrows furrowing.

"One of the hundreds of girls on campus in love with all things Jack Carter." She rolled her eyes and let out a sigh.

I guffawed. "Uh, no. I can't stand the guy."

"Well that's a first," she admitted with a laugh. "We have a million pictures of Jack, but in all honesty, I'd love to see anything you shot."

"Thanks, Dani." I sat up a little straighter and smiled, unable to quell the little rise of pride welling up inside me.

"Now that you saved me from killing myself over this photo, I need to eat. See you later and thanks again." She tossed her purse strap over her shoulder, catching the ends of her ponytail in it before cursing and tugging the strands free.

It took longer than I expected to edit the photos from last night, but I had to admit they were good. They were better than good, actually. My stomach rumbled and I wondered if Melissa was still on campus. I sent her a quick text to which she responded, "Still here. In the SU."

I wrote back, "I have class in a few, but I'm on my way," before inserting the memory card into my camera and shoving it into my backpack. I passed some girls and pretended not to notice when they pointed and whispered Jack's name.

Irritated, I took a detour through campus,

pleased when I noticed the pathway was virtually vacant. I shook my head while I walked, annoyed that Jack's antics had made me the focus of attention I didn't want.

I threw open the heavy glass door and heard the sound of bowling pins crashing. Craning my neck to see the bowler, I smiled when I recognized the guy from my digital foundations class. Quick bursts of light alerted me that he wasn't bowling for fun and I watched another kid from class taking pictures of him.

I diverted my attention and looked around the sparse crowd for Melissa's face. She tilted her head and stuck out her tongue, catching my eye, before I strolled over to where she and Dean were sitting. I flung my pack on the table before plopping down.

"Thought you weren't coming to my game?" Jack slid his body into the seat next to mine, his tone sounding a bit arrogant.

"My roommate threatened to set me on fire if I didn't." I kept my voice cool and avoided his eyes, scooting my body away from his.

"Well, at least now I know how to get you to go out with me."

"I'm not going out with you," I said, turning my head away from him.

"At least give me your number then?"

"No thanks."

"Why not?"

"'Cause I don't want to." I breathed out, still irritated about the way other girls acted around him. It just kept eating at me, which was a good thing, because it helped me resist Jack. *God help me.*

"Aw, come on, Kitten."

"Stop calling me that!" I rose from the table, grabbing my things. "I'll see you later," I announced, my attention solely focused on Melissa.

I flung my pack across my shoulder and slipped hastily out a side door. Dropping my sunglasses over my eyes, I headed toward the tall Communications & Arts Building.

"Kitten! Kitten, wait up!"

I looked back to see Jack racing to catch me, and everyone's attention drawn toward us.

"For the last time, my name isn't Kitten." Hiking my bag strap a little higher on my shoulder, I sped up my pace.

"I know! But you've never told me your real name," he said, slightly out of breath.

I let out a quick sigh. "Cassie."

"It's really nice to meet you, Cassie." He said my name all syrupy sweet and his brown eyes danced. It was easy to see why girls threw themselves at him.

"I'd say it's nice to meet you too, but I haven't decided yet."

He laughed. A real, hearty laugh and I had to stop myself from doing the same. "Anything I can do to help sway your decision?" He scratched his hair, his bicep flexing.

"I highly doubt that."

"Let me take you out, Cass." He said it so honestly, I almost believed he genuinely wanted to.

"No." I stood firm, my tone flat.

"Why not?"

"I enjoy my dates to be disease-free."

*Score one for Cassie.*

*Take that, Jack Carter.*

"As do I," he quipped confidently before giving a head nod to a passing teammate.

Now it was my turn to laugh. "Right. I've heard you're not really particular about who you date."

"Well you heard wrong, then."

"Oh, that's right. Actually, I heard you don't *date* at all. You just sleep with any girl who bats her fake eyelashes in your direction."

"I really need to meet your sources."

He followed me into the white stucco building. When I reached my classroom door, I turned to him and said, "See ya, Carter," as I headed down the stairs to my regular seat.

"Are you going to be this hostile on our date?" he shouted into the packed room.

All heads turned my direction, curiosity overwhelming them. I swallowed the lump in my throat and willed my cheeks to not turn red. *Yeah, like that's going to work.*

Pausing on the stairs, I pivoted and glared at Jack. "Who said I was going on a date with you?"

"Don't make me beg, Kitten." I shot him an irritated glare as the classroom filled with whispers and sounds of shock. "Don't make me beg in front of all these people. It's embarrassing."

"I'll go out with you, Jack," a busty blonde shouted, poking her shellacked face out from behind her seat.

"Perfect! I'm sure you two will have a great time together." I dropped into my seat and slinked lower, wishing for the power to become invisible.

My eyes closed and I took a few deep breaths before warm whispers interrupted my attempt to relax. "I don't want to go out with her, Kitten. I want to go out with you." His breath tingled against my neck, causing the small hairs to prickle with excitement and sending goose bumps shooting down my arm.

"What are you doing? Get out of here," I whispered, my tough facade cracking.

Honestly, I'm surprised it lasted this long.

"Promise me you'll think about it." His voice lowered with insistence, then he gave my shoulder a gentle squeeze.

"Promise you I'll think about going out with the school's biggest player? Oh sure, I'll think about it." *Seriously?*

"Promise me," he insisted.

Either he was actually sincere, or he was a really good bullshit artist and I was completely buying into it. I took one deep breath. I turned my head to the left and looked him dead in the eyes. "Fine. I *promise* I'll think about it. Will you go away now?"

A wide grin emerged and his gorgeous dimples appeared, torturing me with their adorable sex appeal. He stood up without another word and walked out of the classroom. I sat in silence, trying to hear anything other than the sound of my heart banging like wild bongo drums in my ears.

*I'm pathetic.*

When class ended, I walked outside to find Jack surrounded by a group of giggling girls. His eyes met mine and he broke from the circle, running to catch up. "Stalk much?" I said between breaths.

"It's not stalking when you enjoy it," he teased, overconfidence oozing from every perfect pore.

Half of me wanted to punch his gorgeous face, and the other half wanted to make out with it. "I bet you say that to all the girls." I rolled my eyes.

"I don't have to say that to all the girls. You're the only one who gives me crap for things like…breathing."

I rolled my eyes.

Again.

"Well, you're an annoying breather."

"You're an annoying eye-roller," he fired back.

"What?" I stopped walking and turned toward

41

his smug face, causing the pack of girls following us to stop as well.

"You shouldn't roll your eyes like that. Didn't your parents ever tell you it wasn't good for you?" He shoved a hand into his front pocket as girls walked by, begging for his attention. I had his complete interest, whether I wanted it or not.

"My parents said a lot of things," I responded defensively.

"Oh, I get it now." His voice was as sweet as Southern iced tea. "Daddy issues."

"How does any girl stand you?" He made me so mad I wanted to smack his smarmy face, but I just stood there frozen as the wind breezed through my hair.

"It's the dimples." Jack actually delivered the line seriously, pointing at the indent on his cheek before breaking into a big smile.

I couldn't take the banter any more. "At least you're humble," I said, before willing my legs to move.

"Just let me take you out. One date," he shouted at my retreating frame. "And if you hate it and we have a horrible time, you never have to go out with me again."

I stopped walking and turned to face him. "So that's it? Just one date and you'll go away forever?" I laughed, actually considering the idea.

We were making a scene again as girls

whispered and guys waited to observe if Jack Carter would actually get shot down.

"Just one date." He held up one finger in front of my face before involving the crowd. "Help me out here, guys." He turned to face the gawkers. "Tell her to go out with me one time. What can it hurt?"

The crowd roared with encouragement, and I heard shouts like, "Awwww, go out with him!" and "It's just one date! Do it!"

I shook my head and rolled my eyes. "Fine. Just *one*." Loud cheers erupted at my response. You'd think I'd just accepted a marriage proposal the way those idiots were carrying on.

What had I just gotten myself into?

# FIVE

"I cannot believe I agreed to this," I said, burying my face in my hands.

Melissa plopped down next to me on the floor of my bedroom. "This is a bad idea. You should probably call him and cancel."

I lifted my head and let out a deep sigh. "He'd never leave me alone then!"

She nodded. "You're right. Oh my God, you have to go."

I pulled myself up and studied my face in my bedroom mirror. "Maybe it won't be so bad?" I wondered as I brushed powder across my face.

"Or maybe it will?" Melissa bit her bottom lip, her face contorted in thought.

"What are you thinking?"

Melissa grinned mischievously. "If the date is horrible then he'll go away, right?"

"That's what he said," I responded reluctantly.

"Well, then all you have to do is be a crappy date! You know, like what's-her-face in *How to Lose A Guy in Ten Days*!"

I leaned away from her, pondering her suggestion while I dropped the brush and picked up my mascara.

"Oh my God! You little slut! You want to have a good date with him. You love him and want to have ten thousand of his little baseball babies!

Cassie!!!"

"Where do you come up with this stuff?" I asked through my laughter.

"Movies. They have the best lines." Melissa's eyes twinkled, matching the huge grin on her face.

The doorbell rang and my laughter caught in my throat. *Shit*. I wasn't ready for this. My deer-in-the-headlights look grabbed Melissa's attention. "I'll go let him in and keep him occupied until you're ready."

I sighed. "Thank you."

I could hear the sound of our front door creaking open as his friendly voice reverberated down the hall and into my room, causing me to shake nervously. Gripping the fine liner brush tightly with a trembling hand, I finished lining my lips and brushed a soft seashell-colored gloss on top. I smacked my lips together once, then puckered to make sure the gloss was evenly spread.

Before I left my room, I did a quick squat in front of the mirror. I watched as my low-rise jeans went even lower, revealing far too much of my pink underwear. I pulled my black tank top down around my waist and bent over again. My jeans still pulled low in the back, but my top stayed firm.

I rounded the corner and heard Jack's voice stop abruptly when he caught sight of me. "You look adorable, Kitten." His voice practically purred.

"That's it, I'm not going." I threw my hands up

in the air and turned back toward the hall.

He stopped me with his laughing response. "I'm sorry, Cass. I won't call you that anymore."

"I'm not sure you can help it." I eyed him narrowly.

"I might slip up a time or two, but can you really blame me?" He shoved his hands into the pockets of his black and white shorts and then batted his thick eyelashes at me.

"Yes. Don't call me Kitten. It's annoying and it makes me hate you."

"Is she always this argumentative?" he asked Melissa through a one-dimpled smirk.

She smiled coyly at him. "Not usually. You must be special."

*Oh my God! She turned into complete mush in two seconds! Traitor!*

I shot Melissa a shocked and horrified glare and turned to see Jack smiling as if he had won the top prize at the fair.

"Don't give me that look," I threatened through gritted teeth.

"What?" He shrugged his strong, broad shoulders. "You think I'm special. It's cool."

I couldn't resist rolling my eyes at him. "The only type of special I think you are is *e*-specially irritating. Like a rash."

He let out a quick huff. "Come on, Kit...er, Cassie. Let's go. It was nice to meet you, Melissa."

He grabbed her little five-foot-two-inch frame and squeezed until she giggled wildly.

*Traitorous bitch.*

"See you later, Meli." I shook my head and mouthed, "I can't believe you!" at her. She waved me away and blew me a kiss.

Jack led me in the direction of his car. Since I had no idea which one was his, I followed blindly one step behind. He walked over to the passenger side of a vintage white Ford Bronco covered with dents, scratches, and chipped paint.

"Are you sure this thing's legal on the streets?" I asked, eyeing the giant, oversized tires and lack of a roof.

His eyebrows pinched together. "You scared?"

"Are you high?" I squinted toward him. "No, really, do you do drugs 'cause I don't date guys who do drugs."

He turned the key and the door unlatched with a pop and squeaked open. Then he took me by the hand and gently helped me up into the seat, placing his hand firmly on my rear.

"Hands off the ass, Carter," I snapped.

"I was just helping you up. Honest." He feigned innocence as he closed the door behind me. "You sure you're not scared?"

"I'm not scared. This car just looks like something that belongs on a sand dune or in a monster truck rally or a repair shop." I glanced down, noticing the silver-dollar-sized hole in the floor.

"Is it the tires?" he asked sincerely.

"They are massive."

"Just like my—"

"I swear to God," I quickly interrupted and turned away.

"What?" He laughed. "I was going to say *heart*. The tires are as big as my heart." He patted his chest for emphasis.

"You mean as big as the hole in your chest where your heart's supposed to be?" The verbal jab dropped out of my mouth before I could stop it.

"Ouch. Can we at least wait until dinner before you decide I'm heartless?"

"If you insist."

"I do." His brown eyes softened and he grabbed the wheel, put the key in the ignition, and turned. The engine rumbled to life and my seat vibrated under me. I strapped the old seatbelt around my body and gave Jack a wary glance.

"You are scared," he said with concern.

I shook my head defiantly. "I'm fine, just go." I gestured toward the road.

He removed his hand from the stick shift and placed it on my leg. I winced in response.

"What did I tell you about the touching?" I asked, giving him a sideways glance.

"Fifty cents. Don't worry, I got it covered." One

dimple greeted me before quickly disappearing. "You sure you're okay?"

I nodded as he put the car in drive and it rocked forward as he gassed it.

"Shit." He muttered under his breath.

"What is it?" Suddenly I was concerned for our well-being. We were going to tip over from the massive tires and die.

"I meant to ask you this *before* we left, but I got distracted. You're so feisty all the time, you make me forget things." His left arm rested on top of his door panel and he leaned his head into his hand. I watched as his fingers made their way through his hair, grabbing fistfuls as he eyed the road ahead.

"So are you going to ask me, or are you going to make me guess?" I tried to hide the snark in my voice, but failed.

Jack turned to look at me briefly before returning his gaze forward. "I meant to ask you if you eat meat or not?"

I felt my face contort into a look of confusion and surprise. "So you want to know if I'm a vegetarian?"

He let out an exasperated sigh. "Yeah."

"Why?"

"Because I want to buy you a cow. Why do you think?" He tried to keep calm, but his cheeks were slowly turning a nice shade of red.

"I don't know. Where are you taking me?"

"I'm taking you to the best burger joint in town and they don't have a menu for vegetarians."

"Really? They don't serve salads?" I asked incredulously.

"No. They don't." His tone turned serious as he glanced in my direction again.

I couldn't stifle my laughter as I almost choked on my words. "I eat meat."

He raised an eyebrow and eyed me tentatively before I smacked the shoulder nearest me with the back of my hand. "Not *that* kind of meat!" I huffed before looking away. "I'm not a vegetarian! You're so irritating."

"You keep saying that, yet here you are."

"I didn't realize I had a choice." I rolled my eyes so he'd notice.

"What did I tell you about that, Kitten?"

"How many times do we have to go over this whole 'Kitten' thing?"

"How many times do we have to go over the eye roll thing? It's bad for you and I'd hate to see anything happen to those gorgeous green eyes of yours."

I struggled to formulate a comeback as his compliment floated in the air. My breath faltered and my mind stopped focusing on anything but the sound of his voice and the look on his stupid, beautiful face.

"Cat got your tongue, Kitten?"

"The next red light you come to, I swear to God, I'm jumping out of this death trap and walking home."

He chuckled, clearly amused. "Alright, I'll stop."

I narrowed my eyes, refusing to believe his words. When we arrived at the restaurant, I hopped out of the car quicker than he could turn off the ignition. The place was a converted old ice cream shop. The few items they offered were written in chalk on the wall when you first walked in. An old cash register sported a handwritten note that read CASH ONLY, and when I got a look at the number of diners packing the room, my brain quickly went from wondering how they stayed in business to how they kept all their customers happy.

"Is it always like this?" I asked Jack, shocked at the massive crowd.

"Hey, Jack." A gorgeous brunette rushed passed us, reaching out to touch his arm.

"Hey, Sarah. Busy tonight, eh?" he shouted, trying to be heard over the hum of the crowd.

"Always!" she answered with a smile and a wink.

*It figures.* "Come here often?" I asked, annoyed already.

"I told you, it's the best burger place in town."

Sarah reappeared and rested an arm on Jack's shoulders. "Sit anywhere you want, sweetie. You want your usual?"

He glanced at me before answering her. "Cass, you like bacon? Fries?"

I nodded my head. "Mm-hmm."

"Make it two, please. Thanks, Sarah."

She looked at me briefly before turning her attention back to my date. "I get off at midnight," she whispered in his ear loud enough for me to hear.

"I'm on a date," he said harshly.

"Oh, of course you are. Later then." She scurried away, her face flushed from embarrassment.

"Sorry about that." Jack put his hand lightly at the small of my back, leading us to a small booth in the far end of the room. "Oh, I almost forgot! I'll be right back."

Before I could argue, he hopped from the booth and ran out the front door. I watched through the restaurant's large plate-glass window as he opened the passenger side of his death trap and reached into the glove compartment. I fiddled with strands of my hair, tucking pieces behind my ear as I watched Jack's every move. Two water glasses appeared in front of me and I turned to greet Sarah with a smile. She didn't return the gesture as Jack reappeared and slid into his side of the booth.

"First things first," he said, pulling a paper bag from his jacket pocket. I heard the sound of metal clanking against fiberglass as he poured the entire contents of the bag onto our table.

Quarters spilled out in every direction. Several rolled off the table, spilling onto the floor and into my lap, the rest covering portions of the tabletop. "What the hell?"

"Fifty cents a touch, right? This oughta cover me for a while." He grinned, obviously proud of himself, as he folded his arms behind his head and leaned into them.

I welcomed the heat rising in my cheeks. "Cute," I admitted reluctantly, gathering the quarters into a pile at the end of the table, fighting a smile.

*One for Jack Carter. Dammit.*

He didn't respond. He simply sat there smiling, focusing those dark brown eyes on me. "Stop looking at me like that," I said, flustered.

"Like what?"

"Like I'm a slab of meat and you're hungry."

He laughed loudly and relaxed into his seat, slinging his muscular arm over the back of the booth. He rubbed his hand over his face and looked around, letting his eyes roam the restaurant and then his gaze slid back to me as he sipped his water. "You're different."

I rested my elbows on the table and leaned toward him, intrigued. "How so?"

"Well for starters, you're sassy. I never know what you're going to say or do next." He grabbed one of the quarters and flicked it, watching as it spun in circles.

"That's just sad, Jack." I couldn't help but be annoyed that my sassiness was so defiant in his world.

"And you're not impressed by me." *Oh my God...he actually winced.*

"Oh, I know how tough that must be for you. I mean, you are just..." I waved my hands in his direction, "so impressive." My eyes widened sarcastically with the words.

"I mean it. Every other girl is always clamoring to get near me and you're the first girl trying to get the hell away."

I fell back into the booth laughing, feeling my tense muscles relax for the first time tonight. "What can I say? I guess I'm not like every other girl."

He shook his head, burying a smile. "So tell me, Cass, what's your story?"

"What do you want to know?" I took a gulp of water, casting my eyes away to hide the truth I just might be willing to tell him.

"Why haven't I seen you before this year?"

"I went to community college the past two years. I just transferred."

"Lucky me." He took another swig of water and placed it back down. "So where are you from?"

"About two hours northwest of here. Lived in the same house my whole life. What about you?"

"I grew up ten minutes from here."

"Really? So close. Did you even think about going anywhere else? I mean, I'm sure you had a lot of offers for baseball." I was genuinely surprised, considering what I'd seen of his talent and everyone's reaction to it.

He grimaced slightly before his expression softened. "I got offers everywhere. I could have gone to USC, UCLA, Texas, Florida, Georgia, Alabama...you name it."

"So why didn't you?" I leaned into the table with interest.

"I wanted to play for Coach Davies," he explained. "But mostly I wanted to stay near my grandparents." His voice lowered with emotion, his eyes focused somewhere in the distance.

"Oh." I leaned back in shock.

"Not the answer you expected?"

"Not really. I mean, it's sweet and all, but I don't get it. Why your grandparents?" I craved honesty from him. Honest words, honest thoughts, honest emotions.

"They practically raised me and Dean."

I smiled at the mention of his brother's name. "I like him."

"Want me to put in a good word for you? I know him pretty well." Jack sounded like he was teasing, but there was a bit of a sharp undertone to his offer.

"No thanks. He's not really my type. Too nice," I added, erasing the worry lines from his face. "How'd you both get into the same school, anyway?"

"It was one of my conditions."

"Conditions?"

"Yeah. I only agreed to come here if they agreed to let him in too."

My jaw dropped. "You bribed the university?"

He wagged his finger. "No. I just said I'd come here as long as when Dean was old enough, they'd let him in too."

"And they agreed to that?" I asked, somewhat horrified. "I mean, obviously they did 'cause you're both here."

He laughed. "Dean would have gotten in anyway, but I wanted assurance."

"Interesting." I ran my fingers through my hair, tucking the stray strands back in place behind my ear, quietly fighting the sense that this guy might not be so bad after all.

He leaned across the table, inching closer to me. "What is?"

"You're just different than I expected," I answered, focusing on his full lips.

"That's 'cause you're judgmental." He leaned back with a smile.

I closed my mouth and narrowed my eyes, unprepared for the rant that was about to leave my lips. "No. That's 'cause you're a pig. You're typical and selfish and pathetic and you treat girls like shit and…"

"Hey!" he interrupted, his tone offended. "Who says I treat girls like shit?"

"Sorry, Jack, but I don't know anyone who enjoys being fucked one minute and forgotten about the next."

"You make it sound so heartless when you say it like that," he admitted, my words apparently stinging.

"Well it kind of is." I shrugged. "And you wonder why I wanted to stay away from you?"

"You thought I'd do the same thing to you." His eyes widened as understanding settled in.

"I assumed you wanted to."

"Of course I want to sleep with you," he admitted without shame and I felt my inner thighs tingle. "But I'm not sold on the forgetting about you part."

I eyed him warily, my heart racing beneath my shirt. "You probably say that to all the girls."

"I don't have to say that to all the girls."

I sat in silence, stunned by his honesty.

"What are you thinking about?" He reached over and tapped my hand with one finger, bringing me out of my thoughts.

"Honestly?"

"Honestly."

"That I don't trust myself with you."

He folded his arms across his chest. "And why's that?"

"Because I can't tell whether or not you mean the things you say."

He uncrossed his arms and leaned into the table again. "What does your heart tell you?"

"Who cares? My heart's dumb! It believes anything," I said, clutching at my chest above my left breast.

He laughed, his eyes glued to my hand. "Fine. What does your head tell you then?"

"My head questions everything and believes nothing."

"So your head wants proof and your heart wants reassurance?" A small line appeared between Jack's eyebrows.

"Pretty much."

"I think you just made life a thousand times more difficult." He grabbed his head with both hands and squeezed.

"That's why I came up with my boy test...to protect myself."

"Protect yourself from what?" he asked, reaching for another quarter.

"Guys like you."

Our conversation was interrupted by the sound of plates being set on the table. "Here you go, two Titan specials with fries. You two need anything else?"

"I'm good. Kitten?"

I rolled my eyes so hard it hurt. "Can I get a side of ranch dressing, please? Thanks."

My eyes widened at the sight of my burger. It looked like it could feed the entire football team. And the mound of french fries that sat next to it had to consist of twenty potatoes.

"Please tell me you can't actually finish this?" I looked at Jack, my face shocked.

He laughed. "I can. And you better clean your whole plate."

"Clean this?" I pointed to the plate with an incredulous look.

He laughed again before lifting the burger to his face and taking a mammoth-sized bite. Sarah dropped off the dressing and I dipped the hot fries in, biting carefully. "Holy crap, these are amazing."

"Told you," he managed to say, his mouth stuffed with food.

I hated how cute he was. Even with a mouth full of food, he was still irritatingly adorable.

"So tell me about your boy test." He picked up his napkin to swipe at a smear of ketchup on his chin.

"Forget I said anything about it." I waved him off with my hands.

"Come on, Cass. I want to know." He eyed me curiously.

"Fine," I relented. "But you can't make fun of me."

Both dimples appeared on his cheeks and my heart fluttered quickly. "I won't. Promise."

I didn't believe that smile, but I gave in anyway. With a deep breath I rattled off, "They're more like rules. Rule number one: Don't lie. Two: Don't cheat. Three: Don't make promises you can't keep. And four: Don't say things you don't mean."

"That's it?" he asked in disbelief.

"They may not mean much to you, but they mean everything to me." I sighed, slightly embarrassed that I'd shared my list with him.

"I don't mean any offense, Kitten. It's just...well, those seem like pretty normal expectations to me."

"You'd think so," I agreed, taking a bite of my monstrosity they called a cheeseburger.

"But?"

"But most guys can't seem to do them. They lie. They cheat. And most people in general can't keep their promises, or stop themselves from saying things they don't really mean."

"What about you?"

My forehead creased. "What about me?"

"Can you follow your own rules?" he asked, his tone serious.

"I try to live my life following those rules. Otherwise you hurt people."

He took a quick, short breath. "So did people lie to you a lot or something? Some guy break your heart in high school?"

"It's more like my dad can't seem to follow through on anything he says. He always tells me a lot of things, but he never actually does them." I hesitated.

"Like what?" Jack leaned forward, intrigue written all over his face.

"I don't know, like everything. He promised he'd be at my graduation, and then he didn't show. He says he won't be late to things, but he always is. Or how he'll buy me something, but then he doesn't. He makes promises he can't keep. All. The. Time. But it's not just to me, you know? He tells other people things and they believe him. And when he doesn't come through, I'm usually the one left picking up the pieces since he's nowhere to be found."

I paused, suddenly insecure with my admission. "Is that stupid?"

"No. Your dad sounds like an ass." He frowned, his face twisted with disgust.

I looked into his eyes and then down at his mouth before continuing. "Have you ever noticed how pretty and beautiful words can be? How easy it is to say the things you think someone wants to hear. How you can affect a person's entire day with just a few measly sentences?"

My slight smile dropped. "But when you don't follow them up with any action, they're completely pointless. They're just sounds and syllables. But they mean absolutely nothing." My gaze glossed over as my mind wandered.

He reached across the table for my hands, but pulled away quickly before he touched them. I watched as he grabbed two loose quarters from the pile and scooted them over to my side of the table. "Almost forgot." He smiled before placing his hands on top of mine.

I tried not to smile, but failed. Heat swirled throughout my hands at his touch and I tried to tame the butterflies that flapped wildly in the pit of my stomach.

"I knew you had daddy issues."

My smile faded as I ripped my hands out from under his. "You're such an asshole," I said defensively, feeling stupid for sharing anything of importance with him.

"If you stop calling me names, I'll tell you something personal about me."

"I don't want to know." I folded my arms across my chest.

He swallowed his food when loud shouts drew his attention. He looked up from our table, grumbling under his breath.

"What is it?" I asked him, looking around for the source of the shouting. My eyes fell on two muscular-looking guys in baseball hats. "Friends of yours?"

"Not exactly."

I took another bite of my burger when a loud *thwap* diverted my attention. I jumped in my seat and noticed one of the guys had pounded his fist on top of our table, causing the quarters to spill out around me. I reached for my drink, steadying it before it toppled over. I looked at Jack, whose face was slowly turning a shade of purple. His hand flexed, his knuckles whitening with each compression.

"Get out of my face, Jared," he threatened, his jaw tight.

"Not so tough sober, eh Jack?"

Jack looked at me with pleading eyes, as if apologizing for what was to come. Then he glared up at the unwelcome visitors crowding our table. "You're just begging to get your ass kicked twice in one week, aren't ya?"

"Get up!" Jared challenged.

"Can't you see I'm on a date?" He gestured toward me.

Jared glanced in my direction. "Like she matters. Just one of many, isn't that what you always say?"

Jack jumped out from behind the table and puffed out his chest. "Don't talk about her like that. Don't even fucking look at her. You hear me?" He took a step toward Jared, his fist clenched tightly at his side.

Jared noticed Jack's intent and offered slyly, "Another time then."

"I highly doubt that." Jack seethed, the veins in his neck throbbing.

Jared leaned in close to my face before walking away. "At least you're pretty. Come find me after he tosses you into the garbage with all the others. I promise to sleep with you more than once."

My mouth opened to respond when Jared's body was suddenly ripped out of view. Jack pummeled him against the floor with a loud thud. Jared tried to kick, but Jack was too quick, moving out of the way before he could make contact. Jared scrambled to get up, but Jack threw his fist into Jared's jaw as the sound of bones crunching filled the air.

"I told you," Jack said as he punched him again, "…not to talk to her." Another hit and I gasped when Jared's bright red blood splattered across the clean, white-tiled floor.

I shook my head, struggling to make sense of this crazy, unexpected scene. "Jack! Jack, stop!" I scooted out of the booth and pulled at the shirt stretched across his back, begging for his assault to end. Jack delivered another blow to the ribs and I threw my body onto his back, leaning as close to his ear as I could get without getting hit. "Jack, stop."

His head snapped up. He glanced down at Jared, then lifted his head to look around at the gawking crowd and then back to me, his eyes sad. "I'm sorry, Kitten."

It was the first time that name didn't piss me off. I helped him to his feet, my body shaking with shock.

Our waitress, Sarah, hurried over, shaking her head. "You have to go, Jack. Just get your stuff and go."

"Sarah, tell Carl I'm sorry about the mess." Jack wiped his face, still red from anger, and now probably embarrassment as well. He scooped the quarters into their paper bag and tossed two twenties on the table before grabbing my hand and pulling me out the door.

When we reached the car, he opened the passenger door, lifted me in, and then walked over to the driver's side, his head shaking the entire time. I watched his chest slowly rise and fall with each breath he took. "I'm sorry, Cassie. I shouldn't have let him get to me."

"What was that even about?" I asked, eyeing his bloody knuckles.

Jack settled into the driver's seat and looked out his window, avoiding my gaze. "I slept with his girlfriend."

My heart throbbed as his admission caused an ache of disappointment to spread throughout my chest. "Right when I think you might be halfway decent, you say something that fucks it all up."

He gripped the steering wheel tightly and turned to me, his dark hair flopping forward. "I didn't know."

"Don't bullshit me, Jack."

"I'm not. I promise. She said she was single."

I sank into my seat as the breath I unwittingly held escaped from between my lips. "Well, she sucks. That girl."

He forced half a grin. "Yeah, she does."

He started the engine and I felt the rumble violently vibrating my seat. I quickly buckled myself in and said a silent prayer that we wouldn't die on the drive home.

We spent the drive back to my apartment in silence, the radio providing background noise as we each buried ourselves in our own private thoughts. I watched as the lights of the town streamed past in a neon blur, my mind replaying the events of the evening. Jack pulled his deathmobile in one of the spots marked VISITOR in front of my building, and turned the ignition off, but didn't make any effort to move. I reached for my door handle. "You know," he said, "my dad's an ass too." His voice sliced through the warm evening air.

I allowed my hand to slide down the side of the door, releasing the grip I held. I turned my body to face him before I leaned back into the seat. "Tell me."

He avoided my eyes, reluctant to continue. I wondered if he regretted starting to open up to me, but I wasn't about to let him off the hook.

"Please?"

"He took off when Dean was three. He just left one morning for work and never came back. My mom was frantic looking for him. Called every hospital, police station, hotel, but he was nowhere. I remember her tearing through the phone book with such fear and desperation in her eyes. She flipped the pages and tried to dial the numbers, but her fingers were shaking so badly I had to do it for her." He sighed sadly. "We had just celebrated my birthday the week before."

I wanted to reach out for him, but didn't. Thinking that somehow my touch would stop his train of thought and I wouldn't get to experience this side of him again, I kept my hands tucked between my legs and pressed my lips firmly together.

"I don't really remember my dad. But when my mom left…"

I could no longer stay silent. "Your mom left you guys too?" My mouth fell open in shock as my heart literally ached for him.

"Yeah. I distinctly remember her saying that we were *so bad*, she couldn't take it anymore. She said she couldn't raise two bad boys on her own, so she had to go."

"Holy shit. She said that? How old were you?" Each breath I took felt like it was being ripped from my lungs.

"I was eight. Dean was five."

"Jack, I'm so sorry. I can't even imagine." I reached out my hand and settled it on his thigh.

He eyed it for a split second. "Fifty cents, Kitten." I jerked my hand away, shaking my head.

"I was just joking, Cass. Listen, don't say anything to anyone, okay? Not many people know that story and I'd like to keep it that way if possible."

"Of course. It's not my story to tell." I smiled, hoping he believed me.

The moment I thought he was done revealing his past, he continued. "My mom walked out the door just as my grandparents were pulling into our driveway. I remember hearing yelling, car doors slamming, and tires screeching. And I'll never forget the sound of Dean crying and screaming out for her."

His eyes looked like he was a million miles away as I watched him relive his childhood nightmare. "The next thing I remember was my grandmother's smiling face walking through our front door. She told us to run upstairs and pack our things so we could sleep over at her house. I think it was really hard on them, suddenly having two little boys around, but my grandparents never complained. Not once." He scratched the back of his neck.

"Have you seen your mom since?"

"No." His response was sharp.

"Haven't heard from her or anything?" I asked, wondering what kind of mother could just up and leave her two boys and never come back.

"Not a word."

I shook my head in disbelief. "I can't imagine. So, how rotten of a kid were you," I asked with a smile, not really meaning the question.

He reclined the driver's side seat and focused his gaze on the night sky. "Pretty rotten. Dean wasn't, though. I mean, he was, but he was just copying me. He stopped being bad the minute she left. I think he thought if he was the perfect son, it would bring her back. She'd come home if he was extra good all the time," he said as he tilted his head toward me, "...or something."

"What about you?"

"I was so angry. I thought it was all my fault that she left. So I figured if she was never coming back, what was the point in being good? I got into a lot of trouble."

"Like what kind of trouble?"

He took a deep breath. "I got in a lot of fights." He looked into my eyes and shrugged his shoulders. "Guess that hasn't changed much." His stomach moved in and out as he laughed bitterly and I found my eyes drawn there.

"He deserved it," I whispered, reclining my seat as well.

"He did, right?"

I smiled.

"I got in a lot of fights. And I got in a lot of trouble with girls. I basically took on the philosophy in high school that if I could either hook up with a girl at every party, or beat someone up, then they wouldn't talk about the fact that I had no parents. Fucking and fighting were the ultimate distraction."

I frowned, my stomach churning slightly at his bold revelation.

"What?" He turned his head toward me, his eyes concerned.

"It's just that you still sort of act like that, you know?"

"I know. Old habits are hard to break. Plus, I'm good at being bad and screwing things up. Just ask Dean."

I wasn't sure what to say. I honestly wasn't sure how I felt. I'd never met anyone who had lost both of their parents except to death. I couldn't imagine living with that knowledge, or feeling somewhat responsible for it happening.

"When did you start playing baseball?"

His eyes lit up. "My grandparents signed us up for every sport imaginable when we moved in. They thought it would help." A slight chuckle escaped from his lips, his mouth curving upward. "I don't remember, but my grandma said I would cry whenever the season ended."

I laughed, imagining the scene in my mind. "That's cute. You loved it even then."

He released a breath. "Being on that pitcher's mound, it's the one thing I'm really good at. The one thing I haven't fucked up. And when I'm on the field, everything else fades away. You know?" He turned to look at me, his eyes craving understanding.

I smiled and he continued. "It's like my mind is clear when I'm out there. It's not about my mom or my dad or the stupid shit I've done. It's about me, the ball, and the batter. It's the one place in the world where I feel like I'm in control. Like I have a say in what happens around me."

I stopped my head from nodding in agreement once I realized that I was doing it. "I feel that way when I'm taking pictures. Anything that I'm not seeing through my lens fades away in the background. And I get to frame my picture any way I choose. I get to dictate how it looks. What's in it. What isn't. Behind that lens I have complete control in how things are seen."

He smiled, his dimples indenting his cheeks. "You get it."

"I like this side of you," I said, genuinely

meaning it.

He crossed his arms across his chest. "Don't get used to it."

I jerked back at his suddenly defensive tone. "Way to ruin a perfectly good moment with your craptitude."

"Craptitude?" he mocked.

"Yeah. Your crappy attitude." I pulled my seat upright and reached for the door handle again.

"Fuck. I'm sorry, Kitten. Don't hate me. I just really suck at this." His hand gripped my shoulder, pulling me back toward him.

"Suck at what?"

"This." His finger wagged between my face and his.

"What? Having a serious conversation? I know, it's really hard." It was all I could do not to roll my eyes.

"I don't really have serious conversations with girls," he admitted reluctantly.

"That's seriously pathetic, Jack."

"If I haven't conveyed to you by now that I have a hard time trusting people—" he started to explain before I cut him off.

"I know you do. And you have every right. But you have to start somewhere." He breathed loudly and I finished, "Sooner or later you have to let people in."

*And by "people," I really meant me.*

*Shit.*

He leaned toward me and I could feel the warmth of his breath against my face. "I know," he murmured, closing the small space between us even further.

He cupped my cheek in the palm of his hand and looked into my eyes. "I'm going to kiss you." My heart hammered inside my chest as thoughts of stopping him raced through my mind.

"This doesn't change anything," I stammered, my defenses fading.

"It changes everything." He sounded so sure of himself as his soft lips silenced my weak protest.

My eyes closed and I lost myself in the warmth of his kiss. His cinnamon-flavored tongue gently parted my lips as I allowed him to explore my mouth. He was gentle, the flicker of his tongue soft and slow, causing my heart to expand. His fingers tangled tenderly in the back of my hair, tugging lightly. I lifted my hand to the side of his face, my thumb tracing the lines of his cheek down to his chin before gripping the back of his neck and pulling him closer.

My mouth was frantic, all sense of composure lost somewhere in the taste of him. He pulled away, our mouths parting with one final, closed-mouth peck.

"It changes everything," he repeated, still cupping my face in his hand.

"Prove it."

# SIX
## JACK

*- One Month Later-*

*Prove it* were the two words she said to me before hopping out of my car and running through her apartment door that night. She didn't trust people either. Or more to the point, she didn't trust me. Cassie Andrews didn't need rescuing, but I still wanted to save her.

She wanted me to prove that she was different from all the other girls I'd been with. Apparently she didn't realize she already was. I asked her out on a date and I *never* ask girls out. Hooking up at a party or a club was one thing. That's easy. I can do anything with a beer in my hand, or an audience watching.

But asking Cassie out in the daylight, dead sober, with no one around…that was something I'd never done before. She made me nervous as hell. I knew she wasn't like other girls the moment I saw the disgusted look on her face after I called her "Kitten." Most girls would have creamed their pants if I called them that. But not Cassie. She looked like she wanted to punch me in the jaw.

And I've wanted to kiss her ever since.

The first order of business in my prove-to-Cassie-I'm-serious agenda consisted of ditching my usual table filled with random fan-girls to sit with her in the student union. I figured that giving her priority attention in public showed my intent. The whispers and comments were brutal that first month with my teammates bagging on me every chance they got. Not to mention the relentless advances from what appeared to be every female on campus under the age of thirty.

I never realized how exhausting it was to turn women away. It was one thing to hook up with them and then call it a day, but to be off the market completely was something I'd never dealt with before. To put it simply, girls don't like being rejected, especially if it's because of another girl.

But no one knew what it was like to be me. I'd finally met a girl who didn't try to impress me. She didn't care about what I did as an athlete; she cared about what I did as a person. I was jumping into this thing with both feet. Holding on to Cassie with both arms.

Number two on my list consisted of spending as much time with her outside of school as possible. I made myself a regular at the apartment she shared with Melissa, where Cassie and I had become masters at making out.

I never knew you could spend hours just kissing a girl. I never knew because I'd never done it before. In the last month, I'd learned just how erotic kissing could be. Many nights I'd left her place unsatisfied sexually, but completely content emotionally.

*I sound like a fucking chick. I want to go drink a beer and punch something.*

That's better.

With enough food on my tray to feed an army, I passed a group of panting girls in the student union on my way toward Cassie. A sorority chick named Andrea stopped me with a hand on my arm. I moved away from her touch, scowling at her hand. "What?" I asked sharply, uninterested in whatever was about to spill from her lips.

"Our sorority formal is coming up, Jack." She paused, her eyelashes batting at a ridiculous pace. "And I thought you could come with?"

"No." The huge smile fell from her face.

"Why not? Is it because of her?" She sneered in Cassie's direction.

"None of your business, Andrea. And if you ever refer to my girlfriend like that again, I'll find someone to teach you a little respect."

She huffed at me, all offended, and I walked away, noticing Melissa laughing in my direction.

"You girls are a species all your own." I shook my head in disbelief as I nudged my tray against Cassie's.

She glanced around at the girls whispering and watching us. "Tell me about it."

"It's been a month, ladies. Time to get over it already." Melissa waved her hand into the air, her voice raised.

"Sorry to put you in the spotlight, Kitten." I knew she hated it when I called her that, but I couldn't help it. I liked it. I tossed my arm around her shoulder and pulled her into me, my thumb caressing her soft skin. Her hair tickled my neck as it fell around my back and I wished I could hold on to her forever. I kissed the top of her head before letting her go, her green eyes forming half moons as she smiled.

"I guess it comes with the territory." She looked at me, her cheeks tinged with pink.

"The territory of being Jack freaking Carter's girlfriend," Melissa added with a laugh.

"Glad you're on board with this, Melis." I smiled, encouraged by her attitude.

"Jack, you're still an asshole but you've grown on me. And if you hurt Cassie, I'll break your pitching arm. Capisce?"

"Capisce," I responded, purely to humor Cassie's fun-sized best friend.

I leaned into my girl, the smell of her shampoo engulfing my senses. "You know I'd never hurt you on purpose."

Cassie immediately turned to face me, her eyebrows pinched together. "That's not really reassuring. You know that, right?"

"I'm just being realistic. Don't want to make you promises I can't keep," I added, hinting at rule number three of her boy test.

"So you can't promise that you won't hurt me?" Her tone was annoyed and I instantly wished I could take back my words.

"Cass, I don't ever want to hurt you, but I can't promise you that I'll never screw up or make you mad." I paused, trying to make the thoughts in my head come out right.

"He's good at pissing people off. Isn't that right, big brother?" I looked up to see Dean smirking at me, and took a half-hearted swipe at him as he sat down next to me.

"That's the rumor." I nodded with a smile.

"Plus, if he pushes you away, then you won't be the one who left him. He'll be the one who made you leave," Dean added defiantly.

I glared at my little brother for his openness in such a public space. I glanced around, making sure no one was too close to overhear.

"I don't plan on going anywhere." Cassie put her hand on top of mine and squeezed. "So don't try to make me."

Relief coursed through my body with her reassurance. I had spent so much of my life convinced that no girl would ever want to be with the real me, that I'd never given anyone a chance to prove me wrong. If my own mom didn't love me enough to stay, how would anyone else?

"Jesus, I've never met two people more scared to let someone love them than the two of you,"

Melissa remarked with a frown.

I opened my mouth to protest when she continued, her ponytail bobbing from side to side as she moved her head. "And don't even try to deny it. You're both all messed up from your stupid parents. Cassie here," she lifted her hand in Cassie's direction, "with her dad's constant lies and inability to follow through on even the simplest, most mundane thing, has been disappointed and let down most of her life."

Her hand pointed in my direction. "And you, with your mom up and leaving, telling you it was your fault because you were a *bad kid*. You're convinced that no one will ever stick around. That eventually, they'll leave you too. And somewhere in your twisted, screwed-up psyche, you probably think you deserve it."

Melissa had finally dragged my sorry story out of me, late one night when the three of us were hanging out at their apartment. Cassie had kept her promise and hadn't told her best friend, so it was up to me to fill Melissa in. *Damn, it seemed like such a good idea at the time.*

Melissa took a quick breath and then delivered her final assessment. "You're both so screwed up alone that together you're like the perfect mess."

The table fell briefly silent as her rant sank in. I thought about protesting, but wasn't sure she was all that wrong.

"That's an attractive analogy. Thanks for saying I'm screwed up." Cassie's voice was sharp, her feelings clearly hurt.

I shot Melissa a murderous glare before reaching for Cassie's chin and turning her face to mine. "I'll be the perfect mess with you anytime."

Cassie quickly swiped under her eye and leaned her head against my shoulder. She released a deep sigh. "Melissa just doesn't know anything about having messed-up parents. Hers are perfect. She can't relate."

"Hey! It's not my fault I won the parent lottery." Melissa eyed Cassie. "Plus, we both know I'm not strong enough to deal with the shit you've dealt with. I would've had a nervous breakdown by now. I could never handle everything your dad's put you through."

Cassie's body shook lightly against mine as she released a slight laugh, causing the tension in my chest and back to release. I realized in that moment that her feelings affected my own. I'd never let anyone hurt her as long as I was around. And if they did, I'd sure as hell make them pay for it.

"I don't know if it's because I'm strong or because I've gotten really good at turning off my emotions," Cassie commented, her voice soft.

"It's definitely both." Melissa turned to me. "And Jack, I've never seen anyone completely shut off the way this one can." Her head tilted toward

Cass. "If you push her too far, she'll flick off like a light switch. It's scary."

"Really? That's impressive," I teased as my fingers caressed her side.

"You won't feel that way if she does it to you. Trust me." Melissa's face was the scary kind of serious.

"Well, I hope I never have to see it."

"If I didn't compartmentalize, I'd never be able to function! It's the only way I can survive without being a total basket case." Cassie's face was serious as she defended herself.

"I get it, Kitten. Still impressive." I smiled as she looked up at me.

"So when do you leave for Texas?" Dean's question changed the subject and broke the tension. Thank God for little brothers, especially those who can talk around a mouthful of cheeseburger.

"We fly out Thursday morning. Why?"

"Just wondering."

Cassie sat upright and turned to face me. "What do you do when you're there? Like how does it work? Do you practice? Do parents go?"

Cassie always had a million questions about everything, but it turned me on. She was so damn inquisitive and smart. "Well, we typically fly in the day before our games start. We check in at the hotel. We'll have practice and work out and have dinner as a team. Some parents go, but not many."

"Does everyone get their own room?" she asked, her voice half impressed, half shocked.

"No." I let out a laugh. "We share rooms."

"Do you have like bed checks and stuff?"

I nodded and noticed Melissa's elbows planted firmly on the table, her ears taking in every word. "We do. Usually Coach comes by and makes sure everyone's in their rooms by ten."

Her face softened. "Any other rules?"

I felt my mouth form a half smile. "No girls and no drinking," I said with a chuckle.

She shoved against my shoulder. "I'm sure those rules never get broken, huh?"

"Nope. We're all complete angels when we're on the road." My gaze darted between Melissa and Cassie, then fell on Dean, silently daring him to contradict me.

Dean let out a hearty laugh. "Angels, my ass."

"No, wait wait wait!" Cassie's voice broke through the chorus of laughter. "Do you guys sneak girls in your rooms? Like random strangers?"

I felt her eyes pierce mine. She wanted the truth and I didn't want to lie to her. "Yeah."

She rolled her eyes at my one-word response.

"Kitten. The eyes."

"You're such a pig." She shook her head with disgust.

"This isn't news! But I'm a changed man, Kitten. I swear it." I took her chin in my fingers and pleaded, wanting her to believe me.

"We'll see about that." She stared back at me, her smirk evidence of her disbelief.

"Care to make a wager?" I offered, dying to loosen up the tense atmosphere.

Her face crinkled at my suggestion. "Please, tell me you don't need a bet to stay faithful. I swear to God, Jack."

I felt her body tighten as she angled away from me. With one humorous comment, I'd changed her body language completely. It was as though I could feel her replacing the bricks around her heart that I'd already knocked down. One by one, she cemented them back into place where she felt they belonged.

This away series was going to be the first real test in our relationship. She wasn't sure she could trust me. I didn't blame her though, but I was damn sure going to prove her wrong.

# SEVEN
## CASSIE

I paced nervously around the kitchen while I waited for Jack to arrive.

"Why are you pacing? What the hell's wrong with you?" Melissa looked up from her textbook and eyed me.

"I don't know. I'm sorta freaking out," I admitted, taking a swig from my water glass.

"About what? Seriously, Cass, I haven't seen the guy even touch another girl since your crazy date that night." Melissa tried to catch my gaze, her eyebrows raised.

I shook my head and continued wearing down the kitchen floor. "It's not that."

"Then what is it?" She sat up straighter, laying her pencil in between the pages of her book and closing it shut.

I stopped walking, took another drink, and swallowed forcefully. "I just don't get why Dean can't take him to the bus tomorrow. Why does he want me to do it? And why is he leaving me his death machine?"

Melissa sighed heavily. "Jesus, Cassie. Can't the guy do something nice for you?"

"How is that nice?"

"Last time I checked, genius, your car is sitting pretty back at home." She smirked, her head swiveling back and forth in disbelief at my stupidity.

"So?"

"So he's leaving you his. That's nice of him."

"I guess." She had a point, but my defenses were still up. "But why is he staying over?"

Melissa's mouth fell open as she leaned her head back. "I'm such an idiot," she admitted before smacking her palm against her forehead. "This is your first sleepover with Jack. You're scared to spend the night with him. That's what this is about."

My stomach flipped and rolled with her words. I stared at the black-and-white-tiled kitchen counter, my eyes losing focus until the pattern became an unrecognizable swirl of hazy dark and light hues.

"Earth to Cassie, hello?" Melissa snapped her fingers in my direction and my eyes jerked up to meet hers.

"I'm not scared." My stupid voice shook slightly. "I'm just…not ready."

"Why the hell not?"

"Because once you give your body to a guy, there's no taking it back. And once you've done that it opens up feelings, emotions, and vulnerabilities you never knew you were capable of having. I'm not ready to give him my heart. What if he breaks it?"

"What if he doesn't?" Melissa shot back.

The quick knock on the door startled us both and Melissa gathered her composure before I did.

"Come in," she yelled behind her.

The door swung open and Jack walked in, carrying his baseball bag in one hand and an overnight bag in the other. I watched as he dropped the baseball bag next to the door and then disappeared with his overnight bag into my bedroom. I quickly widened my eyes at Melissa before he waltzed back into the room. She stifled a laugh.

"Hey, Kitten." He nuzzled his lips against my neck and I felt my knees begin to shake.

I forced a nervous smile. "Hungry?"

"Starved," he answered, before his lips met mine.

All my thoughts scrambled inside my head as I released them and lost myself in his mouth. Warm cinnamon engulfed my senses as his breath and touch consumed me. No matter how hard I tried to fight it, Jack Carter always turned me to mush.

*So much for that wall of yours, Cass. Kiss it good-bye.*

When he pulled away, I braced my hand against the countertop to steady my shaking body. Once I was certain my legs would carry me without falling, I headed toward the refrigerator and opened the door, tearing through every tray and cabinet.

"Your options are grilled cheese, mac and cheese, or a quesadilla," I announced, somewhat embarrassed by our lack of food choices.

"I can only pick one?" Jack teased. "What if I want them all?"

"Then you can make them." I smirked while holding the door open with one arm. "Jack, tell me what you want!"

"I sort of do want them all. Is that bad? I'll help." His face crinkled as he braced for my reaction.

I couldn't help but laugh. "Fine. You make the mac and cheese and I'll make the rest. Deal?"

I watched as the tension released from his tanned cheeks and those irresistible dimples appeared. "Deal!"

"Look at you two. Cooking in the kitchen like an old married couple," Melissa remarked from a safe distance.

I turned toward her wishing I could suddenly shoot darts from my eyes. "Old married couple, my ass. We haven't even made it through one road trip."

Jack put down the pot he held and reached for me. He wrapped his arms around my waist and held on to me tightly. "Kitten, are you worried about this road trip? I'm not going to fuck up. I promise."

I avoided his eyes, looking straight past him toward the white wall in the distance. His fingers were suddenly caressing my cheek, before they forced my chin upward. "Look at me, Cass," he pleaded softly.

I closed my eyes tight before opening them and focusing on his. It was so hard to put my feelings into words, all my insecurities and fears coiled inside me, eating away at the trust we'd built.

"I don't want any other girl." He brought my hand to his lips and kissed it gently. "You hear me?"

"I hear you," was all I could force out in a whisper.

"But do you believe me?" He cocked his head to one side and raised an eyebrow.

I shrugged my shoulder. "I guess we'll see."

"Damn straight we'll see." He jerked his head playfully. "I'll prove it to you."

I rolled my eyes and he pressed his warm mouth against mine, his tongue parting my lips. I jerked away. "If this is your way of proving it…"

His mouth instantly found mine again, the heat between us hot enough to start a fire. The taut muscles of his abs pressed tightly against my stomach. I found myself suddenly aware of his fingers and their location against the small of my back, pulling me against him. His body grew harder with every moment that passed and my defenses lowered.

I maneuvered my hands underneath his shirt and ran my fingers along the curves of his back. His skin was smooth and soft, yet hard and muscular. I found myself unable to stop exploring as I caressed every inch I could reach of his warm skin. Feeling his body this way sent excited tingles shooting throughout my entire body. He pressed the hardness in his jeans against me and I struggled to catch my breath. And even though I wasn't ready to be one of Jack Carter's conquests, I found it difficult to resist him when I was this turned on.

Melissa cleared her throat. "Jesus, you two. I feel like I should leave a tip after watching that."

I peeled my tingling body away from his and wiped at my bottom lip, lust blurring my vision.

"We take quarters." Jack smirked before leaning in for one last peck.

Melissa's face contorted with confusion at the inside joke I realized I'd never shared with her. "Whatever. I have to finish my homework. Hurry up and make me some food."

Jack impressed me by not only helping cook dinner, but cleaning up as well. He attempted to swat me with the dish towel a total of twelve times. It annoyed the hell out of me, but I'll admit I also found it endearing. I shook my head absentmindedly, lost in thought.

"What are you shaking your head at?" Jack asked, leaning his hip against the counter.

"I was just thinking about us." I flashed him a reassuring smile as I placed the towel back around the handle of the stove.

"Oh, yeah? What about us?" He took a step

toward me.

I put my hand up to stop him. "Just about how differently I feel about you today versus when we met at the party that night."

"And how do you feel about me today?" He grabbed my hand and tucked it behind my back, pulling my body against his.

"Well, I don't hate you today." I smiled, my heart rate picking up speed.

His lips moved toward my face, brushing against my cheek without stopping. "You didn't hate me that night either," he whispered, his breath hot against my ear.

Excited chills replaced my will to playfully fight back. I pushed him and spun on my heels away from his hot body. "I have to get ready for bed."

"I'll come with you," he called out to my retreating back.

I stopped and turned to face him, my eyes narrowing. "No, you will not." I pressed my hand firmly against his hard chest. "You'll stay right here until I'm done. Go watch *SportsCenter* or *Baseball Tonight* or something."

His eyebrows pulled together. "Seriously?"

"Seriously."

His face softened, a half smile appearing. "Okay, Kitten. You get ready for bed and I'll wait here."

I assumed he thought I was up to something, but

the truth was I had no intention of doing anything sexual with him tonight. I wasn't ready and before this night was through, I was going to have to admit that to him. It was a conversation I dreaded having. I washed the makeup off my face, brushed my teeth, and slipped into my pink tank top and white boxer shorts before reentering the living room.

"You can come in now," I announced from the doorway.

Jack's gaze slid over my body, then he pushed himself up from the couch and sauntered toward me, a smile plastered across his cheeks. "Night, Melissa." He smacked my backside with his hand and steered me toward my bedroom.

"Stop it, brat!" I shouted as I ran into the bedroom. I watched as he closed the door behind him and then reached into his overnight bag.

"I brought you something." He pulled an empty mason jar from his bag and handed it to me.

I turned it in my hand, my eyes narrowed in confusion before reading the handwritten note stuck to the opposite side: KITTEN'S QUARTERS. I laughed out loud before placing the jar on top of my dresser.

"These too." He pulled out the bag of quarters from our first date, the sound of them clinking against one another taking me back in time.

"Cute." I smiled as he poured the contents of the bag into the jar.

"You owe me a lot of touches, Kitten." His lips

pursed together, his tone teasing.

"Apparently. Who knew you could be so clever?"

"Everyone except you," he answered in that cocky tone so uniquely his.

"Oh, here we go," I said, rolling my eyes.

"Kitten." Jack's brows pulled together, his voice stern. "What did I tell you about the eyes?" He took two steps toward me and our faces nearly touched. He brushed his hand along my cheek before placing it behind my neck and pulling my mouth to his. His tongue parted my lips and entered. His hand followed the lines of my curves until stopping on my hip with a firm grip. My eyes rolled behind closed eyelids as I lost myself in his touch.

And as quickly as it began, he pulled away, a satisfied smirk plastered all over his face. He bent down near his overnight bag and pulled out a leather pouch filled with his things. "Is it okay if I jump in the shower?"

"Of course. There's a towel under the sink." I smiled, still trying to catch my faltering breath. My eyes refused to look away from him as he ripped his shirt off and dropped it to the floor near my sink. His tanned, well-defined arms caused my insides to stir. He unzipped his shorts before stepping out of them and promptly pressed his body against the counter as he reached for the toothpaste. I forced myself to look away before I started actually drooling at the sight of him in nothing but some well-fitting boxer briefs.

Staying strong tonight might be harder than I thought.

When the shower turned off, he opened the door, my green towel wrapped tightly around his waist. Beads of water dripped from his wet black hair as coils of hazy steam swirled around him.

"Kitten, can you throw me a pair of briefs?"

I tossed off the covers and crept out of bed toward his duffle bag. I opened the flap of fabric and noticed dress shirts, ties, and slacks. "What's with all the dressy clothes?"

"We have to dress up whenever we travel."

"Seriously? Why?"

"Because, Kitten, it's the rules. We have to look presentable. And we're a professional college baseball team. We have to make a good impression."

"Huh, I guess that makes sense," I said, before rooting around for his briefs.

He laughed. "It's a hell of a lot better than a bunch of rowdy guys in t-shirts and baggy shorts."

"That's true!" I rooted around in his bag and grabbed the first pair I could find. "Here," I said, throwing the undergarment toward his feet.

"Thanks, babe," he responded before allowing the towel to drop to the floor. I felt my jaw drop right along with it as my eyes refused to look away.

My insides flushed with heat as he turned his head to face me. He smiled confidently before reaching for the briefs and slipping into them.

*Holy shit. This night might kill me.*

"Like what you see?" Jack teased, his eyebrow cocked as he slipped into bed next to me.

"Why don't you just date a mirror?" I shot back, his cockiness forcing my defensive nature to re-emerge.

"For starters, I can't have sex with a mirror." His mouth formed into a slight smirk that made me want to smack him. Before I could respond his mouth was on mine, his tongue minty from my toothpaste.

My tough defenses faded as the warmth of his skin penetrated my thin clothing, his lower body grinding against mine. The feeling of his hardness working against me caused a slight moan to escape from my lips.

"I want you, Cassie." Jack touched his lips against my neck. His tongue was warm on my skin as he licked his way up toward my ear, his breath raspy and hot. "I want you," he whispered breathily before nibbling on my earlobe, the grinding between my legs continuing.

"Jack." I spoke his name between breaths. "Jack, stop." He stopped moving and I felt his heart thumping rapidly against my chest. His thumb rested on the side of my face as I lost myself in the brown of his eyes. "I'm sorry. I want to…just not tonight."

I braced myself for his reaction, unsure of what it would consist of. In the past, it royally pissed guys off if I'd asked them to stop. They acted as if it was their God-given right to have sex with me, whether I was ready or not. Guys seemed to change into different people whenever their dicks were involved.

All warmth left me as Jack rolled onto his side, his body still facing mine. "It's okay, Kitten. I don't want to do it if you're not ready." He leaned toward me, his lips pressing against the tip of my nose.

"Thanks." I smiled, grateful he didn't seem angry.

"But you'll be ready soon, right?" He couldn't keep a straight face as the words left his lips. "I'm kidding. No pressure." He smiled, his voice reassuring and calm.

I smiled in relief at his understanding as he reached for me. He hugged me tightly before placing my head against his chest, both arms wrapped around me. "Would it help if you knew I was falling in love with you?"

I tore myself from his grip, my eyes locking on his. "Don't fuck with me, Jack Carter."

He stifled a laugh as he reached for me. "I'm not."

I leaned down to kiss him, my emotions

tangling up inside me. "Say it," I begged as my tongue swept across his bottom lip.

"So much for no pressure," Jack teased, his eyebrows furrowing.

"Say it," I begged again.

"I," he hesitated before looking me square in the eyes, his head nodding, "I love you." He pulled at the back of my neck, his mouth devouring every part of mine.

"Jack." I breathed his name as I melted into him, my legs wrapped around his waist. And just like that, those three little words had changed me. Desire overwhelmed me as I longed to be connected to him in every possible way. I wished for the space between us to disappear as I inched my body closer to his. "I want you."

He pulled back slightly. "We don't have to do this, that's not why I said it," he said, running his fingers down my back.

"I know it's not, but I want to." I was actually surprised at myself, my pelvis grinding slowly against his as my desire grew.

"You sure?" He searched my eyes as he asked one last time.

"You trying to talk me out of it?" I teased and rolled away from him.

His eyes widened as he watched me scoot out of my boxer shorts, revealing the light blue thong hidden underneath. He tossed my shorts onto the floor before leaning over and tenderly kissing the top of my foot. He knelt down and worked his hands and mouth up my calf to my thigh, not an inch of skin left untouched. I practically vibrated with excitement and need, but allowed him to continue to explore.

He shifted upward and continued his way up my belly, lifting my tank top off in one swift motion before lightly kissing the space between my breasts. Lowering his body completely onto mine, he pressed his lips against my neck before heading back to my mouth, where I waited anxiously for him.

My hands dug into his back, his muscles hard and tense. I tugged at the waistband of his boxer briefs, trying in vain to lower them. He slipped them off and I felt his excitement grow as his body pressed against mine. "Do you have anything?" he asked before taking the final step.

"You don't?" I asked incredulously.

"I meant to bring one," he explained slowly, his breath hot against my ear. "Just in case, you know?"

I shifted my weight, turning to look at him, "Mm-hmm. Just in case, huh?"

"Well, you can't blame a guy for hoping." His eyebrows arched. "But I forgot it at home."

"Seriously?"

"Seriously," he responded solemnly.

"Well," I hesitated, "I got on the pill when we

started dating."

"You did?"

"Mm-hmm." I smiled sheepishly, embarrassed at the revelation as he pressed his wet lips against mine.

He pulled away slowly. "I've never..." He started to say before stopping short.

"Never what?" My breaths quickened, his hesitance making my confidence waver.

His eyes met mine with longing and uncertainty. "I've never done it like this before," he admitted.

"In a bed?" I teased, unsure of his meaning.

"No." He paused. "I mean like this. Without anything else."

I was almost awestruck when I realized that *like this* meant without a condom. Jack's vulnerability shone through him in that exact moment like a lighthouse beacon in a raging storm. Somewhere along the way, we'd crossed an imaginary line where feelings and emotions blurred into the unknown. A place neither of us dared go before.

"Really? Not ever?" I slid my hand down the back of his neck, his muscles straining against my fingertips.

"Never. If I didn't have one, I didn't do it. There's never been anyone like you, Cassie. There never will be." His admission silenced us both as the weight of the moment sunk in.

"Do you still want to?" I trembled as the words

left my lips.

He shifted and I felt my panties slide down my legs and leave my body in one fluid motion. That was all the answer I needed as my breathing increased with every kiss, every touch, every electric-filled moment. He stopped and cupped my face with both hands. "You know this changes things." His eyes searched mine for acceptance and understanding.

"Prove it," I said with a slight smile, remembering the words I spoke after our first kiss.

"I love you, Cassie." His voice was so sincere that I blinked back the tears pooling in my eyes.

"I love you too," I admitted, my protective walls crumbling to piles of dust around my jagged heart.

His lips were instantly back on mine, his tongue passionately exploring the inside of my mouth. With one easy thrust, I felt him inside me. I inhaled quickly, a pleasure-filled moan escaping my lips.

"Are you okay?" he asked, his movement slowing.

"I'm fine, keep going." I closed my eyes, wanting more.

"Oh my God, you feel incredible." He breathed heavily against my ear. "Holy shit, I may never recover from this."

His hands pressed against my shoulders, his muscles flexing as he worked his body gently in and out of mine. I moved my hips in time with his, causing a throaty growl to escape from within him.

I opened my eyes and raked my fingers through his hair. I followed the lines of his body down his back where beads of sweat were pooling. The muscles in his back tensed as I reached my arms around him. My hands came to rest on his backside and I pulled him deeper into me with every thrust. Another throaty moan and he pressed his sweaty cheek against mine, his labored breathing whooshing in and out of my ear.

His breath was hot against my neck. "I've never loved anyone before, so go easy on me."

I turned my head to face him and pressed my mouth against his. "Jack," I whispered with a sigh. "Don't stop." I continued pulling him to me as our bodies slid against each other. His thrusts caused a tension to build inside me, growing quickly as I felt myself striving to meet them desperately, grasping for something I'd never experienced quite this strongly before.

My body tingled everywhere, from my scalp all the way down to my toes. A heated wave of sensation and emotion swept over me, engulfing me as my body seized in a contraction of pulses, all centered at my core.

His movements quickened with urgency in response to mine, and I lifted my hips to rise and fall in time with his. "Cassie…" He stared into my eyes and I smiled bravely, yet for a moment, I felt completely exposed.

"It's okay," I said softly, and tightened my intimate grip around him. He bit his bottom lip and his eyes narrowed as I felt him explode and pulsate inside me. He quivered before relaxing and allowing his body to fall on top of mine.

"I...can't...breathe," I complained playfully, pushing at his shoulders.

"Sorry." He laughed and rolled onto his side. "That...was amazing," he said between labored breaths.

He leaned into me, kissing my nose before propping up on one arm. "I love you. I'm sure I'll fuck it up because I don't know what the hell I'm doing. Just promise me that you'll be patient with me. Grade me on a learning curve or something?"

"You should really go into sales, you know that?" I teased, rolling my eyes.

"Promise me, Kitten. Patience."

"Only if you promise not to do anything that embarrasses me or makes me look stupid."

"Deal." He grinned and I leaned in to kiss his dimples, my limbs tangled up with his.

I'll admit I was scared. We'd crossed the line and my heart would never be the same, no matter what happened from here on out. But if I wanted him to believe in us, I had to believe in him.

*****

I drove Jack to the baseball stadium at five the

next morning. When we arrived, I looked over at the rumbling bus and Jack's arriving teammates. I laughed when I noticed Jamie, a girlfriend of one of Jack's teammates, driving a monster-sized truck. She looked terrified behind the wheel and her expression brought me relief since I assumed my face probably looked the same. Glancing over at me, she shrugged her shoulders, and I waved in response.

Jack hopped out of his death machine, grabbed his bags, and sauntered over to the driver's side where I reluctantly sat.

"Take care of my pride and joy." He grinned, his dimples making an appearance.

"You know it's just going to sit in the parking lot at my apartment, right?" I shrugged.

He laughed before grabbing the back of my neck and pulling me toward him. "I'll text you when I get there." His mouth covered mine as hoots and hollers filtered into the air. He pulled away, turned around, and flipped off his teammates.

"Amateurs." He laughed.

"It's the first time they've ever been able to give you shit. They're excited." I pressed my lips together and smiled.

He leaned in, giving me one last kiss before walking away, his body disappearing behind his two large bags.

# EIGHT

I sat in my Comm Law class as my professor droned on about the legal regulations of mass communication as it applied to freedom of speech and the press. Instead of taking notes, my mind drifted to thoughts of Jack and our night together. I absentmindedly placed my pen near my mouth and started chewing on the cap, my eyes blurring over.

Maryse, the gorgeous brunette next to me, nudged me with her elbow, breaking my trance. I turned to look at her and she lifted her chin toward the front of the class where our teacher was writing down topics for our next test.

"Thanks," I whispered with a sideways glance.

"No problem." She smiled. "You're dating Jack Carter, right?" I nodded. "Screw this class, I'd be thinking about him too." She giggled quietly.

I stifled a laugh and let out a long, drawn-out breath, knowing I'd been caught. Our professor ended his lecture and Maryse stood up when I did, following behind me as the class dispersed. Once outside, she appeared next to me, her full hair bouncing with each step. "So how did you get the elusive Jack Carter to fall for you?"

"I really don't know. I guess you'd have to ask him that." I smiled and dropped my sunglasses over my eyes.

"Every girl at this school has been chasing him for years," she said, acting as though this was new information to me.

"Maybe that's just it. I didn't chase him."

Her eyes widened. "Ahhh, so he chased you? That probably would be a first for him." She applied a shiny gloss to her lips and puckered before pushing the tube back into her pocket. "Guys love the chase. It's once you're caught that you have to be careful."

I glimpsed at her. "What do you mean?"

"I'm just saying a guy like Jack Carter isn't fit to be tied down. I can see him enjoying a challenge, which is what you were. But you're not anymore 'cause he has you. Where's the fun in that?"

I didn't respond, unsure of what to say in my defense. What if she was right? What if it was all a game to him? At first he couldn't have me, then he got me. Then I wouldn't give it up, but I just did. There were no more challenges.

The pathway split and Maryse peeled away to head in the other direction. "I have another class right now. Media Ethics. Snore." She rolled her eyes. "I'll see you Monday. Don't forget to study!"

"See you Monday," I answered with half a smile as my mind raced.

I wandered toward the student union, noticing the lack of activity that normally bustled around it. It was weird to admit that a sports team had that much of a presence on campus, but they really did. The lack of energy when they were gone was noticeable.

When I opened the door, the usual obnoxious sound of girlish chatter was absent. I glanced around the almost empty space and laughed to myself as I headed toward Melissa and Dean. If the team wasn't here, then the fan-girls weren't either. That revelation was almost as weird as it was disturbing.

I hadn't taken two steps before an overly friendly blonde reached out a tanned arm to stop me.

"Hi. It's Cassie, right? I'm Mollie, and I was just wondering if you and Jack were still dating?" She made sure her voice was loud enough for her three eavesdropping friends to hear.

I pinched my eyebrows together, my body tensing. "Why?"

"Well, it's just that my friend from Texas sent me this photo last night from her cell. That *is* Jack, right?" she asked, holding her phone out where I could see it and giggling while her friends anxiously waited for my reaction.

I leaned toward the phone and squinted at the grainy photo on its screen. It was definitely Jack holding open a hotel room door as a skinny, dark-haired girl walked through it.

"And this one too." She scrolled to another photo of Jack smiling while closing the door behind his new friend.

I fought off the heat rising in my body. "It looks like him." I sniffed in dismissal and forced myself to hold it together while I walked away with my head held high.

The sound of giggling echoed in my ears as I forced back the tears that burned in my eyes. I refused to let the mean girls see me crumble.

I strode toward Dean, my gaze burning holes through him. "What was that?" he asked when I got close enough to hear.

I dropped into a seat at their table. "That was a picture of some chick walking into Jack's hotel room." My eyes began blurring from the tears that threatened to fall. "And then another one of him closing the door behind her. Did I mention the smile plastered all over his face?"

"No way." Dean shook his head.

"Yes, way." Unease quickly spread throughout my body, making itself at home. "Fuck. I'm such an idiot."

Dean put his hands on top of mine and squeezed. "Maybe they're old?"

"What are you talking about?" I yanked my hands away.

"There are a lot of pictures of Jack and other girls out there, Cass. Maybe they're old?" He shrugged.

I winced, suddenly feeling vulnerable in my surroundings as the mean girls watched me greedily like coyotes from several tables away.

"Jack wouldn't do that to you." Melissa attempted to reassure my splintering ego.

"I wouldn't go that far." I choked out the words, my tone cold.

Melissa frowned at me with annoyance. "Why would you say that?"

"Because she knows my brother." Dean glanced at Melissa before looking back at me. "And she's waiting for him to screw up because he keeps telling her he's going to."

"Well, for the record, I want it noted that I don't believe it. Not for one second," Melissa said with confidence.

"I don't either." Dean gave me a soft smile.

"Well, it was definitely Jack in those pictures. And the shirt he was wearing was packed in his bag. I saw it the other night." I could no longer hold back the tears as they rolled slowly down my cheeks. Refusing to allow my tears to be fodder for the mean girls' gossip, I rose from the table and darted into the bathroom.

Once I was safely behind the locked stall door, I let the teardrops fall. My heart ached inside my battered chest. I felt stupid and embarrassed for letting Jack Carter ever get close to me.

A knock on the stall door caused my breath to catch. "Cass?" Melissa asked in a soft voice. Without a word, I unlocked the latch and she pushed the door open. She took one look at my tear-stained face before grabbing me in her arms.

Hugging my best friend only made the tears fall harder. "Why would he do this? I don't understand."

"Cassie, I'm not trying to be a bitch, but you're really jumping to conclusions here."

"You'd do the same thing if you were suddenly dating the one guy who'd never dated anyone before." I winced, my head pounding in time with my heartbeat.

"I know it looks bad, but didn't he call you last night?"

"So what? He calls and texts me all the time. Doesn't mean he can't hook up with some girl after we get off the phone. Doesn't mean he can't send me a text while some random chick is in his room." The logic made perfect sense to me.

"That's true, Cass, but I just think you should give him a chance to explain."

"Explain that I've been a complete idiot? That I got played by the biggest player on campus? You even warned me about him." I buried my head in my hands, my chest literally aching with each breath I took.

"But I was wrong. I mean, I wasn't wrong that he was a jerk to all those other girls. But he's not that way with you. You know that, Cassie. There has to be some sort of explanation."

"Why are you defending him?" I glared at her through my sobs.

"Because I see the way he looks at you. And I hear the way he talks about you." Melissa's forehead creased in sympathy.

"I don't want to look like a fool in front of everyone! Those girls with those pictures…" I paused to gasp a sob. "I'm mortified. Do you know how embarrassing that was?"

"Those girls got exactly what they wanted. They don't care about you. They're so fucking bitter that you're the one with Jack that they'll do and say anything to tear you two apart. Can't you see that?" Melissa tried to reason with me, her voice tinged with disappointment.

But nothing she said made me feel any better. I couldn't get the image of Jack's smiling face as he ushered the girl inside that hotel room out of my head. It was simply that easy to make me question everything and assume the worst.

"I have to go." I pushed past Melissa and stormed out the bathroom door.

My mind didn't stop racing until I got to our apartment and crashed on top of my bed. I begged my brain to shut off and pleaded for my body to find some peace in sleep. The sound of my cell phone beeping startled me. I glanced at the screen, which read *One new text message from Jack*. My stomach dropped as I read his name. I pressed the

Read button. *Heading off to the field. Call you after the game. Miss you like crazy.*

I didn't respond.

I couldn't.

My stomach twisted into pretzel-like knots as my heart yearned for the truth. I curled my body into a ball, clutching a pillow tightly as the pounding in my head resumed. Closing my eyes, I reached for an escape.

The sound of my ringtone blared loudly from the floor, waking me from a dream-free slumber some time later. I glanced at the clock on my nightstand, its red numbers alerting me that almost four hours had passed.

My phone continued blaring the music I'd picked out for Jack's calls.

"Are you gonna answer that?" Melissa yelled from the other room.

I pressed the Ignore button, stopping the music from playing. After a minute, my cell phone beeped, alerting me to a new voice mail. I didn't listen, afraid that if I heard the sound of his voice, my resolve would weaken completely. Another beep followed and *One new text message from Jack* flashed across the screen.

I tried to resist reading it, but my heart wanted to know what he had to say. I clicked Read. *Everything okay, Kitten? We won today. I pitch tomorrow. Call me as soon as you get this. Miss you.*

I turned off the display, tossed my phone back onto the floor, and headed into the living room where Melissa sat watching TV.

"Did you really ignore his call?" she asked without looking at me.

"I can't talk to him right now."

She turned to face me. "You need to talk to him right now."

I shook my head. "I can't have that conversation with him over the phone. I need to be able to look him in the eyes when I ask him about those pictures."

"He's not your dad, Cassie." Melissa's face softened as she placed her hand on my knee.

I dropped my gaze. "I know that."

"Do you?"

"Of course I do."

I knew my tone sounded defensive, because she asked again. "Are you sure?"

"What the hell is your point, Melissa?"

"My point is, Jack's not going to promise the school a popular band for grad night and then disappear, leaving you to clean up the mess and answer all the questions. He's not going to make a bunch of promises to people he can't keep."

I cringed at the memory I'd tried so hard to block out over the past few years. But the truth was, the embarrassment my father caused me was etched deep inside and was never far from my mind. And whether I wanted to admit it or not, I was affected by his lies and inability to follow through on the smallest of promises.

I didn't say anything. I continued to glare at Melissa, angry at her for pointing out the flaws I felt I couldn't change.

"Cass, I just don't want you to punish Jack for the mistakes your dad made." Her voice was soft as she leaned in to touch her forehead to mine.

"How can you even say that? You know what I saw today. Those pictures have nothing to do with my dad." I jerked back, my jaw clenched.

"No, the pictures don't. But the fact that you refuse to speak to Jack unless it's in person, does. I know what you're doing," she stated, her expression solemn.

"Why don't you inform me then?"

"You want to test him. Judge his body language. Watch his eyes, his mouth."

"You're damn right I do. Please tell me what's so wrong with that?"

"Nothing, I guess." Melissa shrugged her shoulders in defeat. "I just thought that maybe you wouldn't *need* to talk to Jack in person to decide if he was lying or not."

"But I do. Don't you see?" I took a long breath. "I don't trust myself when it comes to him."

"Why?"

"Because I'll want to believe anything he tells me over the phone. I'll hear his voice and turn into a stupid girly ball of mush."

"This is about protecting yourself, isn't it?" Melissa rested her chin against her hand and sighed.

I nodded.

"You think someday you'll be able to trust the way a normal person does?"

"You mean blindly?" I laughed harshly before continuing. "Probably not."

The sound of Jack's ringtone blasted from my bedroom again, grinding our conversation to a halt. "Please go answer that, Cassie."

"I can't. I'm sorry." I winced before walking into my room and pressing Ignore once more.

My phone beeped with another voice mail alert, followed quickly by the sound of an arriving text message. This was going to be a long weekend.

*Kitten, I'm getting worried. Please let me know you're okay before I lose my fucking mind over here. I love you.*

Part of me thought, *Good. Lose your mind. Be worried. You deserve it.* The other part of me breathed in with relief that he actually cared. I shook my head, disgusted at my conflicted emotions, and turned my phone off. I couldn't deal with any more text messages or missed calls tonight. Not to mention the fact that I couldn't stop wondering if Miss Thin Brunette would be making another appearance inside Jack's hotel room later. The very thought made my stomach churn.

I heard Melissa's cell phone ring, followed by the sound of her voice. "Cassie, get out here!"

I reluctantly walked back into the living room where Melissa held out her phone in my direction. "Who is it?" I whispered, afraid of the answer.

"It's Dean. Get on the phone."

"Hello," I said, my tone irritated.

"Cassie, Jesus Christ, what the hell is going on? Jack's calling me like a lunatic. He's flipping the fuck out. Says you won't answer any of his phone calls or texts!"

"So what." I pretended not to care.

"You gotta talk to him, Cass. You can't ignore him like this when he's on a road trip, it's not fair."

"Yes I can!" I screamed back into the phone. "He's the one who had a fucking girl up in his hotel room, not me! So don't tell me I have to talk to him, Dean. Don't talk to me about what's fair!"

The tears reluctantly escaped my eyes once more as Jack's betrayal settled into my damaged heart.

"You're so goddammed stubborn! He's going fucking apeshit and you're just going to let him?"

"I just can't call him, okay? I can't talk to him right now." I pleaded with Dean for some sort of understanding. "Just tell him I'm busy with a project for school or something. He'll believe that."

Dean breathed heavily into the phone. "Fine. I'll tell him. But, Cassie, he's not stupid. He'll figure out something's wrong and then I don't know what he'll do."

"What does that mean?"

"It just means that I've never heard him sound as crazy as I did tonight. He was literally flipping the fuck out because he couldn't get a hold of you."

"I guess he should have thought about that before he invited some whore up to his hotel room," I snapped.

"You're completely unreasonable, you know that?" Dean asked, his voice harsh.

"How am I unreasonable?!"

"Because you'd rather ignore this entire situation instead of put an end to it," he snapped.

"I'm not ignoring it! I simply refuse to discuss it over the phone. So what?"

"See? Unreasonable and selfish."

"Now I'm selfish too?" I shouted with a laugh.

"Sort of. You're only thinking about yourself and your feelings. You're not thinking about Jack at all. This isn't just a game to him. This is his future. This is his career. He can't fuck up. Don't you care about that?" Dean's voice was pained.

"None of that matters if he cheated on me," I responded, my tone cold.

"But you don't even know what happened. You don't even know who that girl was. She could be an old friend of his…you have no clue because you won't ask!" He sighed loudly.

"Nope. I won't. Not until he gets home. And don't you dare say a thing to him either, Dean! I don't want you tipping him off so he has an entire weekend to think up the perfect response."

"I'm not saying a word to him. But, Cassie, can you please at least send him a text message? Just give him something so he can focus on the game? Please do that for him."

The phone fell silent between us. Of course I cared about Jack and wanted him to pitch well. No matter how badly I hurt, I didn't want to distract him from the one thing that truly owned his heart. "Fine. I'll text him as soon as you let me get off the phone."

Dean huffed out a small laugh. "Talk to you later then."

"Wait! Dean?"

"Yeah?"

"You know I'm not picking him up on Sunday."

There was a slight pause before Dean sighed. "I'll come get his car."

"Thanks. Bye." I pressed End and handed Melissa back her phone before walking into my bedroom and powering my cell back on.

I quickly typed out a text that read: *Sorry, Jack, been busy with a photography project. I'll probably be pretty swamped until you get home. Good luck tomorrow. You'll be great! xo*

Less than a minute passed before my phone beeped, signaling I had a response. *It makes me crazy to be this far away from you and not know what's going on. I just completely lost my shit on Dean. What have you done to me? LOL Call me if you have a chance. If not, I understand. Good luck with your project. Can't stop thinking about the other night...*

I tried so hard to be strong when it came to him, but even his text messages challenged me. I knew I'd jumped to conclusions about the pictures, but I refused to look like a fool. And in my opinion, only a fool would carry on like nothing had happened. Simply put, I didn't want to be that kind of girl. The kind of girl that needed Jack in her life so badly, she'd overlook potential relationship-ruining material.

But in trying so hard to be unlike all the other girls, I made myself irrational, declaring Jack guilty before viewing the facts of the case. I clung to my principles with both hands so tightly it was the only way I got through the next day and a half Jack-free.

That, and the fact that I'd turned my phone off.

# NINE

Panic set in when I realized that Jack would be arriving home soon. I hadn't communicated with him in any form since the text messages two days ago. I half wondered if I should leave the apartment. But where would I go? I couldn't hide from him forever. The sooner we had this conversation, the better it would be for everyone involved.

I paced back and forth in my bedroom, my thoughts all over the place. It was easier to be the tough girl when Jack was in another state and I could simply shut him off with the press of a button on my cell phone.

Nerves shot through my unsettled stomach as I curled up on my bed and waited. Finally, tires squealed outside and I peered out my window just in time to see Jack come to a screeching halt in one of the parking spots. He appeared to be shouting at poor Dean in the passenger seat before he bolted out of the car and sprinted out of sight.

Within seconds, his knuckles knocked wildly against the front door. "Cassie!" He banged relentlessly as he yelled through the door. "Cassie! Please, Cassie, open up. It's not what you think." *So much for Dean not saying anything.*

My stomach rolled when the door finally creaked open and I heard him ask, "Melissa, where is she?"

"Kitten? I'm coming in," he announced from

behind my closed bedroom door. When he walked in, my heart skipped a beat at the sight of him. His hair was wild and wind-whipped from the quick drive over from the stadium and he was still in his dress clothes from the airport, although his tie was loosened and barely hanging on.

He ran to the side of my bed, dropped to his knees, and reached out for me. I pulled back before he could touch me, my eyes focused on his as he spoke. "Kitten, it's not what you think. That girl wasn't in my room for me."

I refused to move, unwilling to be deceived. "Did you hear me? She wasn't there for me. I roomed with Brett and he met her our first night. He invited her up to our room, but she wasn't there for me. I just answered the door."

"Where'd the picture come from then?" I wondered, the question suddenly dawning on me.

"She came upstairs with a bunch of other girls, but I wouldn't let them in. One of them must have taken it."

"Really?" I asked, my voice filled with more hope than I'd anticipated.

"I swear it." He reached out again for my hands and I allowed his fingers to intertwine with mine. He brought my hand to his lips and he kissed it all over.

"So you weren't with her?" I asked once more, even though I already believed him.

"No. I don't even like brunettes anymore. I'm into this one particular shade of blonde." He gave me a tentative, lopsided smile, and ran his fingers through my hair. "I wouldn't do that to you."

I practically jumped out of my bed and into his waiting arms. He pressed me tightly against his chest before he tipped my head back and covered my mouth with his. "I missed you," he said between kisses. His tongue parted my lips as I melted into him, the self-imposed stress from the weekend falling from my shoulders.

He pulled away before I was ready and asked, "So, tell me exactly what happened."

I collapsed onto my bed, pulling him with me. "Some random chick came up to me on Friday and showed me two pictures of you with this girl going into your hotel room. I pretty much lost it after that."

"And you just assumed the girl was with me?" He looked down, picking restlessly at my bedspread, his voice tinged with sadness.

"You two were the only ones in the photos, so yeah, pretty much." I shuddered, recalling the pictures in my mind.

"That's not fair, Kitten," he remarked, his eyebrows pinched together.

"I know it's not." I looked away from him, embarrassed at my ability to write him off so quickly.

"You have to remember that I've been playing ball here for three years now. I have friends in all the places we travel. And sometimes they come up to my room to hang out. I always share a room with at least one other guy. You can't assume that I'm doing something wrong all the time."

"But what was I supposed to think?" I couldn't help but defend my initial reaction and thoughts. "I saw a girl walking into a room that you were holding the door open for. Then I saw you closing the door behind her, with the world's biggest smile on your face."

"Fuck, Cassie, how about asking me?" His tone changed, anger quickly replacing sadness. "Is that why you never called me? Because you thought I cheated on you the second I left town?" He lowered his voice, the angry tone still present. "We had sex."

"I'm not the first girl you've had sex with, Jack."

"No. But you are the first girl I've ever loved."

"I just couldn't have that conversation with you over the phone," I admitted, guilt careening through my body.

"So instead you had no conversation with me at all?" He eased off the bed and walked across the floor. "Do you know how crazy that made me? I'm trying to concentrate on my fucking baseball game and all I can think about is why the hell the girl I'm in love with is ignoring me. I knew something was wrong when you never called. I tried to shake it off, but I couldn't. You can't do that to me. Don't you understand? You can't fucking do that to me when I'm trying to play ball!"

"I'm sorry, Jack. I didn't think…"

"This is bullshit, Cassie!" he shouted, his jaw tense. "I haven't done anything to make you not trust me." His eyes widened as the realization set in. "But that's it, isn't it?" He nodded his head in understanding, then turned his hurt gaze to me. "You don't…trust me."

I avoided his eyes, the truth in his words resonating deep within me. "Look at me!" His voice rose along with his anger.

I did as he demanded, grateful for the tears blurring my view of him. "What do you want from me, Jack?" My voice cracked with emotion.

"I want you to give me a fair shot, but apparently that's too much to ask." He turned his back to me and threw open my bedroom door. I heard the front door slam shut as I sat stunned in my bed.

"What just happened?" Melissa poked her head through my doorway.

"I think I just royally fucked things up." I exhaled and wiped a tear from my eye. "Hand me my phone, please?" I practically begged, pointing to its location on the bathroom counter.

Melissa snagged my phone and tossed it to me.

"You wanna talk about it?"

"In a minute. Thanks." I tried to smile but couldn't. Melissa nodded in understanding and closed my door behind her to give me some privacy.

I scrolled through my contacts searching for Jack's name and pressed Send. I listened as it rang twice before going straight to voice mail. He was ignoring me. I swallowed my pride and waited patiently for the beep that acknowledged his voice mail recording, but hung up instead. I had no idea what I wanted to say to him that wouldn't sound pathetic or stupid.

How had things twisted into tangled-up knots so easily? I walked into Melissa's room and found her reading a book on her bed. I cuddled up next to her and worked through the emotions churning inside of me.

"You were right about Jack," I started.

She dropped the book to her side and turned to me. "About what?"

"He said the girl wasn't there for him."

"Who was she there for then?"

"Jack roomed with Brett and apparently Brett met her and invited her up." I let out a long sigh.

"Do you believe him?" She leaned her curly brown head against mine.

"I do."

"So then why'd he leave?"

"He got pissed that I didn't trust him." I shook

my head at the absurdity of the situation. "I feel like a crazy person right now. I mean, one second I'm overwhelmed with relief that the girl wasn't there for him. I'm looking at Jack, realizing how much I care about him. And in the next, I'm feeling horrible and guilty for not trusting him. Now he's gone and I'm scared to death that I just screwed it all up."

I forced my eyes closed as I inhaled through my nose. "What if I lose him?" My face twisted in pain.

"You won't." Melissa's voice was stern with certainty.

"How can you be so sure?" I asked, unable to hide the fear in my voice.

"Because Jack's just as stubborn as you are! He's not going to quit on you that easily. But he is right, you know. You don't trust him. And that's not fair." She stroked my hair as she spoke.

I breathed in deeply again. "I know, but it's hard. I mean, I saw those pictures and was so embarrassed. I felt like such an idiot. Like those girls knew something I didn't about my own relationship."

"Trust me, I know how you felt. But you never once questioned that maybe he didn't do it, right?"

"Not really," I confessed.

"I'd be pissed off too."

The sound of the front door swinging open stopped our conversation. Footsteps beat against the floor toward my bedroom before stopping. "Cassie!" Jack's voice echoed throughout the apartment.

"I'm in Melissa's room," I nervously squeaked out.

Jack appeared and leaned against the doorway, his dressy attire now replaced with black shorts and a tight-fitting baseball t-shirt. He buried his hands in his pockets before demanding, "Get up. I want to talk to you."

Fear shot through me as I struggled to move from Melissa's bed. She helped push me to my feet and I eyed her nervously.

"It'll be fine. Go. Apologize," she whispered before giving my backside a light shove.

I stumbled over my flimsy flip-flops before regaining my balance, my eyes searching Jack's for any sign of happiness, but failing. I followed his lead into my bedroom where he slammed the door shut behind me.

"Sit." He pointed at my bed and I did as he requested.

He didn't join me. Instead, he stood in front of me, eyeing me before speaking. "Let me finish before you say anything. Okay?"

I couldn't seem to find my voice, so I simply nodded.

"I want to be really pissed off at you right now. No, forget that, I *am* really pissed off at you." He stopped talking, took a deep breath, and ran his tanned fingers through loose strands of his black hair. "Listen, I know we're both fucked up. We both have trust issues and this thing happening between us is scary as hell." He wagged his finger, his eyes avoiding mine.

"But when I told you I loved you, I meant it. I didn't mean that I'd love you only if it was easy, or only if it was drama-free. I think we both know life isn't like that." I watched his face twisting with emotion as my eyes began to fill with tears.

"I know it's not easy to be with me. Dating me means that you have to deal with some pretty crazy shit that other people don't and I'm sorry for that. All the things you're just now being exposed to, I've had years to deal with. I'm used to it…the crazy pictures, the girls, the fan pages, the blogs, the reporters, the scouts, all the social media stuff."

He shrugged his shoulders as his eyes met mine. "And I know that the past version of me is someone you would never trust. But who I am when I'm with you" he paused, "isn't who I used to be. I don't think I've been that guy since the night of our first date, so it's not fair that you judge me like I'm still him."

He settled his body next to mine on the edge of the bed. "If we're going to do this, then you have to trust me. And you can't shut me out or ignore me when things get uncomfortable."

It felt like hours of silence passed before I asked, "Can I talk now?"

He laughed. "Yeah."

"I'm really sorry, Jack. I know you haven't done anything to deserve my mistrust, but it's just that I saw those pictures and I felt so stupid. I'd just told you not to make me look dumb or embarrass me, and I felt like that's exactly what you did. I went into self-preservation mode where nothing else mattered but me." I tried to explain my craziness in a way I hoped he'd understand. That basically, he was dating someone with serious trust issues.

His arm swept around my back and pulled me toward him. I allowed a few teardrops to fall before wiping them away. "You make me fucking crazy, but I love you." He pressed his warm lips against my temple.

"So you're not breaking up with me?" I asked with a pout.

"You're not that lucky."

# TEN
## JACK

"Kitten, come on, we're gonna be late!" I shouted toward Cassie's bathroom in between paces.

"I'm coming, hold on!" I heard the sound of clanking against the countertop and feet shuffling.

"Okay, I'm ready," she announced as she entered the living room.

My jaw dropped at the sight of her tanned legs in that little white sundress. I scanned every inch of her body, my eyes loving each curve. I shook my head and smiled. She seriously looked like a fucking angel. And I wanted to be her devil.

"Kitten, you're gonna give Gramps a heart attack looking like that."

Melissa's laughter echoed from her bedroom. "Please don't kill Jack's grandpa, Cass. Not a good first impression."

Cassie giggled in response. "I'll do my best." Her bright green eyes focused on mine. "See you later."

I stuffed my cell phone into my pocket before reaching for Cassie's hand. She locked her fingers in mine as I led her toward the door. "See you later, Melissa," I shouted toward her bedroom.

"Bye, you guys. Have fun!"

I ushered Cassie outside with a light slap to her ass and when she turned to smack me, she stopped and simply smiled instead. God, I loved this girl.

"You look beautiful," I said, running my fingers through the soft golden waves in her hair.

"Thank you." She smiled and hesitated at the side of my car before I helped her up and inside.

I glanced over at the girl to my right and noticed her fidgeting with her hair. Shit. She'd actually curled it and I was going to fuck it all up on the drive. I should have borrowed Gran's Honda.

"Here." I tossed my baseball cap into her lap.

"What's this for?"

"Just put it on. It'll help keep your hair in place." I shot her a half smile. "It's better than no hat, right?"

She shrugged her shoulders, saying, "I guess we'll find out," and placed the hat on top of her head. She laughed as it fell all the way down, covering her eyes. "You have a huge head!"

I leaned toward her, grabbing the bill of the hat between my fingers and pulled her close. "No. You have a small head." I ducked under the hat and planted my lips firmly against hers as she giggled. God, she smelled good.

The engine screamed to life as I turned the key in the ignition. "Ready for this?"

"I'm ready," she answered with a nod and I took off, the wind whipping through my hair.

"So, have you ever brought a girl home before?" Her voice cut through the sound of the air and the roar of the engine.

I glanced at her before laughing. "You're kidding, right?"

"No." She shrugged.

"Cassie." I eyed her before shaking my head. "I've never even slept with the same girl twice."

"So? That doesn't mean you haven't brought some random girl home before." She sighed.

I placed my right hand on her knee and caressed her bare skin with my fingers. "You're the first. And the last," I informed her, my expression serious.

She smiled and her whole face lit up. Or maybe it was mine. All I know for certain is that smile lit up even my darkest days.

We drove for ten minutes before I pulled the car directly in front of my grandparents' blue and white one-story house. Gran's yard was meticulous, with manicured bushes lining the front of the house.

"It's so cute," she said, removing my hat and fussing with the tangled strands of her hair.

I smirked in her direction. "Your hair looks perfect, Kitten. Come on." I grabbed the hat she discarded and pulled it on my head, tucking my hair underneath.

I opened the car door and helped her down, my hands resting on her hips and ass. "I think you're trying to kill me in that dress."

"I'm glad you like it," she teased, her eyebrows

raised.

"I'll like you better out of it," I whispered against her neck.

"Jack! Stop it." She smacked my arm and I laughed.

We interlocked our fingers and I led her toward the blue double front doors. One of them shot open and Dean appeared, grinning from ear to ear. "It's about time," he chastised before pulling Cassie against him in a tight bear hug.

"I will hurt you. Get off her." I playfully shoved him away from her.

Cassie laughed at our horseplay, then lifted her chin, sniffing at the air. "It smells incredible in here."

"It's Gran's homemade sauce," Dean said with a smile.

"Welcome home." I beamed, watching as she looked around at all our things.

"Look at all these old pics of you two. You were so cute," she said, pointing at an elementary school photo framed on the wall.

"We're still cute." I led her across the aging beige carpet toward the entryway to the kitchen.

We walked through and I immediately spotted Gran leaning over the stove, her graying brown hair pinned tightly back in a bun. Gramps sat at the round dinner table, reading the newspaper. He looked up when he heard our footsteps, his glasses resting on the tip of his nose like always.

"Oh, Ma, they're here!" Gramps sounded excited. He rose from his chair and walked straight toward Cassie with open arms.

"You must be Cassie. It's so nice to finally meet you." He squeezed her hard against his chest.

I laughed as I headed over to Gran. "Gran, this is my girl, Cassie."

Gran wiped her hands on her apron as Cassie grinned and pulled herself from Gramps' hug. "It's so nice to meet you, Cassie. We've heard so much about you." Her eyes crinkled in the corners as she grinned, a hint of dimples like mine appearing on her creased cheeks.

"It's so nice to meet you both. Thanks for having me," Cassie replied with a warm smile. "Can I help?" She directed the question toward Gran.

"Oh heavens no, dear. I'm almost finished. Go sit down and make yourself comfortable. Jack, you get her whatever she needs, you hear me?" Gran's voice took on the tone she only used with Dean and me.

"Yes, Gran, of course." I leaned toward her and planted a kiss on her cheek.

"Do you need anything, Kitten?"

"I'm fine, thanks."

Gramps pulled out the empty chair next to him and patted it. "Come sit down next to me, Cassie. Or do I get to call you Kitten too?" he asked with a wink.

Dean laughed out loud. "I think we should all start calling her Kitten."

I shot Dean a murderous look, not at all amused. "Only I get to call her Kitten. You'd be wise to remember that."

"Jack, stop threatening your brother," Gran remarked while waving the steam away from her face.

"Yes, Gran." I gave Dean a hard kick under the table.

Gramps leaned on his elbow and tilted his head. "So, Cassie, Jack tells us that you're a photographer."

She glanced at me, grinning before looking back at Gramps. "Well, that's what I'm studying right now. I'd like to start my own business as soon as I graduate."

Gramps slapped his hand against the table. "Well, that's just great! Isn't that great, dear?"

"That is great. What kind of photography?" Gran asked.

"Ideally, I'd like to work for a magazine that focuses on travel and human interest stories. I'd get to travel around the country and meet all sorts of incredible people with amazing stories." Cassie started to explain slowly and loud enough for everyone to hear. It didn't escape me the way her green eyes lit up when she talked about her craft.

"Ooooh, that sounds exciting." Gran squeezed her shoulders up to her ears.

"Now, what would you do for them? What kind of pictures would you take?" Gramps asked as he reached for his glass of water.

"I think I'd either get assigned with the journalist writing the piece, or I'd go by myself to shoot whatever the focus of the article was about. It could be anything from a new hotel opening and its impact on a struggling city, to a town's comeback after almost being destroyed in a natural disaster. But the overall theme is positive and uplifting."

She paused before looking at me, her eyes wide. "There's an internship that I'm going to apply for this summer. Apparently one of the New York-based magazines has an LA office and my professor mentioned it to me today. He said he'd write me a letter of recommendation, so you never know."

I gave her a big smile. "Can't win if you don't play, Kitten. They'd be idiots not to hire you."

"Thanks, baby."

"You should see her stuff, Gramps. She's really good," I added, pride shooting through my body.

"She is," Dean agreed. "But I have a question. The stuff you take pictures of is so creative. I mean, your angles and what you put in your shots… Gramps, she has this one picture of Jack on the mound. You can't see his whole body or even his face. It's the coolest shot! Will you get to take pictures like that for a magazine?"

"First of all, thank you. It's sweet of you to say that about my photos and I appreciate it." Cassie smiled. "I guess it totally depends on the magazine and their style. But the ones I'd love to work for have very beautifully creative photos and I think they give the photographer a lot of control with their shots." She shrugged her shoulders.

"That sounds perfect for you. Your photography is way too beautiful to be defined by someone else's standards. If it doesn't work out, you can always go into sports photography and follow your boyfriend around the country," I suggested helpfully.

"So, I'd just wake up and take pictures of you all day?"

I let out a slight chuckle. "Sounds like a dream job to me."

"Oh, Lord." Gran sighed. "Forgive me, Cassie, I did the best I could with him."

She laughed. "It's okay, Gran, he's perfect just the way he is." Her eyes wandered back to mine as her lips curved in a slight smile.

"Jack, Dean, come help me serve, will you?" Gran asked.

Dean and I jumped up from the table and returned carrying steaming dishes filled with Italian food. The smell of freshly baked bread mixed with garlic tomatoes filtered into the air and my mouth started to salivate.

"Dig in, please. Cassie first," Gramps insisted.

Cassie reached for the bowl of spaghetti and dished out a huge helping before grabbing two piping hot pieces of fresh bread and tossing them onto her plate. Her eyes widened once she added salad, and I gently placed my hand on her upper thigh and squeezed.

"Get enough, Kitten?" I teased.

"I think I got excited in my serving sizes," she admitted, the hue of embarrassment rising in her cheeks.

"Don't worry about it. Just eat what you can."

"This all looks incredible, Gran. Thank you so much," she said sincerely, before digging in.

"You're welcome, dear. Thank you for coming."

"Now, Jack, we need to talk about the draft," Gramps mentioned between sloppy, sauce-filled bites.

"What about it?"

"Well, for starters, who all will be here on draft day besides the reporters from that TV channel?" Gramps swirled some spaghetti around his fork.

Cassie looked at me, clearly interested in the conversation we'd yet to have. I swallowed my food before speaking. "You and Gran, of course. Dean, you'll be here, right?"

Dean nodded and I turned to face Cassie. "And Cass, I'd like you here too."

"Wait. Here for what? I'm sort of lost right now."

"The major league draft. They think I'll go within the first couple of rounds so it will be televised on ESPN."

"Really?" she asked with surprise.

"Really." I mimicked her tone and she glared at me.

"That's crazy."

"You'll come though, right?" I reached under the table again and connected with her thigh, moving her dress up slightly with my fingertips.

"Of course I'll…come," she sputtered before swatting my hand away.

"Great. So, Gramps, it's you and Gran. Dean and Kitten. And of course, my agents, Marc and Ryan."

"You have agents already?" Her face scrunched up as she winced noticeably.

"Not officially. I can't sign with them until I get drafted, but we have a verbal agreement."

"And how many do you have? Don't most people only have one?"

"One's an agent and the other's a lawyer. But they work together and it stops me having to hire a lawyer separately," I explained.

"Oh. We really need to talk more about all this baseball stuff. I feel like I don't know anything that's happening." She bit her bottom lip and I saw the unease on her face; she looked so overwhelmed. I'd do anything to take that feeling away from her. I didn't just want her by my side through this process, I *needed* her there.

"Sorry, Kitten, we've had other stuff going on. And this is all pretty recent. I was going to tell you about it."

"No, it's okay. I'm not mad or anything. I'm really excited for you, but the whole TV thing is a little overwhelming."

"It only happens if you're getting drafted really high. They don't send camera crews to everyone's house," Dean said, and I couldn't read her expression any longer, her face blank.

"Oh. When is it, anyway?"

"The first Monday in June," Dean answered before I had the chance.

"And then when do you leave?" Cassie asked softly, her green eyes searching mine for answers I didn't have yet.

"I don't know for sure, but I think right after," I answered, my chest suddenly feeling like it weighed a thousand pounds.

"Like that day?" she asked, as her eyes started to get that shiny look.

"No. But within a week, I think." Her face twisted at my words.

She was upset. Of course she was upset. I hadn't told her any of this and now it was all being sprung on her without any warning. I could be such an idiot sometimes.

"So what's the plan, Jack? What do your agents think is going to happen?" Gran asked from across the table.

"They think I'll go within the first round and that should come with a solid signing bonus. If we like the deal, then we accept it and I'll have to move to wherever their Single-A farm team is."

"What's a signing bonus?" Cassie asked, her forehead creasing.

"A signing bonus is exactly what it sounds like. It's money used as an incentive to get the player to sign with the team instead of returning to school for another year. The minor league pay scale is barely enough to live off of each month. That's why the signing bonus is so important. But not every player gets it." I tried to clarify without confusing her.

"So not everyone gets a signing bonus, but you will because you'll get drafted in the first round?" she asked, her voice stumbling a bit.

"Exactly."

"How many rounds are there?"

"In the draft? About forty."

"Holy shit, and they think you'll go in the first?" Her eyes widened as I stifled a laugh. "I'm sorry," she said before clasping her hand over her mouth, her face embarrassed.

"We've heard far worse," Gramps said with a

laugh.

"What happens to those guys who don't get a signing bonus?" she asked.

"What do you mean?"

"Well, you said they can barely live off of the money they make without a bonus."

"No one plays this game for the money, Kitten. We play it because we love it so much that the thought of being without it causes unbearable pain. It's a game that one day ends for every single person who plays it, but we all want to put off that ending as long as possible." I took a quick breath. "When you only dream of doing one thing for the majority of your life, it's almost unfathomable to think about doing anything else. You don't know how. It's all you've ever wanted and you'll not only fight like hell to get there, you'll fight like hell to stay."

"I love how much you love it," she said, her eyes beaming.

"I wouldn't play it if I didn't," I admitted, grinning at her.

"Do Marc and Ryan have any idea what team is going to try to draft you?" Dean asked while ripping apart a piece of bread.

"If they do, they haven't told me."

"So you have no idea where you'll be going?" He chewed thoughtfully while he waited for my answer.

141

"Not yet." I smiled.

"The teams are all over the country, right?" Cassie asked, her expression a mixture of excitement and concern.

"Pretty much."

"And you just have to go wherever they tell you to?"

"If I want to play ball, I do," I responded with a playful grin, hoping to lighten the darkening mood.

Gran's concerned gaze swung between Cassie's face and mine. "What will you two do when he leaves?"

"Well, we haven't really talked about it yet, Gran." I ran my fingers nervously through my hair. Cassie placed her hand under the table on my thigh and I quickly reached for it, grateful for her touch.

"Long distance relationships suck," Dean commented darkly.

"What the hell do you know about 'em?" I snapped at Dean, suddenly overwhelmed with the reality of the situation with Cassie and me.

"I've just heard they suck. And they never last." He clamped his jaw shut, a little too late for my liking.

"That's enough, Dean!" Gran swatted him with her napkin. "Long distance relationships can work just as well as any other kind. Sometimes they're even better."

"How so?" Cassie asked, our minds clearly on

142

the same page.

"For starters, your relationship becomes less about the physical aspect, obviously," she said with a laugh, "and more about the things that truly matter in the long run. When you can't see each other for months at a time, the building blocks of your relationship either flourish or flounder. No relationship can survive without trust, honesty, and communication, no matter how close you are."

She stopped for a moment, looking at both Cassie and me before continuing. "Long distance means countless hours talking on the phone. And I mean, really talking. Because it's all you have when you can't simply get in your car and drive to the other person's house. You get to really know each other. The bonds you form during that time apart can be as solid as steel beams."

I found myself completely focused on Gran's words. "She's right," Gramps added with a twinkle in his eyes. "When you only have the telephone or letters, it changes things. All the emotions and feelings are still there, but they're amplified in a way that's tough to explain. That's why the communication part is so important."

Gran glanced over at him with a dimpled smile. "Because it's easy to misinterpret things or jump to the wrong conclusion when the person you love is far away. The only way to fix it is to talk about it. So you end up talking…a lot."

"When were you two apart?" I asked, finally realizing they were both speaking from experience.

"During the war. But I wrote him every day," Gran said matter-of-factly.

"And I wrote every chance I had." Gramps grinned. "Called, too."

"That he did." They exchanged a loving glance and I squeezed Cassie's hand.

"Well, that's enough of that talk for one night. I'm sure the kids don't want to think about all this stuff right now." Gran waved a hand in front of her face before rising from the table, followed by Gramps.

"No, it was really nice to hear. Thank you." Cassie smiled, her hand still holding mine.

"We'll get the dishes, Gran. Go lie down," I suggested with a hearty smile.

"Thank you, Jack. We'll just be in the other room," she said before slowly making her way into the living room.

"You two *are* gonna stay together, right?" Dean asked with a wince.

I turned to look at Cassie, whose eyes were piercing into mine. "She'll probably be sick of me by then." I couldn't help but tease Cassie in a weak attempt to hide my fears.

"Most likely," she kidded back.

At least, I hoped she was kidding.

"You guys seriously haven't talked about any of

this?" Dean questioned in disbelief, leaning back against his chair.

"Not yet." I tried to be cool, ignoring the irritation rising in my body.

"Dude, June isn't that far away. And you'll leave right after the draft. You two are hopeless."

I rammed my foot into Dean's shin with force, my temper flaring. "Why don't you shut the fuck up, Dean, and worry about your own love life. Or lack thereof."

Dean's chair slid across the kitchen floor with a loud squeak. "Ow, Jack! Jesus! I was just saying you two should probably get your shit together and actually start doing that whole communicating thing Gran was talking about. 'Cause the last time I checked, you sort of sucked at it."

I stood up from my chair, my breath increasing with each second that passed. "You're being a real asshole, Dean, you know that?" I seethed, my jaw working as I ground my teeth, trying to control my anger.

Cassie's hand gripped the bottom of my shirt, pulling it tightly toward her. "Jack! Sit! Down!"

I looked at her face, all pinched with fear, and fell back into my chair, my breathing ragged. After thinking a moment, I shot to my feet again and grabbed her arm. "Let's go."

"What? No. We haven't even done the dishes and…"

"We're leaving. I'll do the dishes when I get back," I demanded, leaving her no choice.

"Night, Dean," she said grudgingly, two steps behind me.

"Night, Cass. Sorry."

I stormed into the living room before leaning in to plant a kiss on Gran's soft cheek. "I'm gonna take Cass home. I'll be back in a bit and will handle the dishes then. Okay? Thanks for dinner, Gran. It was delicious."

"Did something happen, dear? What happened?" Gran's voice echoed her concern.

"Ask your other grandson." I smiled at her unapologetically, before giving Gramps a hug, inhaling the scent of tobacco lingering on his clothes.

"It was really nice meeting you both. Thank you so much for dinner. It was fantastic." Cassie smiled softly before leaning in to hug Gramps and then Gran.

"Nice to meet you too, young lady. Good luck with that internship!" Gramps remembered with an enthusiastic smile.

"You're welcome any time, even after he leaves," Gran told Cassie, her eyes tired but kind.

"That's very sweet of you. Thank you so much. I'll see you both soon."

I practically dragged Cassie out of the house by her hand before she ripped it from my grip once we were out the door. "Jesus, Jack, enough! Stop pulling me like I'm a fucking dog or something. I don't even know what you're so pissed off about!"

I came to a sudden stop on the walkway as guilt immediately mixed with my anger. "Did I hurt you?" I asked, my insides battling.

She cocked her head to one side, assessing me. "No. But don't do that again. I don't like it."

I reached for her hand, but she tucked it behind her back. "I deserve that," I said with a nod before walking toward my car ahead of her. I opened her door, but didn't stay to help her up. If she wasn't going to let me touch her hand, she sure as shit wasn't going to let me grab her ass.

Once inside, I pulled open the old ashtray, the sound of jingling change filling the air as I dug around for the proper amount. I glanced at Cassie, knowing that she was pissed causing an aching in my chest I couldn't stand. "Forgive me," I said, before tossing two quarters into her lap.

She glanced down, the corners of her mouth turning up in a hesitant smile as she shook her head. "I hate you."

"No you don't." Relief spread through me as soon as I realized that it would be okay. We'd be okay.

She narrowed her eyes, releasing a long breath. "Just take me home, Jack. That's what you ripped me from your house to do, so just do it already."

My stomach twisted as her tone chased away every ounce of relief I'd just felt. I started the car and we drove in silence the entire way to her apartment, except for the music I chose. As soon as I put the car in park, she hopped out.

"Come on, Kitten. Wait!" I shouted at her retreating back, but she continued walking. "Cassie!"

I realized she had no intention of stopping, so I followed slowly behind her, my mind racing. When I reached her front door, I noticed that it wasn't closed all the way and my heart literally let out a thankful beat.

"Cass?" I peered around the door into the empty living room. I noticed the light on in her bedroom, so I headed that direction.

I walked in and found her looking in the bathroom mirror as she scrubbed the makeup from her face. She turned to me and sighed before looking back at her reflection. I sat on the edge of her bed, suddenly feeling like the biggest asshole on earth. The problem was, I wasn't sure what the hell she was even so mad about, but I was certain it was my fault.

I watched as she gathered her long hair into a ponytail, revealing that gorgeous neck she usually hid underneath. I knew I was in trouble with her, but suddenly all I could think about was kissing that neck. I stood up and started to walk toward her, my other head clearly in charge of my actions.

"Don't," she snapped and I stopped. No fighting back, no response, no arguing. I simply turned my ass right around and sat back on her bed. If I had a tail, it would sure as shit have been tucked between my legs.

I was one hundred percent not in control of this situation. This girl fucking owned me right now. I sat on that bed waiting for her to give me the time of day. I didn't necessarily like this feeling, but I suffered through it…for her. I convinced myself that I'd probably suffer through pretty much anything for this girl.

The water turned off and she walked toward me, avoiding my eyes before sitting down as far away from me as possible. "What the fuck is wrong with you?" Her angry tone caught me off guard.

I shrugged my shoulders. "What did I do?"

"You're kidding, right?" She let out an irritated laugh. I stared at her as she threw her hands up in the air in exasperation. "You flipped out at your grandparents' house. I thought you were going to hit your own brother!"

"He pissed me off!" I attempted to defend my actions. "I didn't like the things he was saying about us. I don't want to hear that shit when it comes to me and you."

She released a loud breath, her shoulders slouching. "Jack, you can't get pissed every time someone says something unflattering about us."

"Yes, I can," I responded seriously, and she laughed.

"Okay, you *cannnn*," she dragged out the word before continuing, "but you shouldn't. Plus, it's not like Dean was really wrong."

"What are you saying?"

"Just that we don't really have the best track record when it comes to trust and communication, is all. We clearly have some stuff to work on." She smiled as she scooted next to me.

I threw my arm around her waist and pulled her into me before kissing her on the head. "So we're not perfect."

"Not even close." She laughed and her eyes danced. "But, Jack?"

"Yeah?" I leaned away from her so I could see her face as she spoke.

"Will you please keep me in the loop when it comes to your baseball stuff? I don't want to be the last to know what's going on with you." She spoke softly and I could see the hurt in her eyes.

"You'll never be the last to know again. I promise." I caressed her hip with my thumb, the feeling that I'd let her down surging through my body.

"So you'll really be gone soon?" she asked, her tone of voice breaking my fucking heart.

I nodded. "But I'll be back in a few months. The

season ends in September, so I come home as soon as it's over."

Her eyes lit up as the worry lines on her forehead subsided. "Really? So it's not like you move away forever?"

The heaviness in my chest lifted. "Is that what you thought? That I got drafted and never came back?"

"Pretty much. I don't know how it works."

"I just go for the rest of the baseball season and then I come home. They've already been playing games since April," I told her, wanting to alleviate her fears.

"And then what? I mean, you go back again, right?"

I smiled half-heartedly. "I go back in February."

She started counting the months between when I come back and when I leave again on her fingers as I braced for her response. "That's not terrible." She smiled and dropped her hands.

"Totally doable, right?" I asked with confidence, but my insides were doing somersaults.

"I'm not ready to give up on you quite yet. I'll try anything with you once." She winked at me before seeing the big grin on my face, then began backtracking. "Well...almost anything." Her cheeks turned rose-colored.

I tilted her face toward mine, lifting her chin with my fingers. "I love you." Her eyes focused on my mouth before closing as I pulled her to me. She tasted like the mint of her toothpaste and her lips were soft as I parted them. The touch of her tongue against mine woke up parts of my body I had no real control over. I tangled my fingers in her hair, pulling her even closer to me.

She let out a low sound and all I could think about was ripping that little white dress off her body. I leaned her against the mattress and positioned myself on top of her. The way her hair spilled out all around drove me crazy. There was something so sexy about seeing it splayed across her pillow as she lay beneath me. "You're so beautiful," I reminded her as I leaned down to kiss her again, pushing the lower half of my body against hers.

I waited for the signal that she was willing to go farther before I attempted anything. Her hips lifted from the bed to meet mine as she pressed herself into me. My hand reached down to her leg before sliding up along her bare skin, bringing her dress with it. I pulled the fabric up to her hip as she wiggled, sensing no rejection to my actions.

I ran my thumb along the elastic of her thong, sliding underneath it. The feel of her skin made me ravenous. I couldn't get enough; all my thoughts consumed in what it felt like to be inside her. "I want you," I admitted, my breath faltering.

She opened her eyes to mine, her mouth

opening slightly as her hands reached for the button on my shorts. Her fingers brushed against me as she fumbled, causing a moan to escape from my lips. My willpower fading, I reached down to help her remove the fabric that remained between us.

I flung off my shorts and boxers as she pulled at me, her fingers digging into my exposed skin. I sat up, my breathing erratic as I tossed my shirt onto the floor. Her gorgeous body, half naked with her white dress bunched up toward her breasts, took my breath away, and I peeled the dress from her effortlessly. Then I reached lower and pulled her underwear all the way down to her feet, where she kicked them off.

The curves of her body called out to me, and I slid my mouth over them, my tongue tasting the salt on her skin. Her breathing was quick and heavy as her fingers slid along the muscles in my back. Every sound that escaped her lips simply made me want her more. "Jack." Her voice was shaky. "I want you."

Her words lit a fire inside me that was hard to contain. I wanted to please her…satisfy her…ruin her for all other guys out there. I wanted this moment right here to be the best part of her day.

Her hands gripped my body as I slid into her. She let out a sigh and I almost lost it right then. I bit down on my bottom lip as I rocked in and out of her, trying to focus on anything other than how

153

amazing she felt.

Her eyes opened and closed as my thrusting continued. No matter how many girls I'd slept with at Fullton, none had ever come close to feeling like this. Nothing had ever felt like this. Not even baseball. "I'll never get over how incredible you feel," I admitted without shame.

She looked into me. "You too. Don't stop, Jack." She panted the words and I crushed her lips against mine. My hips moved with hers, my shoulders burning from the weight of my body, but refusing to falter. She moaned and shuddered as she sucked in a deep breath, her eyes flying open in wonder as her body trembled in spasms. My pace quickened; I knew wouldn't be able to hold out much longer.

Her head thrust back and I kissed along her neck, before finding the sweet taste of her lips. My mouth covered hers, my tongue exploring while I continued working in and out of her. "Cass," I said as my lips pressed against hers. She sighed as her teeth grazed against my ear. I groaned without control and released myself into her.

I gently pulled out of her before falling onto my back, my breathing loud and uneven. She turned to lay her head on my chest and I wrapped my arm across her bare, damp back.

"I love you, Jack." Her breath whispered against my skin as I kissed the top of her head.

"Just don't forget that when I'm gone for three months this summer."

"I'm not the one who's slept with half the school." She laughed, softening the barb a little.

"That doesn't mean half the school won't try to sleep with you the second I'm out of the picture," I informed her, my tone serious.

I've seen the way other guys look at her. I'm not the first guy at Fullton to notice Cassie. I'm just the one who actually got her.

"You're insane." She looked over at me, disbelief written all over her face.

"Let's hope every guy on campus has the same opinion of me."

"I'm pretty sure they do. It's not like you're known for your sweet disposition."

"Good." I smiled as contentment welled within me.

# ELEVEN
## CASSIE

Things with Jack and me were in a good place after all the chaos at Gran and Gramps' house. We spent every spare moment together, which didn't seem like much these days. With the baseball draft nearing, Jack focused more than ever on all things baseball. And I had been working on putting together a portfolio for the internship.

"Hey." Melissa leaned against the wall in our kitchen, clearly wanting to talk. "I was thinking about heading home. Did you want to come with?"

I thought for about two seconds before answering, "No way. The guys don't have games this weekend, just practice."

She smiled. "Then I'm definitely leaving."

I laughed, tossing my hair from my shoulder. "Alone time with Jack...whatever will we do?" I placed one finger in front of my puckered lips before tapping.

"I seriously don't want to know." She rolled her eyes and turned to open the fridge.

"Yeah, you do," I teased, raising my eyebrows.

Her lips turned up in a half smirk. "Sorta. But please don't share." She shook her head as if trying to shake way a disturbing image. "What did I hear about Jack and the softball team?"

"Oh." I shrugged. "Since the guys don't have a game, they asked Jack to throw out the first pitch

156

tonight."

"Seriously?" Her head cocked to one side.

"Apparently it's good publicity. I don't know. Whatever, it's not like he has a choice. He can't really say no to another team at the school, you know?"

"That's still sort of weird."

"I think so too, but whatever. I'll be there."

"You're so supportive," she teased, cupping her hands together.

"Oh, I do try," I said with a fake Southern accent as I fanned my hand in front of my face.

She laughed. "I'll see you when I get back. Want me to check on your car?"

"Oh, yeah. Can you make sure it's still sitting in my driveway collecting dust?" I giggled at the absurdity of the situation.

"You don't need it," my mother had told me during one of our many arguments. "It just gives you a way to leave school when you should be studying or doing homework." I had tried to tell her that maybe I'd need to leave school for a photography project, but then she'd just insist that I take Melissa's car. No matter how many times I tried to tell her that she made no sense, she refused to budge. So there my car sits. At home. Waiting for me. And the truth is, I'm not sure I ever want to go back for it.

"Don't have too much fun with Jack this

weekend. Call you later, 'K?" Melissa gave me a squeeze before grabbing her things.

"'K. Drive safe. Tell your parents I said hi and I miss them." I smiled and waved as she walked out our front door, almost crashing into Jack.

"Have a good weekend, Jack." Melissa winked and he turned to me, his eyebrows raised.

"Uh, you too, Melis," he responded with a half grin before closing the door. "What was that about?"

"She's leaving for the weekend." I tried not to blush but felt the heat rising to my cheeks.

He dropped onto the couch next to me. "The whole weekend?"

"The whole weekend," I said, dragging out the words for effect.

"Sweet. Listen, before I get distracted, Matt wants us to come over before the softball game and hang out at his place. I told him I'd check with you first." Jack rested his head against the pillow on my couch, his hat flopping to one side.

"Fine with me. Who's gonna be there?" I asked absentmindedly, tossing the hat aside and running my fingers through his soft, dark hair.

"A few of the guys from the team. Dean and probably Jamie. I don't really know."

"I like her," I admitted with a smile. "She's funny."

"She is funny. And she's good for Matt," Jack

added, alluding to things I knew nothing about and frankly wasn't sure I wanted to.

"Everyone's going to the game, right?" I asked, changing the subject.

He pushed himself up with one arm until he sat facing me. "Why won't you just come with me when I go?" He slid his thumb down my cheek.

"Because you have to be there an hour before the game starts. For what, I have no idea, but I'm not going that early." I pouted, eyeing him with my best puppy dog impression.

He put his hand behind my neck and pulled me to him, his mouth meeting mine halfway as the overgrown scruff on his face scratched at my bare cheeks. "Seriously, when are you going to shave?"

His lips pulled up into a slight smile. "You know I can't shave until we lose, Kitten. And we're not losing, so probably not ever."

I rolled my eyes. "You guys and your superstitions."

"You love it," he whispered into my ear before sucking at my lobe softly with his mouth, causing my senses to disappear.

"Yep, sure do," was my only response as he continued working down my neck.

He gently pushed me onto my back and leaned on top of me, his dark brown eyes boring into mine. "You are so beautiful. You know that?"

I let out a small breath before pulling his head

down and arching toward his lips. His tongue pushed its way into my mouth with intensity. I ran my hands down his back and slipped my fingers into the waistband of his shorts before lifting his shirt up in succession with my own.

A slight sound escaped my lips at the feeling of his bare skin hot against mine. Chills coursed through me, appearing up and down my legs and arms. His breath was warm on my neck, small kisses being delivered around my ears and cheeks until meeting my mouth once more.

"Cassie." He mumbled my name, his breath ragged.

Without a word, I slipped out from under him and stretched out my hand. He laced his fingers with mine and I led him away from the living room and into my bedroom, where I closed the door behind us.

*****

Jack opened Matt's front door without knocking and led me inside. I watched as five baseball players with hairy faces turned their heads in our direction and smiles instantly appeared on all their faces.

"Carter! What's up, buddy! Hey, Cass," Matt yelled from the round table where they were playing a drinking and card game.

"Hey, Jack. Hey, Cassie." Ryan greeted us without looking up from his hand, his forehead creased in concentration.

Dean picked up his cell phone, checking the time. "Finally! Where have you two been?"

"Not sure I'll ever get used to you holding some girl's hand," Brett added, his blue eyes locked pointedly on our intertwined fingers.

"Get used to it, BT, she's not just some girl." Jack planted a kiss on the side of my face and gently squeezed my fingers.

"I like that you've finally found someone, Jack. And I especially like that she isn't some stupid skank." Matt's girlfriend Jamie walked out from the kitchen with a smirk.

I laughed. "Love you too, Jame!"

"You have to admit my worry was valid!" She pursed her lips together, her brown ponytail bouncing. "Now get in here and help me," she called out, after disappearing back behind the wall.

I looked at Jack and smiled as I untangled my hand from his. He smacked me on the backside when I walked away.

"I love that girl," he said to his teammates before sitting at the table. "Deal me in."

I entered the kitchen before giving Jamie a quick squeeze as I glanced back at the group of guys. "Their facial hair is killing me. They look freaking horrible."

"Please don't remind me. I try to pretend it's all a bad dream," Jamie said, rubbing her palm against her cheek.

"Ahem, ladies." Matt pretended to clear his throat. "We can hear you, ya know!"

"Like we care!" Jamie said with a huff.

"Hey! Don't curse our winning streak!" Cole answered back before slapping his hand over his mouth.

"Jesus, Cole, who raised you? The first rule about the winning streak is *you don't talk about the winning streak!*" Ryan punched him in the shoulder.

"You guys are just lucky we keep kissing you," Jamie said, attempting to steer the attention from poor Cole.

"I second that," Jack belted out, his eyes meeting mine briefly before settling back on his cards.

"Pussy," Brett teased, his eyes focused on the deck of cards in his hand.

"I'll knock you into the middle of next week if you don't shut up, BT," Jack threatened, his jaw rigid.

"He's just jealous 'cause no girls want to go anywhere near him," Cole teased as he removed his baseball hat and tossed it on the floor.

"I can't keep the girls off me. It's you no one wants," Brett chipped back.

The card game continued until Jack checked the clock on the wall and rose from the table. He slammed back a shot of tequila before speaking.

"Kitten, I gotta go. Get out here and give me some loving."

I eyeballed Jamie. "Seriously? Do you hear this guy?" I said with a nod in Jack's direction.

Jamie laughed and gave me a hearty shove. "Get out there."

"You come to me," I insisted, staring him down.

All eyes were on us, entertained by our stubborn battle.

"Gladly," Jack responded and walked hastily toward me. He lifted me up in the air and I wrapped my legs around his waist.

"Keep it in your pants, pal," I whispered into his ear before nibbling on his neck.

"You better stop or I'll throw you on the floor and have my way with you." He yanked my hair back, forcing my head away from his before ravaging my mouth.

"Get a room," Brett shouted.

"We'll just take yours," Jack mumbled between kisses.

"Go or you'll be late." I unwrapped my legs and hopped down.

Jack looked at me one last time before turning to his teammates. "Make sure she doesn't walk alone to the game."

"I don't need a babysitter." I frowned at him, rolling my eyes.

"Dean?" he said sternly.

"I got her, J. I promise we'll all go together. She won't be alone." Dean smiled at me and then looked reassuringly at his brother.

"See you guys at the game." Jack closed the door and all eyes fell on me.

"What? Don't look at me, I'm not the crazy one!" I yelled, shaking my head.

"Just so you know, I've never seen him act this way about anyone other than Gran," Dean said, without looking up from his cards.

I tried not to smile, but failed miserably.

Forty minutes later, the group of us headed toward the far end of campus. The guys were playful as they walked, bumping into one another and knocking each other's hats off. I stopped walking to fall slightly behind when Dean turned around, noticing my absence. I waved him ahead, pulling out my camera and removing the lens cap. When he saw my intention, he rejoined the group with a big smile.

I knelt on the sidewalk, framing the group of guys in the viewfinder, smiling to myself at how happy they all looked. *Click.* Another shot of Dean's hand smacking Brett's hat off. *Click.* Jamie and Matt holding hands from the back was too much for me to resist. *Click.*

"That's a nice camera." A harsh voice startled me and the camera fell from my eye.

I looked up to see a large, beefy silhouette

towering above me, his face shadowed by the setting sun. "Give it to me," he insisted, before taking a swig of something hidden inside a brown paper bag.

I stood up instantly, glancing past the man's shoulder for Dean. I was too shocked to shout. Too nervous to run. You know how you think that if you're ever in a bad situation, you'll be all tough, like in the movies? That's bullshit. You'll freeze, just like I did. All I could do was silently will Dean to look back at me. I prayed he'd notice I still hadn't caught up.

"I said give it to me, bitch!" the man shouted before introducing the back of his hand to the side of my cheek.

His knuckles hit me with such brute force that my head flew to one side, my hair flying out all around me. I whipped my head back to face him in shock, strands of hair sticking to my eyelashes and lips.

*Did he just hit me?*

"That guy just hit Cassie! Hey!" I heard Dean shouting and the sound of feet heading in my direction.

I couldn't move. My body was still frozen with shock. I couldn't believe this stranger hit me.

He struck me again, this time punching me with a closed fist on the other side of my face. As I stumbled with the force of the blow, I looked in the direction of the group, my eyesight crystal clear. Dean sprinted full speed toward me when the man suddenly appeared in front of him. I watched as Dean shoved him, but the man lifted his brown paper bag and slammed it against the top of Dean's head.

Thick green glass shattered and spilled onto the sidewalk as Dean's body crumpled lifelessly to the ground, blood spilling from his head. I wanted to scream, but no sounds came. My mind immediately replayed the scene: Dean's tall, muscular body losing all coordination as it collapsed into a heap on the concrete, then blood. Lots of it. Brett ran to Dean's limp body and quickly pulled Dean's arm around his shoulder, lifting him and dragging him away in the opposite direction.

I watched the rest of the group as they scattered like animals in a forest fire.

*Hey, wait!*

*Where is everyone going?*

I took two steps in their direction before the man suddenly reappeared at my side. "Where do you think you're going, bitch?"

I instinctively bent over and tried to cover my face with both arms. My eyes focused solely on the black and white design of his shoes as they danced around me. The colors blurred to the left where forceful blows crashed against the side of my face and head.

*Please stop hitting me.*

Blurry movement to the right and the other half of my face exploded in pain.

*Please stop.*

His fist interrupted my internal pleas as it collided with the side of my head once more, almost knocking me off my already shaky feet. I was his personal punching bag. Blow after blow, his blasts showed no signs of stopping, the force of each punch only growing in intensity.

*Dear God, please make it stop.*

*I don't care if I die right now, just please make him stop hitting me.*

*Please.*

*It hurts so bad.*

And just like that his shoes disappeared from my view. I glanced up to see him running between two sets of houses in the distance, my camera flailing wildly from the strap wrapped tightly around his hand.

"Cassie!" I jerked my head down the street to see Cole waving frantically at me. "Cassie! Run!" he shouted.

I didn't run.

I couldn't.

My legs were shaking so forcefully I could barely hold myself upright. I stumbled toward Cole, keeping my eyes locked on his face the entire time.

"Jesus, Cassie, are you okay?" His eyes

widened at the sight of me and I couldn't stop myself from spitting, my taste buds revolting at the metallic taste.

I didn't speak. Blood-covered saliva covered the area where I continued spitting. I pressed my fingertips against my cheeks, the pain sharp where my teeth had ripped up the inside of my mouth.

My mind couldn't process what just occurred. I kept thinking, *Did that just really happen? Did he just hit me?* The words kept repeating over and over again in my mind.

"Where's Dean?" I looked around anxiously, visions of his body crumpling to the ground replaying once again in my mind.

"I don't know. Come on, we have to find Jack."

"Where's everyone else? Where were you?" I asked, my tone almost robotic as a metallic taste filled my mouth. I spit and blood spattered the pavement.

"I...I don't know. Everyone scattered. It just happened so fast." Cole winced as his eyes avoided mine.

He tossed his arm around my waist to help steady my incessant shaking. We were walking slower than Cole would have liked toward the campus entrance when I saw Jack. He ran full speed in our direction, his hat gripped tightly in his fist.

"Cassie!" Jack's eyes grew wide when he recognized me. "Cassie!" he yelled, as he quickened his pace toward us.

I stopped moving, tears suddenly filling my eyes. I didn't recognize it at first, the feeling that overwhelmed me at the sight of him. My entire body released the shock it held as I fell into his strong arms. For the first time since this whole mess began, my lungs filled themselves fully with cool evening air as I took a cleansing breath. I looked into his frantic brown eyes and finally relaxed.

I was safe now because Jack was here.

"What the fuck happened, Cole?" Jack shouted, his voice filled with rage.

"I…I don't know, Jack. One minute everyone's together, and the next some guy's hitting Cassie and breaking a bottle over Dean's head and saying he has a gun." Cole's voice shook as he summed up the events.

"He said he had a gun?" I asked, confused.

"He said he was packing. That's when everyone ran away."

Jack's chest rose and fell rapidly against my body as his jaw tightened. "What did you just say?"

Jack eased me from him and began pacing, pulling at his hair with each step. He turned to me, his eyes filled with pain. "Kitten, where were you when they ran?" My eyes darted between Cole and Jack; I wasn't sure how to respond. "You gotta tell me, Kitten, I'm going fucking crazy right now."

I watched as Cole braced, clearly dreading

Jack's reaction. Jack reached for Cole's shirt, gripping it tightly in his fist. He yanked until Cole stood an inch from his face. "Where the fuck was Cassie, Cole?"

"Jack, I'm sorry." Cole winced, unwilling to put up a fight.

I watched as Jack's other hand balled into a fist. "Jack!" I longed to stop this battle before it began. Jack turned to me, my eyes locking onto his. "He took my camera."

I said the words out loud and allowed my tears to fall. This stranger had violated me. He ripped away a sense of security I never knew I had before suffering the loss of it. He struck my body violently and robbed parts of my innate trust in others. And he took the one material thing that I cared about the most and ripped it from my possession.

Jack's anger dropped away for a moment, his eyebrows pinched together in pain. "I'll get you a new one, Kitten. I promise."

I shook my head. "I need my camera. Why'd he take it? Why'd he hit me so hard? And why so many times?" I fell to the curb, sobbing uncontrollably.

"Do you think we should call the cops? The campus police or something?" Cole suggested with a nervous shrug.

"That's where Dean and Brett are now," Jack snapped.

My eyes opened at the mention of his name. "Where is Dean? Is he okay? I saw him fall. He looked unconscious."

Jack leaned next to me, his hand rubbing the length of my back. "Don't worry. He's fine."

"How? His head was bleeding like crazy! And he couldn't even stand!"

"Head wounds do that, Kitten. They bleed something fierce, but it had almost stopped by the time I saw him," Jack told me, his voice calm.

"So he's really okay?" I released a breath.

"He's really okay." His voice reassured me and he kissed the top of my head.

"Hey, Jack." Cole took a step toward us before Jack cut him off with an angry slash of his hand.

"Stay the fuck away from me right now, Cole, or I'll end up doing something I might regret."

I looked into Cole's worried eyes and flashed him a hollow look.

"I'm really sorry, Cassie." Cole's voice echoed softly.

"Shut. Up. Cole." Jack's tone was deadly, and I turned away.

Jack's arms settled underneath my legs and around my waist as he lifted me into the air. "Let's go home," he whispered before kissing the side of my forehead.

I wrapped my arms around his neck and nuzzled into his chest, the sound of his heart beating against my ears giving me reassurance. He carried me in his arms the entire way to my apartment, never once stopping to catch his breath and never slowing his pace.

Once inside, he placed me gently on my bed and kneeled beside it. "We need to get you cleaned up, Kitten. Your beautiful face is a mess." He lightly brushed my hair back with his fingertips.

I hadn't given any thought to how messed up my face might be. My jaw ached and my head throbbed, but other than that, nothing else really hurt. "I'm gonna get you some ice. I'll be right back." He brought my hand to his lips and kissed it.

I heard his cell phone ring and his voice rose in anger at whoever was on the other end of that call. He reappeared at my side. "The police are coming here, Kitten. They need your statement right now so they can go look for this guy. And they need to take pictures of your injuries, so we can't clean you up just yet. I'm sorry."

"It's okay. I'd rather get it over with anyway." I smiled gamely and then winced. "Ouch. Shit, that hurts," I admitted before placing my palm against my cheek.

"I'm sorry I left you alone tonight. I should have been with you." His face twisted with anguish.

My heart ached for his self-inflicted guilt. "Jack, I should be able to walk through a neighborhood without getting beat up and robbed."

"But if I hadn't gone early. If I'd been there…" His head rested on my lap and he clasped his arms around my back.

"I'm glad you weren't there," I admitted.

"Why would you say that?"

"Because I could never live with the guilt if you got hurt because of me."

He grimaced at my admission. "Kitten, I'd break my fucking pitching arm if it meant keeping you safe."

My heart jumped inside my chest. "You really shouldn't say things you don't mean." I gave him a pained wink, reminding him about my list.

"I'm not," he said confidently before a knock on the front door interrupted our exchange. "I'll be right back. Sit tight." He kissed my forehead and I watched him walk out of my room.

My phone beeped, alerting me to a text message. Melissa. *Oh my God, are you okay? Dean just called me. I'm coming back.*

*Don't come back. I'm fine. I'll call you after I talk to the police,* I responded, knowing she'd be sick with worry.

*The police? What the hell? Call me as soon as you can. I'm freaking out!!!!!!!!*

Her text made me laugh. I think it was all the exclamation points. Or the fact that I could hear her voice whenever I read her words. Either way, I typed out another response. *Call you soon. Don't freak. Jack's here.*

"Hey, Kitten?" Jack peered into my room, his hand gripping the edge of the door. "The police are here."

I tossed my cell phone on the bed before pushing my body off. Two uniformed police officers were waiting for me when I walked into the living room. One held a notepad while the other gripped a camera that caught my gaze and reminded me of what I'd lost.

*That asshole stole my camera.*

*I no longer own a camera.*

*I'm camera-less.*

Tears started to roll down my cheeks as I blinked in vain to stop them. Jack rushed to my side and gathered me close, wiping them away tenderly with his thumb. "Are you okay?"

"I can't believe he stole my camera." I closed my eyes tightly as the drops continued to fall, feeling like a hole was opening in the pit of my stomach.

"We really need to get your statement, miss," one of the officers prompted.

I sniffed once and looked up, swiping at the moisture under my eyes. "Okay."

"Your brother already told us what happened, but we'd like you to corroborate his story. He also said that more happened once he left the scene and we'll need you to give us those details as well.

Okay?" the officer asked, while reading from his notepad.

I looked at Jack with confusion before looking back at the officer. "My brother?"

"Yeah. Um, Dean Carter? He said he was Cassie Andrews's brother," the officer noted.

"How's he doing? Is he okay?" My concern for Dean instigated a rush of questions.

"He doesn't need stitches but has a nasty cut on his head, not to mention a raging headache. It probably wouldn't hurt to have him seen by a doctor," the other officer chimed in.

I looked at Jack and he waved his hand to calm me down. They read Dean's statement out loud and I agreed with his account, noticing as Jack clenched his jaw. I reached down for his hand and squeezed it tightly in mine. I filled in the blanks from when Brett carried Dean away until I walked to Cole, watching again as Jack cringed and the veins in his neck bulged. Seeing him in pain caused an ache to form inside my chest. But I'll admit I liked the fact that he was so pissed off about the whole thing. I'd never felt more safe or protected in my life.

The officers asked me simple questions that I had already answered and nothing stumped me until the last one. "Can you give us any idea of what the perp looks like? Would you be able to identify him in a lineup?"

My gaze flashed to Jack, and I shifted uneasily

in my seat. "I could identify his shoes. And maybe his fist."

"I'm sorry?"

"All I saw were his black and white shoes. And his knuckles. He was standing with the sun behind him and I never saw his face." My body shook and Jack released my hand as he stood up and started to pace.

"Are we almost done?" Jack asked defensively.

"Almost." The officer's voice was a little terse before it softened when he turned to me. "I'm sorry, Cassie, but we have to take some pictures of your injuries."

"That's fine." I sighed and then stood up to move in front of the white living room wall. The officer took pictures of my face at varying angles, while I kept my eyes locked on Jack's, refusing to let go of the comfort he brought me.

When the police officers left, Jack walked me into the bathroom where I caught a glimpse of my reflection for the first time that evening.

"That's so weird." I leaned toward the mirror, touching the green and purple bruise on my brow before moving to the similar one forming on my forehead.

"What is?"

"I don't even hurt where the bruises are," I noted, mesmerized by the unfamiliar face staring back at me.

Jack's forehead creased. "Where do you hurt?" he asked, the pain in his eyes evident.

"My cheeks and jaw." I touched them gingerly.

"I'll go get you some ice and ibuprofen. They'll help with the pain and swelling." He grabbed my hand, turning me toward him. "If I ever find this guy, I'm going to fucking kill him for putting his hands on you."

I shook my head, my heart breaking. "I just want my camera back."

"I know," he said before looking away.

"Hey, Jack?" I stopped him. "Why did Dean say he was my brother?" I asked, suddenly remembering what the officer had said.

Jack shrugged. "I don't know. I can only guess that he thought he was doing you a favor. Or protecting you somehow. Why?"

I smiled and quickly winced with the pain. "I just liked it, was all."

His dimples flashed in his cheeks as his lips turned upward. "Oh yeah? And why's that?"

I shrugged. "I liked the way it sounded."

I didn't know it was possible, but I watched as his dimples deepened as his smile grew. "So did I, Kitten. So did I." He walked out and my heart stammered with his confession.

Jack's cell phone rang and it reminded me that I still needed to call Melissa. I walked toward my bed and reached for my cell as Jack leaned in, his hand covering his phone. "You don't mind if Dean stays here tonight, do you?"

"Of course not. I was just gonna tell you to call him. I'm gonna call Melissa real quick," I told him, relieved that Dean was coming over.

He removed his hand from covering the phone before bringing it up to his ear. "She says it's fine. I don't think so. Hold on, I'll double-check."

He looked at me again. "We don't need anything, right?"

I shook my head. "Nope, just get him over here."

"She says no. She won't care. Make sure Gran knows we're both staying here before you leave. Okay, see you soon."

"I won't care about what?" I asked as soon as he hung up.

"If he stays here all weekend," Jack said before straightening his stance.

"Oh. Not at all. I sort of want him here."

"Oh, really? Trading me in already?" He winked at me and I laughed.

"Ouch. Don't make me laugh, it hurts." I grabbed my cheeks with both hands. "No, it's just that I want to be around him 'cause he was there. He knows how I feel because he experienced it too. Is that weird?"

"It makes sense to me, Kitten," he said with a smile.

"I really need to call Melissa before she shows back up here." I started to press buttons on my phone and Jack turned away, closing my bedroom door as he left.

"Oh my God, Cassie! What happened? What is going on? And what took you so long to call me back? I'm freaking out here!" Melissa yelled into the phone.

"Sorry, it's been a crazy night." I held the phone away from my face, taking care to not press it against my cheek like I normally would.

"Is Dean okay? Is Jack there? What happened?" Her questions shot out rapid-fire.

"We were walking to the softball game to see Jack and we got jumped. Some guy stole my camera, beat me up, broke a forty-ounce bottle over Dean's head—"

"Oh, Cass, he stole your camera?" I could hear the sorrow in Melissa's question as she interrupted me, and her compassion for my loss affected me more than I expected.

I struggled to even out my breathing as I swallowed hard. "Yeah."

"I'm so sorry. I know you're more upset about that than anything else."

"You know me well."

"Are you okay? I mean, where did he hit you? Did Jack freak?"

"Jack's pretty…" I paused. "I don't know what

Jack is. Pissed? Sad? Angry? He's all over the place. Oh, but hey, I think Dean's gonna stay here this weekend. Do you mind if he sleeps in your bed?"

"Not at all. Just tell him no funny business in there. I don't want to come back to sheets I have to crack in half or anything." Melissa laughed at her own joke.

"You are so gross." I chuckled, trying not to scrunch my cheeks.

"I know," she responded proudly. Her tone changed as she asked, "How's Dean? Is he going to be okay?"

"Apparently he's going to be fine. He must have a pretty hard head," I joked.

Melissa was quiet for a moment. "I'm just glad you're both alright."

Before I could respond, there was a knock on my door and it opened slowly. "Kitten, Dean's here."

"Hey, Melis, Dean just got here and I really wanna go see him. Can I call you later?"

"Yeah, you go. Tell the boys I said hi and I'm glad they're staying with you."

"I will. Love you."

"Love you more," she said before hanging up, and I tossed the device onto to my mattress.

I emerged from my bedroom and locked eyes with Dean as Jack stood beside him. My eyes instantly watered up at the sight of him. "Dean! Are you okay?" I said, my voice frantic. I ran to him, locking my arms around his back and squeezing.

"I'm fine. How are you? Are you okay?"

I nodded. "You have no idea how scary it was to see you hurt like that." I tried to shake the images from my mind that I was certain were seared there forever.

"You have no idea how horrible it was to see some guy hitting you," he replied, his voice rising in anger.

"Can we not talk about that right now?" Jack's voice sounded angry and I was grateful for the subject change.

I let out a sigh. "I'm just happy you're okay. Does your head hurt?"

"Like a bitch," he muttered.

"Before I forget, Melis said you could stay in her room."

"Yeah? Well I was going to stay in there even if she said I couldn't," he said with a laugh. "It's okay if I take a shower, right?"

"Of course. There's a shower in Meli's room. She has extra towels under the sink." As I spoke, Jack reached for my hand and pulled me toward the couch.

"We'll be out here when you're done," Jack said, before sitting down and pulling me onto his lap. "I'm going crazy inside right now, Kitten. I feel like I'm losing my fucking mind. I'm not going to practice this weekend. I won't leave you alone." He leaned his head against my chest and I ran my fingers through his hair.

"Jack, I love that you care so much about what happened to me, but you can't be by my side twenty-four hours a day. And you absolutely cannot skip practice this close to the draft. Are you out of your mind?"

He glanced up at me, the pain evident in his narrowed eyes. "That's what I'm trying to tell you!"

"When you go to practice, Dean will stay here with me. I won't be alone, okay?" I prayed my suggestion would ease his worry.

He let out a long, exasperated breath. "Okay. He's the only one I trust anyway…" His voice trailed off. "We'll take shifts."

I rolled my eyes, but he didn't notice. "You have to get past this, Jack. You can't take it upon yourself to be my personal bodyguard."

"Yes, I can."

"You'll drive me insane," I snapped, my voice harsher than I intended. "And then I'll break up with you."

Jack's head snapped around as he glared at me with shock and surprise. "What?"

"I don't want a babysitter. I don't want a bodyguard. I appreciate what you're trying to do, Jack, but I don't want to feel like I'm in a fucking cage."

He slid my body from his lap and turned to face me, his forehead creased. "Cass, just give me some time to deal with this, okay? It just happened and I feel like I'm losing my goddamn mind." He cringed as he continued. "Do you know what it feels like to want to beat the shit out of four of your teammates? Four guys I'm supposed to respect and trust. Four guys I trusted completely before tonight."

I watched as his face twisted with his pain, my heart aching. "I can't tell you not to be mad at them, Jack. I don't know why they ran and left me there. I'm sort of conflicted about all that. It did happen really fast, though, I can tell you that. It's like one minute the guy was with me, then with Dean, then back at me." I closed my eyes, my head shaking.

"That's exactly it. You might be conflicted in regards to them, but I'm not."

Dean walked into the room, a towel wrapped around his waist. "Remind me that it's going to fucking hurt next time I try to wash my hair." He smirked. Dean's ability to bounce back so quickly after what happened amazed me and gave me hope.

"I'm really tired. I'm gonna go to bed, okay? Love you both," I said before pushing myself from the couch.

"So much for our weekend alone, huh?" Jack offered me a slight smile.

I looked at Dean before responding. "It's okay.

This is better anyway."

# TWELVE
## JACK

The fact that some stranger had beaten up Kitten and stolen her camera drove me out of my fucking mind. It had been three weeks and her bruises had faded, but my anger hadn't. I never told her, but I cruised up and down that street every day, sometimes before and after baseball practice, looking for the asshole that had touched her. He was lucky I hadn't found him yet.

I also looked everywhere for her camera. I searched online, went to local pawnshops, but it didn't show up. I wanted justice for her...vengeance, really. But more importantly, I wanted to be the one to deliver it. And every day that I was denied that, my anger toward my cowardly teammates grew. I hadn't talked to any of the ones who were there that night, my temper flaring out of control whenever one of them was near.

I walked into the locker room and changed into my practice uniform in silence. "Carter!" Coach Davies shouted from his office. I glanced up and our eyes met. "Get in here," he demanded before turning his back to me. Coach was a good baseball player, but he was an even better man. He was the reason I chose Fullton State over the other schools. I wanted to play ball for someone I respected, and I respected Coach Davies.

I slammed my locker door shut and hustled into Coach's office. "Shut the door." He motioned before leaning back in his swivel chair. "Come sit."

I sat in the old wooden chair, my mind racing before he spoke. "Look, I don't know what's going on between you and your teammates. I heard something about your girlfriend getting beat up and I'm really sorry about that, but your team is your family and you need to work it out."

"No disrespect, Coach, but my family wouldn't let my girlfriend get the shit beat out of her while they ran away and hid."

Coach frowned. "I'm sorry, Jack, what did you say?"

"Four of your guys left her there alone. Brett took care of Dean, but everyone else bailed on her."

"Who does that?" His voice trailed off.

"I'll tell you who. My teammates. My so-called *family*. My *brothers*. I can't even look at them, let alone pretend like I respect them." I threw my hands up in the air, my voice disgusted. "Coach, it takes all of my willpower every single day to not beat the shit out of them. I'm sorry." I looked down.

"I didn't know the details, Jack. I'll take care of it on my end, but you have to promise me you'll work it out on yours. I can't have my team falling apart at the end of the season. And you need to keep your focus." He leaned toward me, his concern genuine.

"I'm focused. I'll be fine." I attempted to reassure him, but I could see he wasn't buying it.

"Don't quit on me, Carter. Don't quit on this team. Don't quit on yourself." His frown deepened.

"It's not in my nature, Coach. I don't quit." And I meant it.

"Alright, get on out there then. Tell Coach Smith I want to talk to the boys before practice starts."

"Yes, sir," I answered before scooting the chair back.

The entire team sat in the dugout waiting for Coach. Since this wasn't our standard protocol, the guys were nervously trying to figure out what was up. I remained on one end of the long bench, while Brett, Cole, Matt, and Ryan sat on the other.

"Alright, gentlemen, listen up." Coach appeared on the field and was immediately greeted with silence. "I know there was an incident that happened off school property with a few of our players. I didn't realize how bad the situation was. I didn't know what happened. But I know now." His stern gaze landed briefly on each player sitting on the bench as he continued. "And let me tell you, I'm not just molding you gentlemen into great baseball players here...I'm trying to mold you into great men. And great men don't run away from a fight. Great men don't leave a girl alone to fend for herself."

He looked at Coach Smith before letting out a long huff of air. "There will come a time in your life when you lose something that matters to you. You'll fight for it and you won't win. But what really matters isn't the war you're waging, it's that you don't lose the person you are in the midst of the battle. You boys lost yourselves that night.

"And I know that some of you are real pissed off about what happened. Some of you are angry, hurt, embarrassed, shocked, and whatever other girly emotion your mommies tell you to get in touch with," he mimicked with a slight snarl. "I want you to take those feelings and use them on the field. Put it all out there and then leave it there. Don't take those emotions home with you at night where they can eat you up inside and rot your soul. This time we have together goes by in a blink of an eye. It's a special thing. Don't let anyone take it from you."

Without another word, Coach turned around and walked out of the dugout and down the field toward the locker room entrance. The silence was deafening as no one moved a muscle or made a sound. I hated being mad at my teammates, but the events of that night twisted me up so fiercely inside, it was hard to ignore. Forgiving them for what happened to Kitten felt almost impossible, even though they asked for it on a daily basis. I didn't know how to move past the anger. The truth was, I wasn't sure how to forgive them.

"You heard the Coach. Work it out, gentlemen. Let's finish off our season as not only teammates, but friends. Pitchers and catchers in the bullpen. Everyone else on the field."

"Coach Smith?" I said loud enough that it stopped the rest of the team from leaving.

"What is it, Carter?"

"Can I have a minute with Brett, Cole, Matt, and Ryan?" I asked, meeting the gaze of each of them as I said their names.

"Five minutes, then get your asses on the field." He turned. "Everyone else out. Now!" he shouted and the dugout cleared.

The guys sat there, unease written all across their faces. I could tell they weren't sure what I was about to do or say. And I'll admit I liked that they didn't know what I was capable of. Matt had called me a loose cannon once before and I happily wore the term with honor, even though he insisted it wasn't a compliment.

"Coach is right. We can't end the season like this." I shook my head. "I can't leave here hating you guys. This anger I have, it eats me up inside," I admitted. "I just need to know what happened."

"I'm really sorry, Jack. Personally, I panicked," Matt confessed, his eyebrows drawing together. "All I thought about was getting Jamie out of there. I didn't even think about Cassie. I know it's fucked up, but it's the truth."

189

I tried to fight the resentment that welled inside my gut. I clenched my fists before unclenching them. "I appreciate your honesty, Matt." My teeth ground together as I forced my tone to stay even.

"I'm sorry too, man. He said he had a gun and I took off. All I could think about was how I couldn't outrun a bullet. I left Cassie there and watched from a safe distance as she got the crap beat out of her," Ryan said as he looked at the ground.

My heart raced with his words as heat began rising in my cheeks. Ryan noticed the anger spreading across my face and quickly continued. "But I'm the one who has to live with that, Jack. I have to live with the fact that when the shit hit the fan, I went running. I let a girl get beat up and I did nothing about it. You might know how it feels to be you, but you have no idea how it feels to be me right now. I let you down. I let Cassie down. I let myself down. And I think about it every single day."

My breathing steadied as his words sank in. "I don't know what to say."

"There's nothing to say. Just know that I'm sorry," Ryan added.

I nodded before looking at Cole and Brett. "When Dean fell, you should have seen it. He was just lying there on the ground and my gut instinct was to get him out of there. Cassie was still standing and I figured that one of the other guys

would get her. But Dean wasn't even moving."
Brett shuddered with the memory.

"Thank you for taking care of him. I appreciate
it." I half smiled at Brett. "Can I ask you guys a
favor?" It wasn't really a question and they all
answered yes in unison.

"If you see the guy who did it, you call me
immediately."

"I've looked for him every day," Cole admitted.
"I drive around looking for him 'cause I saw his
face. I'd recognize him for sure."

"I'd really like to find him." My eyes narrowed
as I imagined beating this animal to a bloody pulp.

"Maybe we can go after practice? See what we
can find?" Matt offered with a shrug.

"I'm in." Brett raised his hand.

"Me too," Ryan noted with a grin.

"Sounds good to me." I was relieved at their
willingness to help, and felt some of the anger
trickle away.

Coach Smith poked his head into the dugout. "If
you ladies are done with the warm and fuzzies, I'd
like you to get your asses on the field with your
team."

"Coming, Coach." I spoke for the group and we
filed out.

We all knew we'd probably never find the guy,
but this was their way of trying to right a wrong.
And I needed that from them to help work past my

anger and disappointment.

*****

We walked the streets after practice looking for him, until my phone rang one evening during the middle of our nightly ritual. "Hold up, guys, it's Dean," I yelled toward my scattered teammates.

"What's up?"

"They got him." Dean's voice sounded solid and relieved.

"The guy?" My chest immediately tightened.

"They caught him trying to pawn Cassie's camera. He's in jail. I have to head down there to identify him."

My head spun as anger, relief, and fury all coursed through me at once. "Can I get her camera for her? Do you want me to come with you? I should probably come with you." My voice changed as my emotions settled on anger and making the coward pay for ever putting his hands on my girl.

"I'll find out about the camera when I get there, but I think it's evidence now, so she still can't have it back." Dean sounded sympathetic before his tone turned stern. "I'm in the police parking lot now, so I'll just head in and identify him. You should go tell Cassie they got him."

I made eye contact with each one of my teammates, who now surrounded me, and attempted to rein in my temper. I ended the call before addressing the group. "They got him. He tried to pawn Cassie's camera and they arrested him. Dean's at the police station now."

"I'll head down there. I got a good look at the guy too, so I can help," Brett added quickly, and took off running before waiting for a response.

"You alright?" Matt placed his arm on my shoulder.

"In all honesty, I kind of wanted to be the one to find him." I shrugged. "I wanted to introduce his face to the pavement," I added, and they all howled with laughter.

"I bet you did," Cole said with a wince.

"It's probably good you didn't, Jack. Knowing you, you would have killed the guy. You can't play professional baseball from jail," Ryan offered, his tone grave.

"I could start a jail baseball league. I'm very resourceful," I suggested.

Matt ignored my sick humor. "It's good they got him. This is a good thing."

"I know. Plus, Cass would never forgive me if I went to jail."

"Or broke your hand," Cole chipped in.

I frowned at Cole and snapped, "Who invited you?"

"I'm just saying!" he defended.

"Nah, you're right. She'd be pissed if I broke my hand." I sighed heavily, feeling the intensity of my anger dissipating. "I'd better go tell her the news. Thanks for coming out with me, guys."

I shook hands with each of them as the damage between us slowly healed. We walked toward our cars as a group before dispersing. I'm sure it looked like a scene out of *Swingers*, that old movie where people drove around the corner because no one walked anywhere.

\*\*\*\*\*

I found Cassie sitting on her bed, so engrossed in whatever she was reading that she hadn't noticed me standing in her doorway. It was moments like these where I could stare at her for hours. I watched as her eyes scanned the words on the page, her forehead creasing and her eyes narrowing with her emotions. I cleared my throat and she looked up.

"Jack! How long have you been standing there?"

"Not long." I smiled and moved next to her bed.

"I didn't know you were coming over. Is everything okay?"

"I just talked to Dean and they found the guy."

Her eyes widened as she carefully marked her page, closed her book, and set it down beside her. "They caught him?"

I sat facing her. "He tried to sell your camera to a pawnshop. They have regulations to check if things are stolen goods or not. The shop called the police and they arrested him."

"Oh my God. Well, that's good. Do they have

my camera? Can I get it back?" Her eyes lit up with hope.

I reached out my hand and felt her relax with my touch. "Sorry, Kitten. The police have it as evidence. It has to stay there until the sentencing is done."

"How long does that take?"

"It can take months."

"Months?" she repeated, her voice filled with disappointment.

"I'm sorry." And I was. Seeing her disappointed, hurt, and sad practically killed me. I repositioned myself next to her before resting my arm on her leg.

"It's not your fault." Cassie tried to smile, but it looked pretty halfhearted.

"Dean positively identified him. So did Brett. He'll most likely be charged with assault and battery and grand theft."

"Wait," she breathed out, interrupting my download from Dean. "Is there going to be a trial? Am I going to have to testify?"

"I was getting to that." I leaned over, planting a kiss on her cheek. "He pleaded 'no contest,' so there won't be a trial."

She shook her head. "What does 'no contest' mean?"

"He's basically saying he did it, without saying he did it. He waives his right to a trial because he doesn't think he'll get off if it goes to a jury. But the other thing about pleading no contest is he can't be sued for any damages he caused and his sentence will most likely be less."

"Less? How is that fair?"

"He's a pussy. He took the easiest and best way out for him."

I watched as the confusion cleared from her eyes before she leaned her head against my shoulder. "So, no trial. You're sure?"

"I'm sure," I answered.

"Good."

"Aren't you pissed off? Or angry?"

Her head lifted and she turned to eye me. "I can't change what's already done. I just want my camera back."

"And I just want to kill him," I said seriously and she chuckled.

"Let's be happy they caught him. I didn't think they ever would." Cassie's voice sounded more relaxed, and I sighed in relief.

"You're right. I am happy they caught him. Now I know where to go to kill him."

"Jack, stop it." She playfully swatted at my hand.

I winked at her and she rolled her eyes. "I won't ever let anyone touch you like that again, Kitten. It won't happen."

"I know. But we have to move forward, okay?

Put it behind us."

"Fine," I begrudgingly agreed as she nuzzled into me and I realized that he didn't matter anymore. I had everything that truly mattered right here in my arms.

# THIRTEEN
## CASSIE

My eyes opened slowly and I rubbed at them, resisting the urge to close them and go right back to sleep. Today was the big day for Jack. I heard my cell phone beep its soft reminder tone and I reached for it. A text message.

*Morning, Kitten. Are you up? Can't wait to see you.*

I noted the time. Six forty-three a.m. That was over an hour ago. I typed out a response letting him know I was awake and pressed Send. My phone immediately rang. "Hi," I answered wearily.

"When can I come get you?" Jack's voice sounded chipper.

"Good morning to you too," I teased.

"I'm coming over in half an hour. Be ready."

"What? No! I'm still in bed and I need to eat and shower and get ready." It was still early and I couldn't help the little whine that crept out in my voice.

"I didn't say we had to leave in half an hour, just that I was coming over. Plus," he paused, "I have something for you."

My pulse skittered. "What is it?"

"A present. I'll see you soon." He laughed before hanging up.

I jumped out of bed and threw open my door in search of Melissa. "Thank God you're already awake!" I shrieked at the sight of her eating cereal on the couch.

"I can't sleep in. You know this." She looked up from her cereal bowl and smiled.

"Um, Jack will be here in half an hour. And he said he's bringing me a present." I cocked my head to one side and raised my eyebrows as I plopped down across from her. Melissa's lips parted as her smile spread all the way across her face.

"Oh my God, you know what it is! Tell me!" I shouted at my best friend.

"No way. I'm not ruining *that* surprise." She shoveled another spoonful of cereal into her still grinning mouth.

"It's not…" I paused. "He's not…"

Her face crinkled as she read my mind. "Not what? Proposing?"

"He's not, right? I mean, we're not there yet."

"Oh, this is fun." Melissa was enjoying teasing me way too much, and I resisted the urge to reach across the table and strangle the truth out of her.

"You suck," I grumbled. "I mean, it's not like I think he's going to, but it did pop into my head. Probably because he's leaving soon, and I'm a girl and…"

"It's not a ring," she confessed begrudgingly. "But what if it was? Oooh, what would you say if Jack asked you to marry him?"

"I seriously hate you. This isn't funny. I hate

surprises." I stood up, rubbing my suddenly anxious stomach.

"You will love this. I promise. Trust me. Trust Jack," she said confidently. "He knows what he's doing. He has your best interests at heart. And that's all I'll say about that."

I released a deep breath. "Okay. Thank you. I'm gonna jump in the shower."

"Don't fall," she shouted, mimicking her father's usual tired joke.

"Ha ha!" I yelled from my room.

After my shower, I wrapped a towel around me and opened my bathroom door, spotting Jack lying with his eyes closed on my bed. If he really was sleeping, I didn't want to wake him, so I quietly tiptoed past him toward my dresser. I shrieked when he jumped from the bed and grabbed me, forcing my towel to fall to the floor.

"Jack! You scared the crap out of me!" I shouted as I reached for the wet clump of terrycloth.

Jack reached it first and snatched it away. "I don't think I'm giving this back. I like what I see too much."

"Stop," I whined, trying to cover my girly parts with my hands while he stared.

"Come here." He extended his hand and when I grasped it, he pulled my dampened body on top of his. "I love you. You know that?" he asked, running his fingers through my wet and tangled hair.

I didn't respond. I looked deep into his eyes and smiled. His fingers ran down my spine, forcing chills to course through my already chilled body. He arched his head up, meeting my mouth with his before pulling my head down. My lower lip felt the graze of his tongue as it entered my mouth slowly, methodically. His tongue darted against mine before leaving and then returning in a sensual exchange. Every touch awoke parts of me until soon, my entire body was screaming out for him.

"Jack." I breathed his name against his mouth.

"Mm-hmm," he responded as his tongue continued to titillate my senses.

"Do we have time?" I reached for the button of his shorts, hoping he'd take the hint.

"Mm-hmm." He grabbed me firmly with one well-toned arm and propped us both up on the bed with the other.

When we were sitting up completely, he reached for the back of his shirt and pulled it over his head in one swift movement. I stared at the muscles in his chest and shoulders, fascinated by the way they flexed with any movement he made. I fumbled with the button on his shorts, trying desperately to get it open, but failing due to our position.

"Just one sec," he said softly before sliding my body from his. I sat next to him as he kicked off his shorts and boxer briefs. "You can come back now." He smirked before lying on his back.

I leaned down to kiss his dimples before climbing back over. I positioned my body on top of his, my legs straddling his hips as I lifted my lower half and placed him inside of me. I allowed my body to lower gently, taking all of him in one motion. "Oh God," I moaned, feeling him reach places in me I'd never felt before. I looked up at my ceiling as I continued to lift and rock my body over and over, feeling him deeper inside each time.

Jack groaned with pleasure as his hands clutched my hips, moving with my body. Up and down. Up and down. His grip tightened as his excitement grew, willing me to speed up my motion, but I refused. I wanted to make it last. I rose and fell, sounds escaping my lips more often than not.

I looked down at him and noticed his eyes fixated on my face. Or more specifically, they were focused on my mouth. I moaned once more, my lips parting and moving with each labored breath I took as he squeezed his eyes shut.

"Why do you always feel so amazing?" he asked, his hips thrusting upward against mine each time I fell.

"You feel so good." I breathed heavily as I bent over him, my body still rising and falling as I swept my tongue across his lips. This new angle caused him to reach different places inside of me and I unwittingly moaned once more, almost unable to take it.

"Oh God, Jack." I breathed his name, my hips pumping faster. His hands moved me forcefully at a swift pace as he let out a throaty growl. I threw my mouth against his, longing for the feel of his lips and tongue against mine. I ravaged his mouth, unable to get enough, my tongue desperate for a dance with his. And when the hot taste of his tongue finally met with mine, I sighed audibly as I felt the beginning of that rush of tingling that I'd worked for.

As impossible as it seemed, I felt him grow larger inside of me as our movements hastened to their final pace. His eyes snapped shut and his face pinched together as he exploded inside of me with forceful thrusts. I shook with the joy it brought, my insides twitching and pulsing. Breathing rapidly, he opened his eyes and leaned shakily up to kiss me. "You're fucking sexy as hell. You know that?"

I collapsed onto his sweaty chest, my thighs burning. I breathed heavily against him before removing our still attached parts from each other. I scurried into the bathroom and when I came back out, Jack was propped up on the bed with both elbows.

"Are you ever getting dressed?" I teased and he smiled.

"Come here." He hooked his finger at me and I ambled toward him, slipping into a pair of underwear before sitting down in front of him.

He reached behind him and lifted a white box tied with a red bow. It was smaller than a shoebox, but bigger than a jewelry box. I had no clue what could possibly be inside.

"Open it," he insisted as nerves exploded throughout my system.

I pulled at the bow, watching as it released its grip on the box wrapped in white paper beneath it. I tore at the taped corners, ripping the paper away as I glimpsed the familiar red font I'd grown to love. My breath caught in my throat.

"Jack." My voice hitched.

"I know it's not like the one you lost, but Melissa said it's better," he started to explain. "She said this is the one you dream about." His proud smile lit up his whole face.

"It's incredible. But…" I shook my head reluctantly. "I know how much this camera costs, Jack, and it's too much."

His smile wavered as he asked, "Do you remember the night your camera got stolen?" His jaw tensed as I nodded. "Do you remember what I said to you?" I shrugged. "I said I'd get you a new one. I promised. Besides, it could be months before the police release yours from evidence."

"But, Jack…"

"But nothing. Kitten, I'm getting drafted today. By the end of the afternoon, I'm going to have more money than I've ever had in my life. I wanted to do something nice for you. And I made you a promise." His voice pleaded, desperate for my acceptance.

"I'll pay you back," I offered, feeling the self-imposed weight subside.

"Consider it an investment in your future." He reached for my face before tilting my chin toward him. "I believe in you. You have a gift. You are so talented. Now you can show the world."

Little tingles pricked the backs of my eyes with his words. "Saying thank you doesn't seem like enough, but thank you, Jack. I can't believe you did this."

"I'd do anything for you," he said before pressing his lips against my cheek.

"I got the internship," I told him softly.

His eyes lit up. "You did? I knew you'd get it! What'd they say? I mean, when they said you got it, what were their reasons?"

"They said I had real raw talent that impressed them. 'A beautiful eye and a unique perspective,'" I quoted, my eyes burning with unshed tears.

"They have no idea how right they are. Congrats, babe!" He lifted me off the bed and swung me around the room in his arms.

"I was going to have to turn them down because I didn't have a camera anymore," I admitted as one tear escaped. "But now I can accept it."

"You can just call me your hero if you want," he taunted, placing my feet back on the ground.

"You're so irritating." I sniffed back the tears and pretended to snarl at him and he laughed heartily.

"I'm just playing. I'm proud of you. You deserve it." He kissed the side of my head. "Hey, bring it with you today. Gramps said he wants to see it in action."

"I love him," I said with a laugh, imagining Gramps limping around with a giant-sized professional camera.

"And I love you. Now hurry up, 'cause we need to get to the house before the cameras do." He pushed me and smacked my behind.

I tumbled forward before gaining my balance. I turned toward my handsome boyfriend and said, "I'm proud of you, you know? I'm excited for you today."

His eyes brightened. "Thanks, Kitten."

"Are you nervous?" I asked, realizing he never expressed any fear when it came to this subject.

"Not really. I'd be nervous if I wasn't sure whether or not I was getting drafted, you know what I mean? If I had to sit there and wait to find out if they were going to crush my dreams or let me hold on to them a little bit longer. Those are the guys who have it rough. Not me." His eyes held mine in a serious gaze.

"So you're one of the lucky ones?"

"I'd like to think so."

"You're not worried about anything? The money, where you'll be playing, or what team you'll get on?"

"I'll be getting paid to play baseball. Paid…to play…a sport I love. I don't care about the team, how much they pay me, or where I have to go to play it. I just want to do this for as long as they let me," he answered, flashing the dimples on his cheeks.

"Well, I think they're the lucky ones," I explained, "whatever team drafts you. They're lucky to have you."

He avoided my gaze as his cheeks flushed with color. "Thanks, Kitten."

I slipped into some white dress shorts paired with an off-the-shoulder tan sweater. I brushed my hair, letting the golden strands fall down around my shoulders. When I stepped back from the mirror, Jack whistled. "Kitten, the whole world is going to be in love with you after this."

"What are you talking about? I'm in shorts and a sweater," I argued, looking down at my attire.

"You clearly don't see the way yourself the way guys do. If I was watching ESPN today, I wouldn't care at all about Jack Carter. I'd want to know everything about Jack Carter's girlfriend."

I felt my cheeks warm. "Shut up. You're totally

embarrassing me."

"Maybe you should stay here. It's one thing to have half the school in love with you, but I don't think I can handle half the viewing population wanting my girl." He sniffed, running his hand through his black hair.

"You're ridiculous."

He inhaled one long breath before shaking his head with his exhale. "I'm gonna have to put a huge rock on your finger before I leave so everyone knows you're unavailable."

My pulse quickened. "You're crazy, you know that?"

"Crazy about you," he said, waggling his eyebrows.

"No, I think you're just crazy." I laughed as I willed my heart to calm down.

*****

Jack led me through the screen door, his fingers intertwined tightly with mine. "Gran? Gramps? We're here!" he shouted into the house.

I looked around as Gran walked from the entryway in the kitchen wearing a light blue floral dress, a short string of pearls resting at her throat. Gramps followed behind her, dressed in carefully pressed brown dress slacks and a tan button-down shirt.

"You two look so nice!" I squealed.

"So do you, dear. Come here and give me a hug." Gramps shuffled toward me with a smile.

I hugged him and he whispered in my ear, "Did you like your present?"

"I did! It's amazing. I can't wait to show it to you later," I said with a large smile.

Gramps clasped his hands together. "Oh good! I want to learn all about it."

Gran reached for me and I leaned down toward her to give her a squeeze. "You look lovely, dear. I'm glad you're here," she said happily.

"Thank you. I'm happy to be here." My heart squeezed with love as I watched Gran meander back into the kitchen, humming happily.

"Have you heard anything about that internship yet?" Gramps asked, his wrinkled face looking hopeful.

"I got it!" I shouted, then winced a little at how overexcited my voice sounded.

"That's great, dear. Oh, that's just great news." Gramps beamed at me with a wide smile.

"You got the internship, sis?" Dean's voice cut through the noise in the room as he appeared, rubbing his tired eyes.

"I just found out. I wasn't going to take it, but now I can." I shot a thankful glance toward Jack before finding myself wrapped in Dean's arms.

"Congratulations. That's awesome." Dean caught me up in a tight bear hug, then released me with a proud smile.

A quick rap at the door reminded us all why we were gathered there in the first place. Jack pulled the curtain back and peered toward the porch. "It's just Marc and Ryan."

He opened the front door for his two well-dressed agents, who sauntered in with their hands filled with paperwork, a bottle of champagne, and a box of baseballs. "How you feeling, champ?" the taller of the two asked Jack.

"Good, thanks," Jack responded confidently, reaching out his hand to help carry the load.

"Hey, Dean. How you doing?" Dean smiled at the men as they playfully boxed in the living room, almost dropping their things.

I resisted the urge to pull my brand new camera out of my bag and shoot the interaction. The taller man stopped as he noticed me and walked in my direction, his arm outstretched. "You must be Cassie," he said before shaking my hand.

I smiled and nodded. "I'm Marc and this is my partner in crime, Ryan." He gestured toward the other gentleman.

"It's nice to meet you," I responded politely.

"It's nice to meet you too. Jack, you held back on how good-looking your girl is." Ryan winked at Jack with a chuckle.

"Settle down. I haven't signed any agreements with you two yet." Jack smirked before wrapping his arm around my waist and pressing me against him.

"This is fun!" I wiggled my shoulders with excitement, then leaned into Jack's hard chest.

"Oh, you like this, do you?" He dropped his arm and started to tickle my side.

I screamed and ran away, pretending to hide behind Dean for protection. "Save me, Dean," I shouted, grabbing his arms and cowering as he moved his body to block me from Jack's playful attack.

"What's going on?" Gran's voice echoed into the living room before she popped her head in. "Oh dear, stop it! Come sit at the table...that esspen will be here any minute now!"

I laughed at Gran's pronunciation of ESPN. She said it like it was a word, instead of separate letters. No matter how many times everyone told her it was E, S, P, N, she still insisted on pronouncing it *ESS-pen*.

"Are you okay, Gran?" Jack dropped a kiss on the top of her head before enveloping her frail frame in his strong arms.

"I'm just a little anxious is all," she admitted, her voice cracking.

"It's going to be great, isn't it, fellas?" Jack narrowed his eyes toward his soon-to-be agents.

"Of course it is," Ryan reassured.

"This whole thing is nerve-wracking," Gran

declared. "Why aren't you nervous?" she asked her grandson, and I watched the smile take over his face.

"Because there's nothing more I can do. I've worked my ass off and I've left it all out on that field every day for years." He shrugged one shoulder. "It's out of my hands at this point."

Her cheeks scrunched as she beamed with pride. "How'd you get so smart?" She cupped his face with both hands and planted a kiss on each cheek.

"I learned it from you. Now come sit with us and relax." He led her by the hand toward the kitchen table when the chime of the doorbell stopped them. "You sit, Gran. I'll let them in," Jack told her sweetly.

The chatter of voices filtered from the open front door and into the kitchen where we all sat waiting. Jack walked in followed by two cameramen, a reporter, and a producer. They discussed how things would work—that we would basically be filmed waiting for the phone to ring and for Jack to get his offer. They would film the reaction when the call came, and then interview Jack and possibly us after. And they kept reminding us not to look at the cameras and to act natural.

I laughed and all eyes turned to me. "What? It's not natural to have huge cameras following your every move and filming your private expressions. I'm a lot more comfortable *behind* the lens than I am in front of it."

"I know it's a little weird. Just do your best to pretend that the cameras aren't here," the director told me.

We sat around the kitchen table making small talk while the cameras filmed mere feet from us. Waiting for a phone call to come was nerve-wracking enough, but being filmed while you were waiting was a completely different experience entirely.

I jumped when the phone clanged to life, the sound startling me and waking up my dormant emotions. Fear suddenly ripped through my body, followed quickly by nerves, and then elation. My stomach twisted as Jack walked toward the old yellow rotary phone.

"Hello?" His eyes scanned each of our faces, but never the camera. "Speaking." A huge grin spread across his face making the dimples I loved even deeper. "Thank you so much. Yes, sir. I'll be in touch. Thank you."

He slammed down the phone before turning toward us. "Arizona!" he shouted and everyone cheered, including me. I wasn't sure why we were cheering, but I screamed and clapped along. "I'm a Diamondback!"

"Bonus amount?" Marc asked, leaning his elbows against the table.

"Hold on," Jack said before walking over to his

Gran and kissing her cheek. Then he squeezed Gramps and Dean before leaning down to kiss my mouth and I instantly forgot we were surrounded by cameras and strangers.

"Congratulations, babe. I'm so happy for you." I looked into his soft brown eyes and noticed the peace there.

"Thank you," he whispered into my ear before pressing his lips against my neck.

"Carter, come on. Do we have to call these guys back and negotiate or what?" Ryan interjected in a vain attempt to get Jack's attention.

"They said five," Jack answered with a smile, refusing to look away from my face.

"Yeah? Did they say five?" Ryan's eyes lifted.

"That's what they said."

"Well, alright! How do you feel? Should we push?" Marc asked as he scribbled notes furiously onto his pad.

He turned. "I think five is more than fair. I'm happy with it," Jack acknowledged.

"I know it sounds like a lot of money right now, Jack, but you'll lose half in taxes, we take our cut, and you won't be making much for the next few years in the minor leagues. We could probably get them to budge some," Marc suggested, still writing.

"I'm happy with it. I just want to play ball." Jack's tone was firm.

"Alright then. We'll accept the deal as is.

Congrats!"

Jack pulled his chair next to me and tossed his arm low across my back. "Five million isn't a bad signing bonus, right? Am I being naïve?"

I almost choked. "That's what it is? Five *million* dollars?" I asked.

"What did you think?" He laughed, his eyebrows pulling in.

"I don't know, but I didn't think that. Holy shit, Jack, that's incredible." I was so stunned I had to remember to close my mouth since my jaw kept dropping open.

"I should sign, right?"

"Absolutely. I mean, have your lawyer look over the contracts, but of course you should sign! Why wouldn't you?" I grabbed his face and pulled him to me before planting a loud kiss on his lips. "You're awesome. My baby's a Diamondback!"

The reporter tossed Jack a Diamondback jersey and hat and asked him to put them on while they interviewed him for a piece to air later that day. I watched as he tossed the jersey over his black shirt, buttoning the top button before placing the cap firmly on his head and tucking the stray hair underneath.

"How do I look?" he asked, modeling the crimson red jersey with D*BACKS written on it.

"Like a ball player," I responded with a smile.

"Like a million bucks." Gramps punched the air.

Dean grinned. "More like five."

"Can I get my camera? Are we allowed to take pictures?" I asked, longing to use my new camera for this special moment.

The producer turned to me. "As soon as we stop rolling. Otherwise the shutter sound of your camera will filter into the sound bytes."

"Okay," I responded with a huge smile, turning my camera on and exploring its new features so I'd be ready when it was time.

When the television crew cleared out, I grabbed Jack and his family and posed them in the backyard, under a giant oak tree. I took a few group family shots and then individual ones.

"Let me take one of you and Jack, dear. Do you trust me to use your camera?" Gramps asked with a laugh.

"Of course! Be careful, it's a lot heavier than it looks," I noted, handing him my weighty equipment.

"Oh, this is heavy." He carefully placed the camera strap around his neck.

"Okay, now you have to look through it like a regular, old-fashioned camera." I paused, realizing that Gramps had probably never used anything but an *old-fashioned* camera.

I placed his index finger on top of a round, smooth knob. "Then you press this button halfway down so that Jack and I come into focus. Once we're focused, you press it all the way down and you'll hear it click. And that's it!"

"I can do that." Gramps gave me a confident nod and I scurried over to Jack's side.

I glanced sideways, taking in his new hat and jersey before wrapping my arm around his middle. He pulled me tight. "This is exciting, right?"

"Understatement of the year." I shivered with excitement and grinned up at him.

We stood still for what felt like an eternity while Gramps maneuvered us and played with the camera. "Oh, Gramps, can we get one more with Dean?" I looked at Dean and waved him over. "I don't have any pictures of the three of us. I really want one. Or twelve," I said with a chuckle.

"This is fun! I see why you like doing this, Cassie. You can't screw up because you can't run out of film."

"It's pretty cool, huh?" I asked, removing the camera from around his neck.

"Pretty cool indeed," he answered with a wink.

# FOURTEEN

Jack left for Single-A ball a few days following the draft. Dean drove up north with him in his deathmobile, and then spent a few days there with him. It had been twenty-seven days since I last saw him, not that I was counting or anything.

He told me before he left that the minor leagues consisted of Single-A, Double-A, Triple-A, and then The Bigs, which was another word for the Big Leagues, the Majors, The Show. Although signed by the Diamondbacks, Jack would have to work his way up through a succession of teams that funneled players to the Diamondbacks, starting with Single-A.

The Diamondbacks' Single-A team was in a small town in Northern California and even though Jack didn't have to leave the state, he still had to leave where we lived in Southern California. The truth was that when it came to matters of the heart, distance was distance, no matter the number of miles. I was confused at first why he wasn't going to Arizona, but after Jack explained to me how it all worked, it made sense that he would be going to Northern California instead.

It was hard having him gone. I'd become so used to Jack's physical presence that his absence was unavoidably felt and missed on a daily basis. I was thankful for e-mail, Facebook, and our cell phones, but nothing replaced his actually being here. It was weird too, being the one left behind. Jack moved, his life now filled with new experiences, friends, teammates, and adventures. But I was still here, doing the same things I did before he left, seeing the same people, living pretty much the same life.

Yeah. It was definitely weird being the one left to live in the memories of what used to be. Fortunately for me, I kept myself busy with my new summer internship. I'd finally convinced my parents to let me bring my car to school for the summer, since I needed to drive to and from work five days a week. They agreed, but only with the understanding that once the fall semester started, my car had to return to its dust-collecting spot in the driveway.

Seriously? Who were these people claiming to be my parents? They felt like such strangers with whom I had absolutely nothing in common, least of all common sense.

My personal ringtone for Jack blared as I sat outside with my co-worker, Lesslie, watching the surfers during our lunch break. I fumbled through my purse looking for my phone, a smile plastered across my face. "Babe!" I shouted as soon as I answered.

"Kitten," his voice purred in response. "I miss you so much. How's the internship?"

"It's so freaking cool. I love it. I'm learning so

much." Seagulls cawed in the background as I pressed the phone closer to my ear so I could hear Jack better.

"You'll have to tell me all about it when you get up here." Jack's voice was upbeat, his excitement confusing me.

"When I get…what?"

"I wanna fly you up for the weekend."

"Really?" I shot Lesslie a glance.

"Yes, really. I'm pitching on Saturday night and I want you to meet the guys. And I fucking miss you like crazy."

"I miss you too."

"Check with your boss to see if you can take Friday off. E-mail me and let me know what he says, okay?"

"Okay. I'll ask as soon as I get back from lunch," I responded, suddenly not hungry anymore.

"Maybe you oughta remind him that your boyfriend has a bit of a temper, so he probably shouldn't tell you no," he teased with a laugh.

"Oh yeah, I'll definitely make sure to threaten him. That stuff usually works on normal, sane people." I rolled my eyes, safe in the knowledge that he couldn't see me.

He laughed and I pictured his face in my mind. "Seriously though, if he says no, I'll fly you out after work on Friday night or first thing Saturday morning, okay?"

"Okay! Oh my gosh, I'm so excited! Thanks, babe."

"Me too. Talk later, love you." I could hear Jack's smile in his voice as he said good-bye. I smiled back and dropped my hand holding the phone, before tilting my head toward Lesslie.

"Was that your superstar boyfriend?" she asked with a grin, her straight brown hair blowing in the breeze.

"Uh-huh," I responded, my mind a million miles away as I thought about what to pack for the weekend.

"So what are you asking about after lunch?" She elbowed my arm.

"If I can take Friday off or not. He wants to fly me up there for the weekend."

"Oh, Tom's not going to care. Offer to work a half day, and he'll tell you to take the whole thing off."

"Really?"

"Really. Don't even stress about it," she said and I exhaled with relief. "That's sweet of your boyfriend to fly you up. Most guys probably wouldn't want their girlfriends around, let alone pay to bring them there."

I stiffened. "Why would you say that?"

"Oh, I don't mean anything by it. It's just that I know that scene. And there are a lot of girls waiting in the wings to get in on that action," she said with a crooked smile.

"The groupies." I nodded my understanding.

"Yeah." She nodded back, frowning her disapproval.

"I know. I've already dealt with my fair share of them at school. They're pretty brutal." I winced at the memory.

"And those girls are nothing compared to the ones who chase after the professional ball players. Consider the girls in college amateurs and strap your big girl pants on, 'cause you ain't seen nothing yet." She gave my shoulder a friendly squeeze.

"How do you know all this?" I asked, my thoughts drifting.

"I used to photograph a minor league team in town. I saw a lot of things I wish I could un-see." She laughed with a shudder. "I'm just saying be careful. I'm sure your boyfriend's a stand-up guy and all, it's just those girls definitely aren't."

"And you definitely haven't met my boyfriend or you wouldn't describe him as a stand-up guy," I joked with a snicker, doing my best to change the subject.

"Well, you have the right attitude. I'm sure you two will be fine."

"I'm not really worried about it," I lied.

"We should head back in." She stood before reaching out her hand to help me up.

\*\*\*\*\*

I headed down the escalator in the airport and saw Jack standing there holding a sign that read: ANYONE SEEN MY KITTEN?

I laughed so loud when I read it, I scared the poor guy in front of me. "I'm sorry," I whispered to the irritated stranger before quickly covering my mouth with my hand. I stepped off the moving stairs and ran into Jack's waiting arms.

I knew that I missed him, but being in his arms reminded me just how much. He tilted my chin and leaned down to kiss me. "I've missed you," he said with another kiss, his lips brushing against my ear.

"Me too." I wrapped my arms around his body and squeezed, the sound of suitcases rolling past us.

"Do you like my sign?"

My body let out a loud, quick *ha* that could wake up an entire building. "It's adorable. And hilarious," I answered, trying not to laugh but failing miserably.

He reached down, grabbing my carry-on bag with one arm and swinging it behind his shoulder. "Do you have a suitcase?"

"Just this." I smiled, pointing at the bag he carried.

"Really? You're my dream girl." He tossed his free arm around my shoulders and led me out of the airport.

I shivered when the cool morning air hit my body as we exited. "Holy shit, it's cold up here."

"Yeah. The weather's a little different than back home." He lifted an eyebrow as he led me across the street toward the first row of cars.

I scanned the area looking for the familiar white death trap when he clicked the unlock button on an unfamiliar black Acura. I stopped walking and tilted my head back. "Whose car?"

"My roommate, Tyler's. He let me borrow it since I'd knew you'd freeze in mine."

"Thanks," I said, moving into the chilly leather seat.

Jack slid his muscular frame into the car and turned to look at me. His face twisted into a sexy smile, his dimples appearing. "I'm so happy you're here."

I felt my cheeks warm with his words. "Me too. Thank you so much for flying me."

"Gotta see my girl!" he said with enthusiasm before the engine purred to life.

"So tell me about your new roommates and your place and stuff," I asked, even though he'd told me a lot of those things before.

"Well, you know we have a house that we rented. We each have our own room. The guys are Tyler, Nick, and Spencer. Tyler's girlfriend Amanda's in town too. You'll like her, she's cool. And you girls can go to the games together and stuff, so that worked out."

"What worked out?" I asked, wanting

clarification.

He glanced at me before looking back at the road. "Well, I was sort of going crazy before I knew that Amanda would be here. I didn't want you going to the field by yourself. I'm not sure if you know this or not, but I really fucking hate leaving you alone. Especially after what happened." His tone tightened with irritation.

"Jack." I sympathized as I flashed back to the night of the beating.

"I know I have issues. But I can't let something happen to you again." He exhaled through his nose. "So I was happy when Tyler told me that Amanda would be in town. Now you don't have to be alone."

I smiled and rested my hand on his thigh. "Sounds good."

Jack pulled the car into the driveway of a gorgeous two-story house. "Jack, this house looks brand new!"

"I told you it's only a few years old. The guy who owns it has like twelve properties or something. Wait 'til you see the backyard." His eyebrows lifted as he smirked.

"I've seen the backyard." I hinted at the many cell phone pictures he'd sent me.

"Well, wait 'til you see it in person."

I walked on the cobblestone pathway to the oversized front door and headed inside, where music blared in an empty room. "Jesus. Sorry,

Kitten, I'll turn it down." Jack ran to the stereo and flipped the switch off.

"Hey!" A rowdy voice yelled from a distance and I peered around the wall into the perfectly manicured backyard. Green trees, bushes, and plants surrounded the back side of the pool, making it appear lush and tropical. Earth-colored stones and matching boulders accented the area, bringing out the blue of the water.

One of Jack's roommates sat floating on a neon pink raft as another tumbled down the built-in slide. "Wow, you were right. It's much better in person."

"And you can't even see the hot tub from there," he whispered before running up the stairs. "Come on, Kitten."

I followed Jack up before colliding with a girl I assumed was Tyler's girlfriend Amanda, knocking her twisted hair loose. I watched as the light brown strands fell from the once messy bun, into just…a mess. "I'm sorry! Are you okay?" I asked as I helped her up.

"Yeah. You must be Cassie? I'm Amanda," she said, grabbing and twisting her hair back into place.

"Nice to meet you." I smiled, my tone cordial.

"You too. Okay, I really have to go before I pee my pants." She laughed, ran into the bathroom, and slammed the door shut.

*****

The thought of going to my first professional

baseball game alone didn't really appeal to me, so I was thankful Amanda was in town. We arrived at the field, parked, and headed toward the Will Call ticket booth. I gripped my camera tightly as we walked to our seats next to the visitors' dugout.

The stadium was much larger than the one at Fullton State, but the crowd was similar. There were a lot of families with kids and a ton of girls. When our team was announced, the crowd went wild. And when they broadcasted Tyler's name, groups of girls screamed and some stood up, showing their jerseys with his number on the back.

It was nothing I hadn't seen or heard before. I glanced at Amanda, noting the discomfort on her face as she fidgeted in her seat.

"You okay?" I asked, nudging her arm.

Her hazel eyes glanced around the stadium before returning to mine. "There's a lot of fan-girls here." I nodded. "I'm not really used to this," she admitted as she crossed her legs.

"Which part?" I asked, finding it hard to imagine that this scene was completely new to her.

"The girls, mostly. The crazy screaming like that for Tyler. The jerseys with his number. I hate it."

"Really? It wasn't like that for him in college?"

She shook her head. "Not even close. Was it like that for Jack?"

"Oh yeah." I chuckled.

227

"Wow. You're much braver than I am." She swallowed.

"What do you mean?"

"I was just talking to Tyler about this last night. I think it takes a certain kind of person to date a professional athlete. I don't think just any girl could do it." She paused, glancing toward the field. "I'm not sure I'm cut out for it."

"Don't say that," I reassured her as I put my arm around her shoulder. "You can do it. You love Tyler, right?"

"Of course, but it's not about that."

"Yes it is. It's about exactly that." I smiled at Amanda and she gave me an obviously forced smile in return. "He doesn't want these other girls. He wants you. You have to remember that."

She nodded, pressing her shoulder into mine. "You're right. Thanks."

The game wasn't nearly as entertaining when Jack wasn't pitching, but it did give me time to photograph other players and things. I took a lot of pictures of Jack's roommates, knowing full well how much the guys tend to enjoy photos of themselves playing. I even snuck in a couple of Amanda on my way back from the bathroom. Her fingers were intertwined and twisted in a weird way as she pressed them against her lips, staring intently toward the field. I framed her fingers and her mouth in one shot, the focus of her eyes in another, and then her whole body language in a third. She looked so uncomfortable and unhappy.

When the game ended, Amanda and I walked down a ramp that led us underground toward the locker room. The walls were cement and kept the air chilled in the breezeway where we stood, waiting for our boyfriends to emerge. I glanced at the others waiting—some younger girls like myself and other folks a bit older that I assumed were parents—and resisted the urge to walk over and introduce myself. I wasn't sure why, but instead of being friendly, I stood with my arms crossed over my body. The steel gray door flung open with a bang as Jack walked out grinning.

I smiled at the sight of him, his chocolate-brown eyes holding my gaze. He kissed my cheek and grabbed my hand. "Tyler's almost done. We'll see you at home, 'K?" he informed Amanda, leading me away from her.

We walked hand in hand down a long cement corridor before Jack pushed against the metal release bar of the outer door. Once outside, we found ourselves surrounded by squealing girls. They stared at Jack, then at me, then back to Jack. A few asked for his autograph, while others asked for something else entirely. This is exactly what Lesslie from work had warned me about.

"Hey, Jack, call me," a blonde-haired floozy said, shoving a piece of paper into Jack's free hand.

I snarled, offended at this girl's incredible behavior. "Really?" I said to her bitterly.

"What?"

"I'm standing right here," I bit back, my jaw clenching.

"Well, I'm sure you won't *always* be standing right there." She smirked and Jack gripped my hand, knowing I was about to lose it.

"You disrespectful little—" I started to shout, trying to wrench my hand free as Jack's grip tightened and interrupted me.

"Cassie, don't." Jack shook his head and swallowed hard before turning toward the blonde. "You dropped this," he said, crumbling her number up into a little ball before flicking it past her.

I choked back a laugh as he pulled me toward his car. There were scraps of paper scattered on the front seat and envelopes under his windshield wipers. "What is all this?" I asked, reaching for the papers.

"Phone numbers, mostly. Some pictures too."

"Seriously?" My eyes widened as I leaned into the seat.

He scooped up the loose papers, grabbed the envelopes from under the wipers, and placed them all in a stack on his lap. He turned the key and the engine roared its familiar sound. We drove a few feet before he hopped out and tossed the stack of papers into a blue garbage bin.

"Does this happen every night?" The surprise in my voice still lingered.

"Pretty much." He leaned his head toward my face before reaching across the seat and pulling my mouth to his.

We drove the short distance from the stadium to his house and Jack hopped out before opening my door for me. "I don't want to socialize tonight, okay? I just want to go straight upstairs."

"Jack, jeez." I smacked his arm.

"No, I don't mean because of that. I just want to spend time alone with you. I hate not seeing you every day."

"Me too," I admitted, partially relieved.

The noise of the housemates filtered through the front door and they erupted in cheers as we walked through. "Hey, guys. Sorry, we're going to hit the sack," Jack informed them with a wink.

"No, don't go to bed yet! Come on, Jack," Nick shouted before he chugged a beer.

"We'll see you ladies tomorrow." Jack laughed and slung an arm over my shoulders.

"Goodnight, you guys," I said with a shrug before heading up the carpeted stairs.

We shared the same space in the bathroom as we got ready for bed. I washed my face, brushed my teeth, and quickly changed into a tank top and boxer shorts as Jack stripped down before hopping into the shower.

"I'm gonna go get in bed, okay?" I called out into the steam-filled air.

"I'll just be a minute," he responded, his wet face peering from around the white shower curtain. "Come here."

I narrowed my eyes at him before leaning toward him. "What do you want?"

"A kiss." He puckered his lips together, beads of water falling from them as I leaned in, pressing my mouth to his.

"Ugh, you're all wet." I pulled away, wiping the water from my lips.

"See you in a minute." He disappeared behind the curtain.

I shut the door to Jack's room and hopped into bed, noticing the framed picture of the two of us from the day he got drafted sitting on his nightstand. I reached for it, running my fingers across the glass as he walked in.

"I love this picture." I smiled up at him before placing the picture frame back on his nightstand.

"Me too. It's one of my favorites," he admitted, his voice sincere.

"I had an interesting talk with Amanda tonight," I noted as he slid his well-defined body into bed next to me.

"Yeah? What about?" He threw his arm around me and pulled my head against his chest.

"She just said she thinks it takes a certain kind

of girl to date you guys. And she wasn't sure if she could handle it."

"Really? Well that would suck for Tyler, but she's not wrong."

The muscles in his abs tightened as he twisted down to look at me. I pushed my body up and sat, angled toward him. "How so?"

"It takes a certain kind of girl to date any athlete," he started to say. "Most girls can't handle the stress of it. It's hard to deal with other girls throwing themselves at your man constantly. But you're already used to that." He winked and I smacked his shoulder, rolling my eyes.

"Kitten." He pointed at me, his voice rumbling before he continued. "And a lot of girls can't handle the amount of travel we have to do. We're gone a lot and even when we're home, we're not really home. Baseball is our job so it's our number one priority. It has to be or we'll get cut from the team for someone younger, faster, or better than we are. The amount of dedication it takes is more than most girls can handle."

"I've never even thought about it like that before," I admitted, my eyes drifting past his face, landing on the earthy tone of his wall.

"Because you can handle it," he stated with confidence.

I tilted my head. "You're that sure, huh?"

Jack frowned. "Aren't you?"

"I don't know. Tonight was sort of crazy with all the phone numbers and the girls waiting outside for you and stuff..." My voice trailed off as he reached for my chin, tilting my face up.

"I know it's not easy, but please remember that I've been dealing with this craziness for a long time now. It's not new to me like it is with some of the other guys. They have fucking stars in their eyes when they walk out those stadium doors at night."

"And what about you?"

He huffed out a breath, as if surprised at my question. "Honestly? All I'm thinking about when I walk out those doors at night is how long it's gonna take me to get home so I can call my girl."

"Uh-uh." I shook my head and tried to hide a smile.

"It's true." He bent forward to kiss the side of my head before leaning back into his pillow.

"You're not even tempted? At all? Some of those girls are really pretty." I hated like hell to admit that, knowing that Jack could hear the disbelief in my voice.

"Why would I be tempted by any of those girls when I have you?" He grinned before his expression fell flat. "What I should be worried about is someone stealing you away while I'm out of the picture."

"Oh please, like anyone will even come near me. They know better, Jack. You trained every male on campus well."

He let out a loud hoot before smacking his palm against the bed. "That's fucking awesome."

"I'm glad you're so pleased with yourself."

"Do you know how shitty it would be if I had to worry about that kind of stuff? I want to go out of my mind right now just thinking about it."

I placed my hand on his thigh. "Then don't. There's no point."

"We're good, right? Me and you?" His voice faltered slightly and I noticed the clouds forming in his eyes.

"I love you." I longed to reassure whatever unpleasant thoughts were creeping into his mind.

"And you're happy?" His eyes tensed.

"Extremely." I smiled at him.

He exhaled. "You're my game changer, you know that?"

"Game changer?" I shook my head, unsure of his meaning.

"The one girl who changes everything. The one you'd give it all up for." He brushed his thumb down my cheek.

"I don't want you to give anything up."

"I know that. But here's the thing about baseball, Kitten. There's an expiration date for every single one of us who plays and we all know it. Eventually my baseball career will come to an end, and I can live with that. But I can't live without you."

I blinked back the tears forming in my eyes as I leaned into his chest, his warm arms wrapping around me. "The only time I feel safe is when I'm with you," I admitted.

"Because you know I'll kill anyone who hurts you. Because I'm a superhero," he said seriously, his fingers twisting locks of my hair.

"You're something, alright." I laughed into his bare chest, my eyes closing.

"I'm your something…" His voice trailed off into a whisper as I drifted off.

I woke up the next morning to the sound of Jack's alarm beeping relentlessly. I shook Jack's shoulder and he grumbled before flipping over.

"Jack, get up. Turn it off," I whined.

He rubbed his eyes before slamming his palm down on top of the clock radio. "I don't want to get up. I need sleep."

"You get to pitch today," I reminded him, my voice groggy.

"I get to sleep today." He laughed before grabbing me in his arms and squeezing.

"You're going to kill me," I choked out sarcastically. "I'm dying. I can't breathe. Hello? Earth to Jack?"

"Clearly you're not dying if you're still flapping your gums." I wanted to smack him, his grin was so wicked.

"I hate you."

"No you don't."

*****

The rest of our weekend together consisted of two more baseball games, floating around the pool, and the constant reminder of how much we enjoyed being together. Jack's pitching was amazing during his outing on Saturday, which prompted rumors to spread that he'd get moved up to Double-A soon. Which was fast, even by baseball standards.

When he dropped me off at the airport on Sunday evening, I cried. It was like saying good-bye to him for the first time all over again. Seeing him made it harder to be away, which was sort of fucked up, if you asked me.

"I hate saying good-bye to you. It sucks." I buried my face against his shoulder.

"I know. Me too." He kissed the top of my head as his fingers caressed my back.

I pushed myself away from the protection of his arms. "I'll call you as soon as I land, okay?"

"You better," he teased before cupping my face in his hands. "I love you." His mouth pressed against mine as his tongue swept across my lips.

"I love you too," I said, pulling away from him.

I shut the car door before walking through the sliding glass doors of the airport entrance. I headed toward the security checkpoint, thankful that it wasn't crowded. Once my bag and my body were cleared, I found my gate and plopped into an empty chair, the weekend's activities catching up to me. I yawned as my cell phone rang with Jack's song.

"What's up, babe?"

"Cassie," he shouted, the wind whipping through the air, forcing the reception to crackle. "Can you hear me?"

"Sort of. Are you okay?" I grabbed my bag and looked for a more private setting.

"I just got off the phone with Coach. They're pulling me up to Double-A. I leave for Alabama in two days!"

"Oh my God, babe, that's amazing! Congratulations. I've always wanted to see Alabama," I added, so happy for my guy.

"Is that so?"

"Yep."

"In that case, I can't wait to fly you out." He laughed. "I've gotta call Dean and Gran. I just wanted to tell you first."

"I'm so glad you did. Congratulations again, babe. I'm so proud of you."

"Thanks, Kitten. Love you. Call me when you land." He hung up and I couldn't stop my face from grinning.

# FIFTEEN
## JACK

The state of Alabama welcomed me with open arms. That was the good news. The bad news was that the air there was so thick with humidity I thought I might choke. I'd never experienced heat that felt almost solid in form, hitting you in the face when you stepped outside. But the people were friendly and the city boasted that small-town feel I thought only existed in movies.

All the shifting in the Diamondbacks organization caused a group of guys on my team to lose a roommate. This worked out perfectly for me, considering I was looking for some. I moved in right away, taking not only the other guy's room in the house, but his spot on the roster too.

I braced for resentment from the other players that would never come. Instead, I found myself playing with a group of extremely supportive guys. The competition was fierce, but this was still a team sport, no matter how you sliced it.

"Hi," I said as Cassie picked up her phone.

"Hi, yourself," she said back, her voice making me smile. "How are you? How's the team?"

"I'm good. The team is insane."

"What do you mean?"

"Everyone's just really fucking good." I sighed with contentment.

"Like better than your other team, or how?"

"Just in every way possible. It's a whole different level of ball."

"You expected that though, right?" Her voice suggested if I hadn't, I should have.

"I guess I didn't really think about it. They're definitely better hitters and my pitches don't intimidate them."

"So pitch around their bats and make your pitches scary," she suggested with a giggle.

"I'm trying, Kitten."

"Jack, you're an incredible pitcher. You'll figure it out. This is all part of the process and in the end you'll be a better player for it."

"When'd you get so smart?"

"Probably the second you left town." I could practically feel her eye-roll over the phone line.

"Brat."

"I gotta go, Jack. I'm sorry but I get to sit in on a call with the New York offices! Yay!" she screamed into the phone.

"That's great, babe. You go. I'll talk to you later." I chuckled, her excitement making me smile.

"Wait, Jack?" she shouted and I fumbled.

"Yeah?"

"Good luck tonight."

"Thanks. Love you," I said before hanging up.

\*\*\*\*\*

I took a deep breath as I kicked at the dirt mound beneath my cleats. The fans were all on their feet cheering, but I could barely hear anything above the sound of my own heart pumping adrenaline through my veins.

"You got this, Carter," I heard my shortstop shout. I glanced at him briefly, our eyes meeting in a hopeful exchange. The cheers grew louder when I stepped onto the mound. My catcher flashed signs between his legs and I nodded in agreement, then gripped the ball in my left hand, the baseball's string seams pressing against my fingertips. With another focused breath, I lifted my right leg into the air before delivering a piping hot fastball right down the middle.

The batter swung and I held my breath, hoping he wouldn't send that pitch into no man's land. The sound of the ball crashing against the catcher's glove echoed into the evening air, as the umpire screamed, "Strike three! You're out!"

The crowd erupted into cheers and rushed the field before my teammates lifted me on top of their shoulders. Cameras flashed from all around, the quick bursts of light blinding me briefly. Hands reached out from every angle, pulling and tugging at any exposed body part. Everyone wanted a piece of me.

I had just pitched my first perfect game in Double-A ball. The feeling you get when that happens is hard to describe. It's like an unbelievable high. I accomplished something that happens so rarely in the game of baseball. Not a single person from the other team got on base. I didn't walk one batter. No one was hit by a pitch. Just me and my boys on our field for nine straight innings. Tonight, we'd be celebrating. And all I could think about was her.

I peeled myself away from the gaggle of fans and journalists and headed inside the locker room. "I'll sign more after I shower," I shouted toward the group of people wanting my autograph.

I opened my locker, grabbed my cell phone, and dialed.

"Hey, babe!" she answered, her tone excited and bubbly.

"Did you hear?"

"I watched the game online. Congratulations!" She squealed as I pulled my cell phone from my ear. "I'm so proud of you, baby!"

I leaned my head against the wall and closed my eyes, visualizing her gorgeous face. "God, I miss you," I breathed out with a sigh.

"Me too. I wish I was there." Her quiet, wistful tone tugged at my heart.

"I wish you were too. More than anything I wish you were celebrating this night with me."

"I'm so happy for you, Jack."

"Thanks, Kitten. I should probably go. I'll call you later, okay?" My teammates filed out of the showers, eyeing me and pointing at their wrists.

"Have fun tonight. I love you," she said and I grinned.

"I love you too. Night," I replied before shutting my phone off.

*****

The local bar seemed packed to capacity by the time we sauntered in. I walked through the front door with two of my teammates and the entire bar broke out into hoots and shouting. Before I knew it, drinks and shots were being handed to me from all directions. I downed the first three shots without hesitation and held on tightly to a bottle of beer. I looked around to thank whoever sent them over, but the dim lighting made it virtually impossible to distinguish individual people in the thick crowd.

"Great game tonight, Jack," a petite brunette remarked as she grabbed my arm.

I looked at the hand touching me before removing it and placing it at her side. "Thanks."

Her hand wrapped around my waist. "The name's Chrystle."

I removed her hand again more forcefully. "I didn't ask."

"Figured you'd want to know," she said, inching her body closer to mine.

"And why's that?" I asked, laying on the bored tone I usually used to discourage groupies.

She got on her tippy toes and leaned closer. "'Cause you'll be screaming it later," she whispered in my ear with a smile.

"Not a chance." I frowned and turned my back to her before wading through the crowd toward a table in the back.

I reached my excited teammates and quickly sat down. "I'm starving! Please tell me there's food here." My stomach growled on cue and I looked around, noticing the insane amount of tequila shots covering the tabletop.

"Hell yes, there's food! It's just not here yet. So drink up, man. That was a hell of a game tonight, Carter!" My first baseman, Logan, slid a shot in my direction to celebrate.

The rest of the table erupted in similar congratulations and compliments, followed by high fives and knuckle-bumps, as we all grabbed a shot and drank a toast. I looked up from the table and noticed Chrystle eyeing me from the other end of the bar. She winked at me before taking a swig of her beer.

I elbowed Logan, who'd played on this team the past two seasons. "Hey, man. Who's that chick at the end of the bar?"

"Which chick?" he asked with a chortle.

"The little brunette staring at us over there."

"Oh, Chrystle? She's basically a groupie on a mission. I'd steer clear of her if I were you," he warned before downing another shot of the amber liquid.

"Trust me. I'm trying."

"Here. Drink these." He slid two shots over and I downed them one after the other, wincing after I swallowed. "You're definitely on her radar." He pointed at Chrystle engrossed in conversation with our head coach as both sets of eyes stared in our direction.

"I don't want to be on any chick's radar," I answered, my temper starting to rise.

"Well, good luck with that. She's relentless, by the way."

"Yeah, I've noticed." I glanced quickly toward her before looking away. The last thing I wanted this groupie to think was that I was the least bit interested in her.

Logan handed me two more shots and I drank them effortlessly the tequila no longer a shock to my system. "I really need something to eat," I mentioned to no one in particular before noticing the basket of bread across the table.

"Can I eat this?" I asked, reaching for it.

My teammate, Vince, looked up from his cell phone. "Huh? Oh yeah, Carter, here." He shoved the basket toward me. "Eat up, man."

"Thanks." I nodded before ripping apart the bread and shoving a huge piece in my mouth.

It was too late and I knew it. My attempt to put something in my stomach was feeble at best. It was too little, too late…the bread no match for the alcohol that already assaulted my system. I couldn't remember the last time I'd drank this much.

I elbowed Logan. "Where's the pisser?"

"What, man?" He turned to me, his eyes already showing signs of how wasted he was getting.

"The bathroom? Where?" I shouted.

"In the far corner behind the jukebox." He pointed, his finger unsteady.

"Thanks." I pushed away from the table and stumbled. Shit, I was already drunk. My eyes squinted toward the corner of the bar and my legs headed in that direction.

Not even ten steps in and Chrystle stood at my side. "Where you going, Jack? Can I come?"

"No." I tried to sound as disinterested as I could muster.

"You don't mean that." She bit her bottom lip seductively and I suddenly noticed her tight-fitting top. She caught me staring. "You like what you see?"

"Nothing I haven't seen before."

"I don't believe you." She pressed her chest against my stomach and wrapped her arms around my lower back.

"Get the fuck off me," I shouted before shoving her away from me.

"What's your problem, Jack? I just want to make you feel good. Help you celebrate the big game."

"I have a girlfriend. Why don't you go celebrate with one of my single teammates. Or have you fucked them all already?" My lips formed a snarl as I walked away, leaving her behind.

A few minutes later, I exited the bathroom, my face wet with the water I'd splashed on it to help me feel less drunk. It didn't work. And Chrystle still stood there waiting for me.

"I forgive you," she said with a grin before blocking my path with her petite frame.

"Who gives a shit? Get out of my way." I stared blearily at her perfectly made-up face.

"Come home with me."

"I'm not interested." I shook my head, suddenly feeling woozy.

"At least let me buy you a drink?" she offered and I narrowed my eyes, unsure of her intentions. "Come on, Jack, it's just a drink."

I glanced toward Logan for backup, only to see him crashed face-down on the table. I laughed. "Fine. One drink."

When we reached the bar, I watched Chrystle lean across it, trying to catch the bartender's attention. The hem of her shirt rode up her back, revealing the tribal tattoo above her ass. I shook my head at the obvious cliché. Of course a chick like this would have a tramp stamp.

"Hey, Chase!" she shouted at the surly bartender's back. He turned around, meeting her eyes with acknowledgement. "Two shots of whiskey."

"No no no," I yelled and Chase turned to eyeball me. "No more shots," I said, my vision hazy.

"Fine. Two Jack and Cokes," she shouted before turning to me. "How's that?" She nudged me with her elbow.

"Better. I think," I offered up wryly.

"You'll be fine. Now tell me about this girlfriend of yours." She batted her thick-coated eyelashes sweetly.

"I like to keep my private life, private," I slurred, feeling suddenly protective of my relationship with Cassie.

Chrystle looked around the crowded room before whispering, "Well, she isn't here, right?"

"Does it look like she's here?" I threw one hand in the air, glancing to my side.

"What she doesn't know won't hurt her, and I'm not going to tell."

"Thanks for the drink." I grabbed the tall glass that had just appeared on the bar in front of me, before hightailing it away from her.

"Jack, wait! I was just kidding!" she shouted, but I refused to stop. That girl was trouble and I was fucking hammered enough.

I heard her footsteps racing after me as I beelined straight for Logan. "Jack, wait!" She grabbed my shirt with her free hand.

"Stop grabbing me. What the hell do you want?" I spun to face her, my head feeling like it weighed a hundred pounds as the room spun around me.

"I just want to hang out with you," she said, her voice innocent.

"I don't think that's a good idea. You're not very good at accepting the word *no*," I spat, noticing the blue of her eyes.

*Fuck.*

*This isn't good.*

*I'm drunk.*

*And she's hot.*

"You can teach me," she teased, a playful smile spreading across her face.

"Chrystle. Leave me the fuck alone. I'm gonna stop being nice."

"This is you being nice?" She winked before slapping my ass and heading onto the dance floor.

I hurried to the booth and scooted in. "Keep that bitch away from me." Logan lifted his head in a daze as I elbowed him in the ribs.

He laughed. "I already told you to stay away from her."

"Well, it's hard when she follows me everywhere."

"Then stop going places. Sit still. Drink this," he said, before pushing another tequila-filled shot glass toward me.

"You don't have to get me drunk to take advantage of me," I joked.

"Shut up, dickhead. Drink."

I downed the shot quickly. "You're going to have to carry me out of here."

"Shit. You're going to have to carry me," Logan stuttered.

"Maybe they'll let us sleep here." I laughed and pulled out my cell phone.

"No! No cell phones tonight, man. You just pitched a no-hitter! We're getting fucked up!" Logan shouted before sliding my cell phone down the length of the table.

"Dick! Hey, Chance, gimme my phone, will you?" I shouted toward my teammates on the other end.

Chance looked down, his eyes widened, and he pushed it forcefully. I watched as it practically flew and landed in my lap with a thud.

"What did I tell you?" Logan yelled, his eyelids half closed.

"I'm just gonna text Cass, then I'll shut it off," I promised my drunk friend. I typed out the text as quickly as I could, which wasn't very quick considering how drunk I was.

*I miss yo9 os fukkeng mucb. Wish u wede hefd.*

I stared at the text message before pressing Send. I knew I'd spelled words wrong, but I was too drunk to care about fixing it.

I couldn't remember the last time I felt this fucked up. My vision blurred, my head spun, my legs shook as I walked, and my defenses were definitely down on the floor somewhere with my good judgment. I spotted Chrystle on the dance floor and suddenly couldn't tear my eyes away from her tiny little body as she shook it. She watched me watching her and I knew I was in trouble.

*Look away, you idiot.*

Hot prickles shot through my body, but I ignored their warning, watching Chrystle grind her tight little body against another girl's. Her hips dipped and moved in perfect rhythm and I suddenly couldn't stop thinking about fucking her. If she moved like that on the dance floor...

The song changed and she ditched her dance partner and headed toward me. "I knew you liked what you saw earlier. You were just playing hard to get."

"I didn't like it earlier, but I like it now." I slurred my words.

*'Cause I'm fucking loaded and I can't think straight.*

"Is that right? Earlier you had a girlfriend." She toyed with me, pressing her sweaty body against mine as I instantly became aroused.

*Cassie.*

"Earlier you didn't care."

"I still don't," she sassed before grinding her

hips into me.

"You better stop doing that or it's gonna get you in trouble."

*I want to give her some trouble.*

*Some good, hard trouble.*

"Maybe I wanna get into trouble?" She turned her body around and pressed her ass against me before bending over to pick something up off the floor. "I dropped this. Sorry."

*Fuck. Me.*

I grabbed her wrist and pulled her to me. When our bodies were pressed up against each other, she reached down and placed her hand on my zipper. "Take me home, Jack."

"You know this doesn't mean anything, right? It's just sex." Drunken truth spilled from my lips.

"You sure know how to romance a girl," she pouted as her bottom lip jutted out.

"Fucking isn't romantic. And that's all we're gonna do." I grabbed her hand and attempted to pull her toward the exit. "You can drive, right?" I asked as I struggled to stay upright.

"I'm sober as a judge." She dangled her keys in the air.

"I don't know what that means, but let's go."

She giggled as I followed behind her.

*****

I rolled over, my head throbbing and my eyes refusing to open willingly. I thrashed my arm across the bed before hitting someone and I jumped.

"Stop, Jack. Let me sleep," a girl's voice spoke.

*No, no, no, no, no, no.*

This wasn't happening. I was going to turn and look at the other half of my bed and it was going to be empty. This was all going to be a bad dream. I squeezed my eyes before turning and opening them.

*Fuck.*

*Fuck. Fuck. Fuck.*

A head full of brown hair lay splayed across my pillow, a naked female body accompanying it. My stomach dropped to the carpet as I moved to sit on the edge of my bed. I threw my pounding head into my hands before looking down. I tugged and pulled at the recesses of my mind where the memories of last night were hiding. There's no way I did this. Maybe she came home with one of my roommates and needed a place to crash? I love Cassie. I love Cassie so goddammed much I'd never do this to her.

*Fuck.*

The memories started pouring in swiftly and unabashedly. I remembered. Now I wished I could forget.

I grabbed my cell phone and stood up before realizing I was naked. A pair of boxers and a sweatshirt later, I sat on the balcony in the early morning dew, dialing Cassie's number.

"Hey, babe," she breathed tiredly into the

phone.

I didn't know what to say so I stayed silent, knowing that these would be the last few moments that everything between us would be okay.

*Hang up, you idiot.*

*Hang up the phone.*

*She'll never know what happened if you don't tell her.*

"Jack?" she asked. "Hello? Jack?" She sounded so concerned. "I can hear you breathing, dummy." She yawned into the receiver.

"Kitten?" I muttered.

*Too late to hang up now.*

"I wish you could see me roll my eyes," she responded with a chuckle.

"That's not good for you." My voice came out slowly.

"What's wrong? Are you drunk?"

"I think I still am, yeah." I tugged at my hair.

"Did you drive?"

"No."

"Good." I heard the smile in her voice. "Are you okay?"

*I can't do it.*

*I can't lose her.*

*Not over this.*

*Everyone makes mistakes.*

"Yeah, Kitten. Sorry for calling so early. I just wanted you to know how much I love you."

*I am such a pussy.*

"I love you too." Her voice was perfect. She was perfect. I couldn't lose her.

My stomach balled into knots. "Go back to bed. I love you. I'll call you later," I said, swallowing the baseball-sized lump in my throat.

She giggled. "Night, Jack. Congratulations again on your perfect game. I'm really proud of you."

"Thanks, babe. Bye." I pressed End, squeezed my eyes shut, and buried my head in my hands, wishing I could bury the guilt instead.

How could I undo this? Cass couldn't ever know this happened. I'd do anything to make sure of that. I vowed to never drink excessively again. I'd never put myself in that kind of a position where I could willingly be so stupid. Anger quickly filtered through my pain as I remembered the girl sleeping in my bed. I stormed into my room before slamming the door shut with a loud bang.

"Get the fuck up and get out," I shouted. She was on her stomach, sprawled spread-eagle over three-quarters of the bed. Still naked. *Shit.*

Chrystle moved slightly, her eyes opening to look at me. "What? Why are you so angry?" She whined and it made her even more annoying.

"Get out." I reached across the bed, grabbing her by the forearm and pulling.

"Ow, Jack, jeez! I'll get up. What's your

problem?" She sat up, not bothering to pull up the sheet to cover her nakedness, and her eyes narrowed as she glared at me.

"You're my problem. Get out of my bedroom. Get out of my apartment. Get out of my life," I demanded, my attitude void of any respect or kindness.

"You sure weren't saying that last night," she commented coyly and my temper flared.

"Get out or I will throw you out."

"Sounds like foreplay." She bit her bottom lip suggestively and my stomach churned.

"For a twisted slut, maybe." I scowled darkly and flung venom-filled words designed to hurt her.

"Oh, so now I'm a slut?" She swung her legs over the side of the bed and began to wriggle back into her clothes from last night.

"I'm sure you were always a slut," I responded coolly.

"Well, you sure as hell weren't complaining last night. And I'm sure you won't complain again soon." Her confidence oozed through an arrogant smile.

"Sorry to disappoint you, but I don't fuck the same girl twice. Not really my style." In desperation, I went for my worst asshole tone of voice.

"We'll see," she said smugly before heading out my door and closing it behind her.

I tore the sheets from my bed and threw them in the corner, half tempted to light the damn things on fire. I opened the window as far as it would go, trying to air out the sick smell of sex from my room. Images of my idiocy replayed in my mind and I wished I could reach through my head and rip them from my skull.

I walked down the hall to turn the shower on, my reflection in the mirror forcing me to stop short. I turned to face myself, my bloodshot brown eyes staring back at me. I balled my hand into a fist and lunged toward the mirror, stopping just short of striking it.

*You idiot! You pitched a perfect game last night. A perfect game in baseball. And then you almost took your perfect relationship and flushed it down the toilet. This is your future, you asshole. Don't ever be that careless with your future again.*

# SIXTEEN
## CASSIE

The last few weeks of summer flew by as the fall semester approached. The magazine extended my internship and I convinced my mom to let me keep the car, promising that I wouldn't use it to do anything crazy other than drive back and forth to the magazine offices. She was reluctant at first, but when I screamed that she was ruining my life, she relented. I'd have to use that tactic more often.

Jack would be home shortly, depending on if his team made playoffs or not. I'd fallen into a comfortable routine of working and reading while he'd been away, surpassing my self-imposed goal of getting through twenty books in the summer. *The Opportunist* was my twenty-fifth and I was completely engrossed in the story, wishing the main character's mental anguish on no one...except maybe the sorority girls who enjoyed making my life hell.

I walked through the door of our apartment and shouted Melissa's name. No response. I tossed my purse and car keys onto the counter before opening up the refrigerator door and grabbing a bottle of water. My cell phone rang, blaring Jack's song, and I sprinted to reach for it.

"Hey!" I answered with a smile in my voice.

"Hey, Kitten." The flat tone of his voice caused unease to spread in my empty stomach.

"What's wrong? Are you okay?" I asked, unprepared for what came next.

"I fucked up, Cassie." He swallowed hard.

"What are you talking about? Are you okay?" My stomach twisted as the ominous sound of his words settled in.

"I have to tell you something." His voice was so unnatural, it hardly sounded like Jack.

My body slid down onto the cold kitchen floor as I fought against the bile threatening to rise up into my throat. "I'm listening," was all I managed to get out.

"Oh God. Okay." He took a quick breath. "Remember the night a few weeks ago…" he paused, "the night I pitched my perfect game?"

"Yeah," I responded, my lips barely moving.

"Remember when I called really early and woke you up?"

"Uh-huh." My chest tightened and my stomach heaved.

"I kept saying no, Cassie. I swear. I told her no at least a hundred times," he rambled, not really making any sense. "I was mean as hell to her, but she didn't care."

"What happened, Jack?" I couldn't stop the shaking in my voice.

"She was just so fucking persistent. She wouldn't take no for an answer and I was really fucked up."

"What did you do?" My tone was harsh, the tears already welling in my eyes.

"I called you that morning because I made a mistake and I wanted to tell you. I wanted to be honest with you, but then I heard your voice and I couldn't do it. I knew I'd lose you and I wouldn't lose you for some girl who meant nothing." His voice trailed off into a whisper.

"What are you saying?" I demanded.

"I told you I'd fuck up, Kitten. I ruin things," he whispered.

"No. You don't get to do that. Tell me what you did!"

"I slept with someone. I'm so sorry. It didn't mean anything. I made a mistake. I just wanted it all to go away. I wanted her to go away."

My world spun around me at breakneck speed as my heart literally felt like it was shattering inside my chest.

"Cassie? Say something," he begged.

"How could you? *Why*?" I shrieked through my sobs.

"There's more."

"More?" I froze. My head whirled, unsure of his meaning.

"Fuck." He breathed hard and I remained silent for a full minute before he finally continued. "She's pregnant."

He said it so low, my ears barely registered the

sounds. But my shattered heart not only heard the words, it digested them, processed them, and promptly left the spot in my chest where it used to reside and fell to the ground at my feet and turned to dust.

"Are you there, Kitten?"

"Don't ever call me that again," I whispered through my pain.

He breathed loudly into the phone. "I don't know what to do."

"Well, I'm not going to tell you what to do." Bitterness and resentment swept over me and carried over into my voice. As much as Jack hadn't sounded like himself earlier, I knew I didn't sound like myself now either.

"I knew I'd fuck up, but I never meant for this to happen."

"You don't get to do that. You don't get to blame this on anything other than your own inability to keep your dick in your pants. You got drunk. You brought another girl home with you and you slept with her. I deserve better than that." I ranted at him loudly, my voice catching.

"You're absolutely right. You do," he agreed without argument.

"Yeah, well it was supposed to be you, Jack, because you *are* better than that." I was frozen in place, vibrating in shock as my future crashed around me.

"I'm scared."

It took everything in me to put my pride, feelings, and emotions aside and not hang up the phone. I didn't want to care that he was scared. I didn't want to care about anything other than my own breaking heart.

But I couldn't ignore his pain.

"What is she going to do?" I asked first, before the obvious tore through my mind like a tornado. "How did you get her pregnant?" He huffed out a quick breath. "I know *how* you got her pregnant, but, tell me you didn't, Jack. Tell me you didn't sleep with her without protection."

If I thought my heart couldn't break any more, I was wrong. Because that realization sent earthquake-sized cracks shooting through me with such ferocity, I thought I might pass out.

"I was really drunk that night, Cassie. And I don't keep condoms anymore," he said weakly in his own defense.

I didn't respond. I couldn't. The pain of this was too much. Everything hurt so bad...even breathing. It was all a reminder that I was still alive and this nightmare was really happening.

"She wants to keep it, Cass. She wants to have the baby."

"And what do you want?" I asked sharply.

I heard him inhale before blowing the air out long and slow. "I don't know." I could picture him in my mind. He was probably shaking his head, his brow furrowed. "I mean, I just want to play baseball. I'm not ready to be a dad. Especially not with this chick. But then again, I don't want to be the kind of dad that my father was. You know, absent. I'm all mixed up inside and I don't know what the right thing is."

I couldn't take it anymore. I couldn't listen to him talk about having a baby with another girl while I was so fiercely in love with him. "Jack, I can't be the one you talk to about this. I have to go."

I didn't wait for his response.

I couldn't.

I knew that if I waited for him to answer me, he'd change my mind. I'd stay on the phone with him for as long as he needed me to. And I couldn't be that for him. Not right now. Not with this.

I turned my phone off and stared blankly ahead, my thoughts all-consuming. I pictured him saying things to this girl that he said to me. Kissing her the way he kissed me. Touching her the way he touched me. The thoughts made my stomach churn as tears ran unchecked down my face.

My throat burned and I sprinted to the bathroom, losing today's lunch in the white bowl. I leaned against the bathtub, wiping beads of cold sweat from my forehead with the back of my hand. Made-up images crept into my subconscious, threatening to make me sick again unless I forced them away. I curled up into a ball on the shaggy bath mat and cried.

I never realized until the moment it disappeared how much I truly trusted Jack. It took seconds to annihilate the foundation we'd worked so hard to build. In its place were piles of powder, jagged bits of concrete, and shards of my broken heart.

The front door slammed and I heard Melissa shout my name. When I didn't respond, she wandered through the apartment looking for me. Her brown curls fell against the wall as she peered around the bathroom door. Her eyes widened once she caught sight of me.

"Cass? Are you okay?" The sound of her voice prompted more tears to fall. "Oh my God, what is it? What happened?"

I tried to focus, but Melissa turned into a big blur of brown through my watering eyes. "Jack cheated on me."

"What? When? I'll fucking kill him."

"The night he threw his perfect game. He said he got really drunk and this girl was really persistent and he gave in." I could barely say the words out loud. "Why would he give in?"

"'Cause he's an asshole. And he's stupid. He's a stupid asshole." Melissa's eyes welled up.

"She's pregnant."

"Who's pregnant?" she asked before releasing one of those surprised and horrifying gasps that just slip out uncontrollably. "You're kidding?"

"I wish." I grabbed my stomach as it cramped once more.

"I'm so sorry, Cassie. I can't believe this is happening." Melissa kneeled down and wrapped her arms around me, her warmth penetrating my chilled body. "Are you going to be okay?"

"Eventually. Just not right now."

"Does Dean know?" She leaned her head against mine.

"I have no idea."

"Come on, get up." Melissa stood and linked her arms with mine.

I shuddered. "I'm afraid to move too far away from the toilet."

"I'll grab you a trash can. You need to lie down." She carried the brunt of my weight on her tiny frame, practically falling with me once we reached my bed.

I crawled on top of my dark blue comforter and plopped my head on the pillow, Jack's voice replaying in my mind. "What if I can't sleep?"

"If you can't sleep, we'll figure it out. I bet you're more exhausted than you realize. You've had a traumatic day," she said, her fingers brushing against my hair.

I nodded. "It's been a little rough."

"Try and sleep. I'll be in the living room if you need me." She leaned down to give me a half hug before leaving my room.

I crawled under the comforter and snuggled into my bed, wrapping my covers into a safe, warm cocoon around myself as I begged my body to shut down. Implored my mind to turn itself off. I knew I'd only be able to find non-vomit-inducing peace in sleep.

Later, I opened my eyes to the sound of the alarm buzzing. I hit the snooze button before the reality of my situation crashed down all around me. That split second before I remembered was so peaceful, then it was gone. There would be no more peace for me today.

I looked at my cell phone, half tempted to turn it on and throw it against the wall. I ignored it as I shoved out of bed to get dressed.

"Cass, you up?" Melissa hollered from the other room.

"I'm up." My voice was so hoarse from crying, I had to try twice to get the words out.

"I can't believe you just woke up." Melissa walked into my room, her concern for me apparent in her expression.

"Me either." I cleared my throat, longing for some warm tea with honey to ease the burning there.

"Have you heard from him at all?"

I shook my head. "I haven't turned my phone on."

"You don't have to. And you don't have to go to class either, you know?"

"I can't sit here and cry all day," I whispered through my pain. "I need a distraction."

"Okay." She gave me a quick squeeze before leaving me alone.

*****

The next few days were a blur as I found it difficult to concentrate on anything other than my failed relationship. Classes were a great distraction...*in theory*. But the reality was that everything reminded me of Jack, and no matter how many lectures I heard on Visual Reporting or Comm Law, nothing held my attention with greater force than my own destructive mind.

My phone stayed off until my mom called Melissa's cell phone, frantic that I was either kidnapped or dead since my phone kept going straight to voice mail. When I finally did turn it on, seven new voice mail notifications appeared. All seven were from my mom, each one increasing in overdramatized panic.

The blue text message envelope lingered at the top of my screen, begging for me to press it. Eight new text messages from Jack. Eight.

*I am so sorry, Cass. Please tell me you know how sorry I am.*

*How did I screw us up this badly?*

*I love you. I love you so fucking much.*

*I feel like someone ripped out my heart and smashed it with bricks. It hurts. I hurt. And I'd gladly take your hurt too if it meant that you'd be okay. I'd do anything for you.*

*Cassie, please respond to me. Tell me to fuck off. Anything! Your silence is more hurtful than your anger.*

*I deserve this. I deserve anything you want to do to me. I sure as hell don't deserve you.*

*I'm losing my fucking mind. I've already lost my heart so I guess in a way that makes sense. I'm so fucking lost without you.*

*I love you. I'll never stop loving you. And I'm so sorry for everything. I'll never stop telling you how sorry I am.*

But eventually he did stop.

It had been over two weeks since his last attempt to contact me. And as hard as it was to not respond to his texts, it was even harder to stop getting them. I wanted him to want me. I needed him to still need me. Because I was still so desperately in love with him, my heart ached with each beat it pumped.

Of course, Melissa knew. "Jesus, Cassie, you look like hell. When's the last time you've eaten something other than toast? Or brushed your hair?"

I shrugged. "I don't know." My voice was hollow, void of emotion.

"You need to eat, okay?" Melissa cocked her

head to the side, her expression soft.

"I'm not hungry."

"Which is exactly why you need to eat something," she responded, which made no sense to me at all.

Jack's name suddenly appeared on my cell phone. My body started to shake as my gaze swung around to meet Melissa's.

"Jack?" she asked, her tone surprised. I nodded. "Don't answer. Unless you want to. No, you shouldn't." Melissa fought with herself as I pressed *Decline*, sending his call to voice mail.

He'd stopped leaving voice mail messages around the same time he stopped texting. So I jerked my head back in surprise when the *One new voice mail* notification appeared on my screen.

I hesitated before pressing Send, tears already filling in my eyes.

His voice mail was short and to the point. "I know you hate me and never want to talk to me again, but I really need to tell you something." He exhaled before whispering, "Kitten, please. I wouldn't call if it wasn't important." Then he hung up.

I still loved him no matter how hard I tried to pretend like I didn't.

"What did he say?" Melissa asked.

"He asked me to call him. Said he had something he needs to tell me. As if I can take any more of Jack's news." I shook my head, the tears no longer hesitating to fall.

"Well, shit. I wonder if Dean knows. Want to call him for the heads-up first?" she suggested.

"That's actually brilliant, but I don't think so. I'll just call him and I'll be right back." I gave her a half smile before heading into my bedroom and closing the door behind me.

I scrolled through the missed calls list on my phone and pressed on his name before touching the Send button.

"You called," he said as he answered.

"You said it was important."

"I'm really sorry, but I wanted you to hear this from me." Jack's voice was so flat it sounded robotic.

I couldn't take much more of this. My heart was so fractured already. "What is it now, Jack?"

"I asked Chrystle to marry me." He choked on the words and I almost swallowed my tongue.

"You *what*? You're kidding, right?" I instinctively looked at the calendar on my wall to make sure it wasn't April first.

"It's the right thing to do."

I let out the biggest, loudest, most sarcastic *ha!* I could manage. "The right thing to do? How is marrying someone you don't even know the right thing to do?" My head spun as a dizzy feeling overwhelmed me.

"I won't be like my parents." His voice faltered. "I have to be there for my kid."

My voice softened when I heard his pain. "Jack, you'll never be like your parents. But you don't have to marry some stranger to prove that." My lungs felt like they stopped functioning, and I forced myself to suck in a breath.

"It's the right thing to do," he repeated.

"You already said that." I started wondering who he was trying to convince. "Jack, no kid should grow up with two parents who don't love each other, let alone even know each other. This isn't right!"

"I'm sorry, Cass. I'm sorry I'm such a fuck-up." He sniffed.

"You're not a fuck-up, Jack. But please, don't do this." I begged for him to see reason. "It's one thing to have a kid with someone, but it's another thing to *marry* them."

"I already asked her," he admitted reluctantly.

"What? Jack, no," I said as the tears spilled. Breaking up was hard enough to deal with, but marrying someone else was truly putting the final nail in the coffin of *us*. "Have you talked to Marc and Ryan?" I asked through my desperation, assuming his agents would have the ability to talk logic into his clearly illogical mind.

"I have."

"And?" I practically shouted. "What did they

say? I'm sure they told you not to do this."

"They pretty much said exactly that."

"Jack. If everyone is telling you the same thing," my breath hitched, "we can't all be wrong."

"It doesn't matter. I refuse to continue the fucked-up cycle my parents started. We're getting married in two weeks."

"Two weeks?" I could barely say the words aloud.

"Chrystle doesn't want to be showing in the wedding pictures."

I hated her. Right when he made that statement, I felt pure hatred toward this strange girl. How was some random chick getting to marry the one guy I'd loved in my entire life?

"Kitten?"

"Don't…call me that," I said, my breath shaking.

"Cassie." His voice wavered. "I never meant for this to happen. I never imagined marrying someone who wasn't you."

Resentment replaced the sadness coursing throughout my body. "How is that supposed to make me feel? Huh? You can't say that to me! It's not fair, Jack. I can barely get through the day without breaking down."

"I'm sorry, Cassie, but you're not the only one hurting here. You're not the only one who has to try to make it through each day. I lost us too, ya know?"

I felt the breath I was holding escape with a *whoosh* as I struggled for air. "I don't know how to get over you."

"I'll never get over you."

"Then don't do this. Jack, please don't marry her," I pleaded, my voice breaking.

"I have to."

"You don't have to!" I screamed into the phone and he didn't respond.

Melissa barged into my room after hearing my raised voice, her face contorted in confusion and sympathy. I waved her over, not wanting her to leave, so she positioned herself next to me on the bed with her back leaning up against the wall.

"Do you still love me?" I asked him, squeezing my eyes shut.

"I'll love you until the day I stop breathing," he answered, his voice cracking.

"This isn't how our story was supposed to go, Jack. We weren't supposed to end like this."

"You think I don't know that? Our story wasn't supposed to end at all."

"I guess we're really over." I tried to accept the finality of it all.

"If I had the power to take it all back, I would. I'd give anything to undo this."

I broke down. I bawled uncontrollably into the phone, my misfortune spilling out in teardrop form.

"Please don't cry, Kitten." His voice shook.

"Don't call me that any more. You don't get to call me that any more." I could barely speak for sobbing.

"You're right. I should probably go."

"Good…bye, Jack," I moaned before pressing End, not waiting to hear another word. I dropped my head into my hands, my tears soaking the comforter.

"What was that? What's happening, Cassie?"

"He's getting married." I could barely choke the words out.

"He's doing *what*?" she shouted, her face angry. "Why?!!"

"He says it's the right thing to do."

"I'm calling Dean." Melissa shot up from my bed.

"What? No! Why?"

"Because someone has to talk some sense into that idiot and it can't be you!" She stomped out of my room.

My world went black and the next thing I knew, Dean was sitting at the foot of my bed, clearly uncomfortable with the way I carried on. Even with my face buried in my pillow, my muffled wails were loud enough to wake the dead. He tried to comfort me by patting my calves, and I turned my head to look at him before swatting his hands away.

"Say something, Dean," Melissa insisted,

jabbing at his shoulder.

"What do you want me to say?" he asked through clenched teeth.

"Make her feel better. Tell her you talked to Jack. Something!" Her voice sounded so frantic.

I jerked my head up at the mention of his name. "You talked to Jack?" I choked out, my chest heaving.

"Yeah." He frowned.

"And?"

"He's completely irrational. I can't talk any sense into him at all," he admitted, his voice frustrated.

"What about his agents? I mean, what good are they if let him go through with this?"

"They tried, trust me. I guess I should be thankful they got him to agree to a pre-nup," he said and lifted one shoulder.

"They did? That's good." I sniffed.

"They tried to get him to wait. They told him to get confirmation that the baby was his, but you know Jack," he said with a huff.

I nodded with understanding before allowing my head to fall back into my pillow.

"I'm sorry, sis. I tried to tell him this was wrong. I tried to talk him out of it, but he won't listen. He's so stubborn and he's convinced himself that what he's doing is right." He tugged at his brown hair, his eyes closing.

"Gran even tried to talk to him," he whispered, his eyes still tight.

"What? What'd she say?"

"She told him that it doesn't take becoming someone's husband to become a good dad. She told him that one has nothing to do with the other. That being a dad was a choice. That anyone could father a child, but a real man *chooses* to be a dad. She told him that being a husband was something that should be reserved for the person you truly want to call your wife."

"Gran's good." I couldn't hold back a slight smile, awed at Gran's wisdom.

"What'd he say to that?" Melissa chimed in.

"He wouldn't listen to her, either." Dean's head shook and my smile faded. "He told her that his child wouldn't grow up in a broken home. That sometimes you have to be unselfish and compromise even if it's not what you want because it's not about you anymore."

"There's no getting through to him. How are they doing?" I asked, referring to Gran and Gramps.

"They're both really sad. They're worried for him. And they're worried about you." The skin around his eyes pulled tight with his stress.

I nodded, no words necessary.

"He loves you, Cassie. He doesn't give a shit about this girl, he's just so fucked up from our parents that he can't see reason."

"I feel like you wouldn't do this though, and you both grew up in the same house." Melissa folded her arms across her stomach.

"Yeah, but he was older so he remembers things that I don't. He was the one who had to hold it together while our mom fell apart. He remembers the day our dad didn't come home. Honestly, he really lost it when Mom left. He was never the same after that and he's been fighting his demons ever since."

Dean shrugged, picking at the fabric of his shorts. "I never thought he'd let anyone in. We would fight like crazy about it until I realized there was no changing him. I don't think it's that he didn't want someone to love him—he just didn't want to risk loving them back."

He paused, exhaling through his nose. "Then you showed up and everything changed. You changed him."

"He changed me too."

"I'll say," Melissa added, her arms dropping to her side. "She never let anyone in either. I knew the night she saw Jack that something was different." Her blue eyes pierced into mine. "I could literally see it. Watching the two of you interact, it was like watching fireworks light up the night sky. You two burn brighter when you're together."

"Even fireworks burn out," I said, my voice solemn.

## SEVENTEEN

The next few days were hell as the local newspapers and websites focused on the "Upcoming Nuptials of Our Very Own Jack Carter!" and "Hometown Hero Marrying Southern Sweetie!" I couldn't escape the news. No matter what I did or where I went, his one night of screwing up was always right there, *screaming* in my face.

I stopped checking e-mails the day an anonymous person sent me a link that led to a picture of myself underneath a caption that read, "The girl Jack left behind. Why he's marrying someone else."

And I closed my Facebook account the moment after I logged in to see over a hundred and fifty messages from my so-called "friends," asking me if everything they were reading online was true or not.

If I didn't rely on my cell phone to communicate with my job and my parents, I would have shut it off as well. The texts alone were a nightmare. Each time one beeped, my heart jumped. Part of me wanted the messages to be from Jack, wanting to know how much he hurt, how sorry he was, and how he wished it had never happened. But the other part of me could barely stomach it. His words were like knives in a heart already overflowing with stab wounds.

My phone rang and I looked down to see DANI–

TRUNK MAG flashing on the screen. I hadn't been to the offices at *Trunk* since the semester began. I pressed the Answer button, resting the phone against my ear. "Hey, Dani. What's up?"

"Hey, Cass." Her voice sounded cordial. "I'm really sorry about you and Jack."

"Thanks." This had become my standard response. I simply accepted people's condolences for my now-dead-and-buried relationship and tried to move on.

"Um, I really hate you ask you this, but BC is insisting the school wants to do a follow-up feature on Jack since the draft. He says everyone and their mother has their panties in a wad and can't read enough about him."

BC was the editor of the magazine. Half the time I thought he was an idiot, but his ideas usually won us awards, so I stopped questioning his ridiculous demands months ago.

"He freaked out when he looked at our collection of Jack photos." She snickered.

*We had a collection of Jack photos.*

*Who has a collection of photos of one person?*

"We don't have anything recent and he told me to ask you if you had anything from the summer when he was playing. I'm sorry, Cass, I tried to argue with him, but he was adamant that you'd be *professional* about this."

I swallowed the lump in my throat. Going

through photos of Jack wasn't something I was sure I could handle at this point. But BC was right. I needed to be professional.

"You don't have to do this. I can tell him you didn't have any." Dani's sympathy and regret sounded sincere, and I found myself feeling bad for the position she was in.

"No, it's okay. I'm sure I have something you can use. How many do you need?"

"Just e-mail me a few of your best shots. I trust your judgment." I could hear the relief in her tone.

"Okay. Deadline?"

"Tomorrow by noon. I know it's tight but BC wants it to go out in the Welcome Back edition."

"No problem." I sucked in a lungful of air.

"Thanks, Cassie. You're a lifesaver."

I ended the call, reaching for my backpack and stuffing my textbooks inside. I slipped my sunglasses over my eyes, tossed a hat on my head, and headed out the door toward campus.

I strolled along the sidewalk before cutting to the left, entering the well-manicured campus. I marveled at how green the lawn was even though I couldn't remember the last time it rained. I passed two girls in hand-painted sorority shirts and I swear I felt a few brain cells spontaneously combust in my head.

A larger crowd appeared up ahead and my chest tightened as I neared. The stares were less subtle now and the whispers sounded less like whispers and more like shouts. I hated the fact that everyone on campus felt the need to talk about me like I was some freak in a circus sideshow.

My phone vibrated in my pocket and I reached in and pulled it out. Text from Melissa. *My fucking savior.* I walked with my head down, my attention focused on my cell phone instead of the gossiping people I passed.

*In the SU with Dean. It's not crazy crowded.*

With my heart in my throat, I turned in the direction of the student union and punched in a response.

*On my way.*

If I continued to hide, it would only make things worse. I'd be giving them more things to talk about, instead of less. I had to show them I wasn't falling apart. That I could survive without Jack in my life. Whether or not I believed it wasn't the point—I needed everyone else to.

I threw open the glass door before stepping into the familiar smells and sounds. I pretended not to notice as the girls watched my every move, their faces painted with fake sympathy.

I spotted Dean and rushed over, my pace not even slowing as someone called my name. By the time I reached the table, I was practically hyperventilating.

"You're okay. It's okay." Melissa reached

across the table, touching my hand with hers.

My eyes pooled as I squeezed them shut to force the tears to recede. Dean slid next to me, tossing his arm around my shoulder and pulling me against him as I struggled to even my breathing.

"I guess if Jack dumped me, I'd date his brother too." A curvy blonde motioned toward us with a snide smile.

"Shut up, you stupid tramp," Melissa shouted, her face reddening. "All of you just shut the hell up and leave her alone!"

I was silently thankful for her outburst. Thankful she had the guts to say what I wanted to, but was too terrified of actually doing. My actions were so scrutinized that any flare-up would most likely end up on YouTube. It was hard enough simply getting through the day without adding fuel to the wildfire that showed no sign of stopping its ravenous burn.

Cole and Brett grabbed their trays and headed toward our table. When random girls tried to follow, the guys shoved them away and announced loud enough for everyone to hear that they weren't welcome.

Cole sat down on the other side of me, his eyes still holding the pain I recognized from the day of the beating. "We're all really sorry about you and Jack, Cassie. And if there's anything we can do, just let us know. You're still our family."

Brett dropped his tray on the table with a crash. "Girls are such bitches!" he shouted before plopping his muscular body across from me, causing the whole table to vibrate.

"Hey!" Melissa smacked his shoulder.

"Present company excluded of course," he continued with a wink in her direction. "Good to see you, Cass." He smiled, shoving a monster-sized sub sandwich into his mouth.

I laughed and my body welcomed the emotion, embracing it like an old friend it hadn't seen in years.

"There's the smile I love." Dean nudged my arm with a grin.

"Are you still working at that magazine?" Cole asked, flicking an unopened bag of chips across the table.

"Yeah. They extended my internship another semester." I smiled, feeling the excitement course through my veins as I talked about my passion.

"And they're sending you on an assignment!" Melissa squealed.

"They're what? You didn't tell me that." Dean cocked his head to the side as his face pinched a little.

"She just found out, Dean, don't get all pouty about it." Melissa pretended to whine and he threw a grape at her.

I nudged Dean with my arm. "I think it's a test.

They said they want to see what kind of emotions I can evoke in readers with my pictures."

"What kind of what?" Brett's mouth twisted in confusion.

"You're such...an idiot." Cole teased, shaking his head.

"They said they wanted to see how I viewed the world." I shrugged my shoulders. "So they're giving me a chance to show them."

Cole leaned over the table toward me. "That's so cool. Do you think they'll hire you?"

"I don't know. I guess if they like what they see, but I still have a lot to learn. The photographers they have on staff are mind-blowingly talented. I only hope I'll be that good someday. Plus, their main offices are in New York. The only people they have in LA are the head of sales, a research and development exec, some freelancers, and me."

"Would you move to New York?" Brett looked stunned, lettuce and meat falling out of his open mouth.

My eyes met Melissa's as curiosity crept across her face. "Why not? You only live once, right?"

"Because it snows there, that's why not!" Melissa shouted and jutted out her bottom lip.

"New York seems pretty cool." Brett shrugged before finishing off a sports drink and tossing it toward the plastic can a few feet away. When it hit the edge and fell to the ground, everyone at the table broke into laughter and shouting about how much Brett sucked.

I almost felt normal.

And then the moment passed.

Jack was engaged to marry someone else. He had sex with a strange girl without using protection. Something he had never done before us.

*Us.*

"Hello?" Melissa waved both arms like she was signaling a rescue chopper.

"I'm sorry, what did I miss?" I asked and the table roared with amusement once more.

I glanced at my phone, noted the time, and started to gather my things. "I have to go. I have class in ten minutes and it's on the other side of campus."

"I'll walk you." Dean stood as I did, his actions causing the table to fall silent as we left.

"You don't have to walk me to class, Dean. I'm fine."

"I know, but I wanted to talk to you," he said, each step perfectly timed with mine.

"What's up?" I glanced sideways at him as he tugged at his brown hair the same way Jack used to do.

"I just wanted you to know that I'm going to the wedding."

My legs started to tremble as his words surged through me with ferocity. I stopped walking and silently begged myself not to lose it. "Of course you are. You're his brother."

"I know, but I feel like I'm betraying you somehow. Standing up there with Jack, it's like saying that I agree with what he's doing. And I don't. I don't agree with it for one second, but he's my brother and I love him." He lowered his head as he kicked at the ground with his foot.

I threw my arms around him, squeezing hard until he returned the friendly gesture. "I love you for caring about me, but of course you should be there for Jack."

"I just wish I could talk him out of it." He tugged at the corners of his eyes, a yawn escaping.

"Are Gran and Gramps going?" The question alone forced my knees to resume trembling.

"They're not. Gran can't fly for that long and Gramps refuses to go without her." He shrugged. "But honestly, I don't think they have the heart to watch him go through with it."

"Does Jack know they aren't coming?" I suddenly found myself caring for Jack's well-being.

"He knows. I think he's relieved, actually. He feels like he let them down, you know? He's dealing with a lot of guilt right now."

I swallowed hard as my throat burned with repressed emotion. "I'm gonna be late to class. I have to go. Thanks for telling me." I turned on my heel and walked away as fast as my quivering legs would move me.

*****

I paced in the living room, my body a bundle of nervous energy as I waited for Melissa to get home from night class. The door flung open as a gust of wind practically blew Melissa inside. She pushed her small body against the door, shutting it with a loud slam before turning to face me, her hair tangled across her face.

"I hate the wind." She jutted out her bottom lip and blew a huff of air against the pieces covering her mouth.

I frowned. "Me too." I plunked down on the couch and picked nervously at the edge of a cushion. "I need to talk to you."

"So talk." She flipped the kitchen light on, searching the cupboards for her bag of butter-flavored pretzels.

"I want to go out there."

"Go out where?" She turned and squinted at me in confusion.

"Alabama. I need to see him, Melissa. Or maybe he needs to see me? I don't know, but what if I can stop the wedding?"

"Why would you want to stop the wedding?" Her head cocked to one side as she crunched on a pretzel.

"Because."

"Because why, Cassie? This guy cheated on

you. And he lied." Leave it to Melissa to press the issue, forcing me to examine my heart.

"I know. And I always believed that cheating was an unforgiveable act. That once you broke down that foundation of trust, it could never be rebuilt. But I was wrong. I don't want him to marry someone else, Melissa. I don't know that I can get past what he's done, but I'm willing to try."

She stared at me like she'd known this all along and was simply waiting for me to figure it out.

"So why are we still talking about it?"

"Because I don't have the money for a ticket." I sighed, plucking at the frayed edges of the throw pillow. "And I was wondering if I could borrow some? I'll pay you back, I swear."

"How will you pay me back? You don't even have a real job." Even though she was telling the truth, I still wanted to smack her.

"I didn't say I'd pay you back next week, but I will pay you back." Irritated at her reluctance, I squeezed the pillow to my stomach, trying to push back at my emotions.

"I'm just messing with you. Let's go book you some flights!" She tossed the bag of pretzels into the air before heading into the bedroom. I laughed as they spilled out onto the floor.

"And a rental car. And a hotel," I shouted.

"Yeah, yeah. I've got it covered. Get in here!"

\*\*\*\*\*

The lights at the baseball stadium flicked off as the last of the fans pulled out of the gravel lot. The opposing team piled onto their bus and the engine roared to life with a loud puff of smoke. I stood next to my rented Ford Mustang and watched as the home team players sporadically filed out of the locker room. My legs were shaking like crazy, my nerves completely frayed.

I noticed Jack immediately. He was freshly showered, his black hair still dripping wet. A smile crept across my face and I knew without a doubt that if my eyes could sparkle like stars, they would have. Seeing him almost brought me to my knees.

I watched as his eyes scanned the parking lot for his car, before they stopped on me. He looked away and then quickly jerked back, his hair spraying water from the force of the turn.

"Kitten?" He dropped his bag, running.

"I hate when you call me that," I half shouted with a smile.

"What are you doing here?"

I leaned my back into the car as he kissed the side of my face and then stood far too close. I felt my stomach drop to my knees. And my knees drop to my feet. And my feet…well, they could barely stand. He wrapped his arms around me and I nuzzled into his neck, breathing him in. I stopped my fingers from running through his wet hair. I stopped my hands from gripping the back of his neck and pulling him to me. I stopped my mouth from attacking his.

God, I missed him. What was left of my broken heart belonged to him. Every jagged shard had his name written all over it in permanent black ink.

He gently pulled back from our embrace before asking me again, "What are you doing here, Cass?"

"I just…" I hadn't thought about what I was going to say, which was really stupid. I'd just been so consumed in the process of getting to Alabama so I could see him, I hadn't really thought through what I was going to say once I got there. "I just wanted to talk to you."

"You could have called." His teasing tone was so familiar, bringing memories crashing back that made my throat start to burn.

"I wanted to see you in person."

He suddenly shifted his weight and his eyes widened. "Are you okay? Everything is okay with you, right?"

I smiled at his protectiveness. "Yeah. I'm fine."

I watched as he regained his composure with a shaky breath. "That's good. I don't know what I'd do if something ever happened to you, Kitten."

"Like if I was marrying a complete stranger tomorrow?"

His body stiffened. "Is that why you're here?" I watched his shoulders and head drop as the realization hit.

"Jack. It's a mistake. You shouldn't do this. Please don't do it…don't marry this girl." My left hand balled into a fist and rested between my breasts. "I'm begging you. I am literally begging you to not do this."

I started crying. The ugly, uncontrollable kind of crying. His eyes glistened and I watched him blink back his own tears.

"It's too late. Her whole family's in town." His face pinched with pained emotion.

"It's not too late. Tomorrow at whatever time you're supposed to marry her is too late. Tonight isn't. Please." I reached for his shirt and gripped, balling it tightly in my fist. "Please don't do this to me."

"I'm sorry you flew all this way." His eyes looked away from mine.

"So that's it? You won't even consider not going through with it?"

"I already made my decision."

"Do you love her?" I asked, my heart beating as if the next pulse depended on his answer.

His body suddenly pressed against mine as he cupped my face with both hands. "You're so beautiful."

I struggled to breathe. "Do you love her?" I choked out the words.

His dark eyes narrowed. "She's not you."

His breath was a mixture of warmth and

cinnamon from his long-gone breath mint. "What does that even mean?" I asked, my tears spilling over his fingertips.

His hands fell from my face as he breathed in and out through his nose, his temper rising. "Fuck, Cassie. What do you want to hear? How much I hate myself for getting drunk that night and losing the only girl in my life I've ever trusted and truly loved? How I called Dean fifty times a day for weeks begging him to tell me how I could get you back? Do you want to hear how fucking weak and pathetic I think I am for not being able to tell her no that night, when I knew what was at stake?"

His eyebrows pinched together and his jaw tensed as his emotions spilled out into the night air. "Do you want to hear how I tried to talk her out of keeping this baby so that it wouldn't fuck everything up? How I begged her not to keep it, told her I'd pay for everything, I'd drive her there and give her money after it was all over, just to please not do this to me. And then how much of an asshole I felt after that too? Who tells someone that?"

I watched as he paced back and forth before falling to his knees, his hands covering his tortured face. His hands fell as he glanced up at me, tears reflecting in his eyes. "I am so fucking in love with you I can't see straight. I don't love her. I'll never love her. But I fucked up and now I have to pay for it. I'll never forgive myself for hurting you," he said. "Or losing you."

I fell to the ground next to him, my teardrops staining the dry concrete below. I reached for his arms as he wrapped them tightly around my waist and pulled me in. There was no space between us, our bodies sharing the same air. Our foreheads touched and I closed my eyes. "Knowing you're marrying someone who isn't me," I squeezed my eyes tighter to fight back the pain, "is literally killing me."

"You don't hate me?" he asked tentatively.

I opened my eyes to him, my pulse racing at his nearness. "I flew to Alabama to tell you not to get married, dummy. I'm pretty sure I don't hate you." I forced a small laugh.

"How about one last kiss then?" He grinned, his dimples illuminated by the moonlight.

"My heart's already shattered beyond repair, what more damage could it do?"

My eyes closed as his lips pressed against mine. My broken heart sputtered to life as those pesky butterflies in my stomach flapped the dust off their wings. My mouth opened slightly and my tongue was immediately greeted by his. His lips softly opened and closed as our tongues danced with one another as if thrilled to have reconnected. Everything in the background faded away and nothing existed except that kiss. Nothing but the feel of his lips, the taste of his tongue, the smell of his sweet, cinnamon-scented breath. His lips closed gingerly as he pulled away.

"I don't know how to recover from this…from you," I admitted, embarrassed.

"How do you think I feel? Do you have any idea how hard of an act you are to follow, Cassie Andrews? I will never be the same."

He stood up before reaching out a hand to pull me to my feet. I took a shaky breath, suddenly distracted by the sound of tires screeching and the flash of headlights bouncing in our direction.

"Shit." Jack looked at me apologetically and then back toward the oncoming car.

"Who is that?" I asked, and then suddenly I knew. "It's her, isn't it?"

I swallowed hard as the car came to a sudden stop and the driver's side door flew open. Without turning off the ignition or closing the door, a petite, pixie-like brunette sprinted toward Jack. "When you didn't come home, I got worried. All the other players are home already." She flung her arms around Jack's shoulders and squeezed, the massive diamond on her finger flashing. I looked away as my stomach lurched.

"What are you doing?" she asked as her eyes looked past Jack and fell onto mine, her eyes widening as realization set in. I eyed her tiny five-foot-one-inch frame and wished I could tackle it to the ground.

She pulled back from Jack's arms. "What's she doing here?" Jealousy was written all over her pinched little face.

Jack glanced at me before turning to face his future bride. "She came to see me. She wanted to talk."

"She's trying to stop the wedding, isn't she? She doesn't want us to be together, Jack! She's trying to take you away from me and the baby!" She clutched her stomach before throwing her head into Jack's chest.

"She just wanted to talk, Chrystle. Calm down." Jack glanced at me as he awkwardly tried to console her.

She pulled her head from against his body and glared at me. "Don't even think about showing up at the church tomorrow. You will not ruin this day for me! He's not yours anymore!"

"Chrystle. Stop it." Jack scolded her like a child as I looked around the empty parking lot to make sure her threats were really meant for me.

"Excuse me?" I said with a defensive snarl.

She placed a hand on her hip, her thigh jutting out to one side. "You think I don't know who you are?" she asked before jerking Jack's hand possessively into hers.

Anger swept over me, effectively blocking all the other emotions swirling around inside me. "I don't give a fuck if you know who I am or not. Just be thankful you're pregnant."

Her jaw dropped slightly. "Or what?"

"Or else I'd be beating your tiny little ass right now for being a disrespectful slut who sleeps with other people's boyfriends. You're the worst kind of girl."

"And what kind of girl is that?" She tried to sound tough and I had to hold back a smirk.

"The kind other girls can't trust. You're a backstabber, a liar, and a manipulative skank. You have no respect for boundaries or other people's relationships." *Damn, it felt good to finally say those words to her face!*

"You don't even know me! Jack, say something!"

Before he could speak, I lit into her once again. "You didn't care that Jack had a girlfriend back home, did you? And no matter how many times he told you about me, you told him I wasn't there and what I didn't know wouldn't hurt me. You manipulated him that night into sleeping with you."

She eyeballed me, unsure of how to respond, so I continued. "So you tell me…what kind of girl does that?"

"Cassandra, that's enough," Jack said sympathetically.

I cringed inwardly at the sound of him using my real name. No one called me that. Ever. To hear it spill from his mouth, in his voice, it sounded all wrong.

"None of it matters now, does it? I'm pregnant and we're getting married, so you'll just have to find someone else." She looked at Jack for approval, but he refused to tear his eyes from mine. "Have a nice life, Cassie. I know we will." She smirked at me and then tugged at Jack's arm.

Jack whispered, "Good-bye, Kitten," loud enough for me to hear before she dragged him away. I stared down at the concrete, willing the pain to subside, when I heard footsteps bounding back in my direction. I glanced up to see Chrystle standing a few feet away, a smug look on her face.

"I'm the kind of girl who gets what she wants, and what I wanted was a professional baseball player for a husband. And that's exactly what I'm getting. Maybe you'll be a little more resourceful in your next relationship." She patted her flat stomach again before running toward her car.

My jaw unclenched as it fell open.

*****

I drove the short distance to my hotel, tears blurring my vision the entire way. It's amazing I didn't have a freaking wreck. When I pulled into the hotel parking lot, I turned off the engine and dialed Melissa's number.

"Tell me everything," she screamed into the phone.

"Well, I didn't stop the wedding," I admitted,

my voice cracking.

"Oh God, what happened? Did you see him? Did he see you? Did you talk to him?"

"I saw him. We talked. I told him not to marry her. He said he loved me, and then he left with her. He said he couldn't call off the wedding, that this was something he had to do." I choked back a sob as I stared out the windshield into the night, seeing nothing.

"I'm so sorry, Cassie. I honestly thought that if he saw you, it would change things."

"Me too."

"Hey, I'm proud of you. I'm really fucking proud of you. The old Cassie would have never done this. She would have never put aside being wronged to try to win him back."

"Well, the old Cassie never had Jack Carter to lose."

"No regrets, right?"

"No regrets," I repeated.

# EIGHTEEN
## JACK

It killed me to leave Cassie standing alone in that empty parking lot. I watched her as I drove away, tears streaming down her beautiful face. It took every ounce of my self-control to keep my foot on the gas pedal, when all I wanted to do was turn around and be with her.

Seeing her tonight almost broke me. I'd do anything for her, be anything she wants me to be. Because she deserves nothing less than everything.

But I always find a way to fuck things up. And Cassie Andrews was no exception. I had the best damn girl in the world, and I threw it all away. Just like that jerk Jared said I would, the night of my first date with Cassie.

I pulled my car into the garage next to Chrystle's and hopped out to look for Dean. "Hey, little brother! Where are you?" I shouted from the entryway.

"What's up?" Dean yawned as he walked out of the guest bedroom, his dark hair sticking up in every direction.

"Can I talk to you out back?" I glanced at Chrystle, who pretended to yawn.

"You won't be long, will you, Jack?" she asked, her voice nauseatingly light and airy.

"Go to bed without me, Chrystle. I'll be there soon." I forced a smile, dreading each moment I had to spend with her.

Dean and I walked out into the warm Alabama air and sat in two lawn chairs side by side.

"You nervous for tomorrow?" Dean asked with a slight grin.

I turned to look at him. "A little." Then I cut to the chase. "Did you know Cassie's here?"

I watched Dean's eyes widen. "Excuse me? What do you mean, she's here?"

"She was waiting for me in the parking lot after my game tonight."

"Shit." Dean looked at me with worry.

"You didn't know? I was certain you knew."

"I had no idea, Jack. I swear. I would have given you a heads-up or something if I knew." His eyes widened. "Which is why, of course, they didn't tell me."

"They who?"

"Melissa and Cassie. They were acting weird all week, but they didn't say why."

"Does she ever talk about me," I asked, putting my brother on the spot.

"Not when I'm around," he answered and I nodded with understanding. "So what did she say?"

I shrugged my shoulders and leaned toward him. "She asked me not to get married tomorrow."

"She flew all the way out here to ask you that? She could've just called." I watched as Dean eyed the second-story window where my bedroom was.

His eyes searched for something before landing back on mine.

I laughed. "I told her the same thing."

"That sucks." Dean shook his head. "I know this is killing her."

I felt my face tighten with his words. "I'm pretty sure it's killing both of us."

"Then why are you doing it? I mean, don't do it. Don't marry Chrystle." I knew it was hard for Dean to be supportive of my marriage to Chrystle, but sometimes his irritation with me bubbled over, like now.

"It's a little late for that, don't you think?"

"Look, I get why you're doing it. I just wish you wouldn't. I know you still love Cassie."

My eyes narrowed and I clenched my jaw. "Of course I fucking love Cassie. But I cheated on her and got someone else pregnant. I'll spend the rest of my life loving the one person I can't have. That's my punishment for hurting her."

Dean squinted as he shook his head. "What kind of fucked-up logic is that?"

"The only kind of logic I can live with. My pain is my punishment. I brought it on myself. I deserve to hurt since I hurt her. And I don't deserve to have her after what I did."

"You're seriously whacked. You know that, right? You could be with Cassie right now if you wanted to!" Dean whisper-shouted to me harshly.

I breathed in and out through my nose, refocusing my thoughts. "I can't."

Dean stood up, shoving the chair out from under him before leaning close to my face. "You're still hurting her. Every day you aren't with her, you're hurting her. And following through with this stupid wedding is probably going to fucking ruin her!"

He went back into the house and slammed the sliding glass door shut with a *thwack*. I replayed the conversation in my mind, convincing myself that he was wrong about one thing. Eventually Cassie would heal and get over me. She'd find someone new to love…someone who deserved her.

But me? I'd never find another girl like her. And I'd never love anyone the way I love her. My pain would last a lifetime and hers would one day become a distant memory.

*****

The church was a combination of newly updated renovations mixed with the original structure built in the early eighteen hundreds. I had no idea that the tall building I drove past on the way to the ball field was an actual church until Chrystle forced me inside one day.

It honestly looked like an oversized mausoleum from the outside. But once you walked through those massive doors, it was a different story. Maybe it was the impressive stained glass windows that guided you down the aisle. Or the white and black swirled marble staircase. Whatever it was, I found myself understanding why people found comfort here.

The pews filled up quickly with my teammates and Chrystle's family and friends. I stood at one side of the altar with Dean next to me, and Chrystle's best friend, Vanessa, waited at the other. The large white doors opened as organ music filtered from the enormous pipes.

Chrystle appeared in a skintight white dress, the fabric hugging every inch of her body as her smiling father walked her down the aisle. What a fucking sham. He had to know this wasn't real. If I had a daughter, I'd never let her marry some schmuck who didn't even love her.

I wanted to throw up. Beads of sweat began to accumulate behind my neck as my heart started pounding. Dean leaned over and whispered, "We can still leave," and I actually considered it. My stomach flipped as I struggled to hold back the sickness that threatened.

What was I doing? This should be Cassie walking down the aisle toward me. I shouldn't be marrying this girl. I don't love her. Hell, I can barely stand her. The mere idea of spending every day with her made me want to vanish into thin air.

I imagined having the power of invisibility and how freaked out everyone would be if I suddenly disappeared. *Poof, gone*. The crying and screaming that would overwhelm the church. Some would insist that demons took me. Or that maybe I was the demon. I forced back a laugh as I glanced toward Vanessa who eyed me, her expression wicked.

I glimpsed back at Chrystle just as she placed her free hand on her stomach and rubbed it with a smile, as if reading my mind. I swallowed my broken laugh and remembered why I was standing there in the first place. I had an obligation to my unborn child. A duty as a father.

I ~~couldn't~~ *wouldn't* leave my baby. I would follow through with this because it was the right thing to do. My kid deserved a family that was whole, not broken, not incomplete, not separated. He deserved to grow up in a house with a mom and a dad who loved him. I refused to be the reason why he switched houses depending on the day of the week and I was unwilling to only see him on those days. Kids should grow up with their family and I wouldn't abandon mine.

I forced a smile as she neared, a part of me suffocating with each step. She looked pretty, but all I saw when I looked at her was the reason I'd lost the one thing I ever loved. I glanced at Dean, his face pained behind the happiness he faked, as Chrystle sidled up next to me. The preacher read vows and we repeated them to each other, my heart slowing with each word until I was certain it would stop beating altogether and I'd drop dead.

Couldn't everyone in the room tell I wasn't in love with the girl standing next to me?

I felt hollow. Empty. Devoid of all emotion as I said, "I do," when I really wanted to shout, "Hell no, I don't!"

The words, "You may now kiss your bride," echoed in my mind as Chrystle's grin widened. I leaned in to give her a peck, refusing to close my eyes, but she grabbed the back of my neck with both hands and refused to let me go. I pulled against her tight grip as my temper flared.

"That's enough," I whispered through a tight smile.

"Ladies and gentlemen, may I present Mr. and Mrs. Jack Carter," the preacher shouted with enthusiasm, and I pulled at my tie, willing its chokehold to loosen.

"You okay?" Dean leaned in with a whisper.

"I gave up being okay the day I lost Cassie," I admitted, Chrystle's hand gripping mine as she pulled me from the altar.

# NINETEEN

After the wedding Chrystle wanted to buy a house, insisting that our child needed a neighborhood and a backyard in order to be truly happy. We fought for weeks over it, until I finally got it through her thick skull that we weren't going to live in Alabama forever.

"I can get moved up or traded at any time, Chrystle! Then we'll have to move right away. It doesn't make any sense to buy a house here when we're most likely not staying," I shouted, trying but failing to hold back my temper.

"But I want to live here in the off-season. Don't you?" she cried.

"Hadn't planned on it." I longed to feel any emotion for the tears she shed, but couldn't find it in me.

"You're not even trying."

I released an exasperated sigh. "What are you talking about?"

"This marriage. *Us.* You're not even trying, Jack. I deserve for you to try." She stomped her foot on the floor. "I'm carrying your child. We both deserve for you to try."

There was the emotion I so desperately needed. Guilt. Welcome home, old friend. "You're right. I'll try harder," I promised, and she cried again.

"Sorry. Being pregnant makes me really emotional." She wiped at her face with the back of her hand and I reluctantly pulled her into my arms.

\*\*\*\*\*

I walked through the front door carrying my baseball gear before I shouted, "Chrystle? I'm back!"

I refused to say that I was *home* because Cassie was my home. But I'd lost that, and her, forever, so I'd never truly be home again.

"I'm up here," she shouted from upstairs, her voice sounding odd.

"Are you okay?" I yelled before craning my neck to hear her response. "Chrystle?" I yelled again, dropping my bags with a thud.

I could make out the soft sounds of crying as I rushed up the stairs to our bedroom. Chrystle was curled into a ball surrounded by pillows and used-up tissues. While no feelings existed for the woman I was married to, my feelings for what grew inside of her were immeasurable.

"What's wrong? What happened? Is the baby okay?" I asked, overwhelmed with worry.

"Oh, Jack." She broke down into tears. "I lost the baby this morning."

My stomach dropped and on its way down it grabbed a hold of my heart. "What? What happened?"

"The doctor said it's common. I woke up and started bleeding really bad. I was so scared." She threw herself into my arms and sobbed against my

307

chest.

Devastation ripped through me. Somewhere along the way I'd grown used to the idea of being a father. I'd made plans and looked forward to a future that no longer existed.

There was no more baby. I brushed under my eye and stared at Chrystle's stomach, resting my hand there.

"I can't believe I lost our baby. I'm so sorry. All I wanted was our baby. Our child." She looked up at me through her tears.

"I know. Me too," I admitted as a tear escaped my eye. "Can I get you anything? Do you want some water or something?"

"I'm okay. Where are you going?" She clung to my shirt as I climbed to my feet.

"I'm just going downstairs to grab a drink. I'll be right back, okay?"

She nodded and I flew from the room, my emotions taking over. I hopped over the last two stairs before rushing into the tiny bathroom and slamming the door shut. I fell to the floor, my head falling between my legs as I grieved for the child I'd lost.

My chest heaved with pain before a sliver of hope crept in.

*You can leave Chrystle now.*
*Get a divorce and go fix things with Cassie.*
*Spend your life making it up to her.*

Relief washed over me, quickly followed by guilt, my new best friend. How could I feel relief at a time like that? This isn't the time to find happiness. What the fuck was wrong with me?

I steadied my heartbeat before pushing my body up from the floor. I poured a glass of water, grabbed some headache medicine, and slowly crept back up the stairs.

"Let's make another baby, Jack."

Her request caught me off guard. "What?"

"Make love to me," she begged.

"No," I told her staunchly, the very idea made me want to punch something. I hated the relief I felt, but the truth was, I'd just dodged a bullet. I wasn't about to load the gun again.

"Why not? Now that we're not having a baby, you're going to leave me? I can see the headlines now…'Jack Carter Leaves Heartbroken Wife After She Loses Baby.'"

I winced. "Calm down, Chrystle."

"Say you won't leave. I can't handle you leaving on top of what I already lost." She sobbed, her face flushed.

"I'm not going anywhere," I conceded.

I woke up the next morning, my head throbbing as if I'd drank too much the night before. But it was the ache of loss that ripped through my skull. I glanced at Chrystle, her arm possessively clasping mine. She whined as I removed it from her grip and flipped over, but continued sleeping as I crawled out of bed.

I brushed my teeth, splashed water on my face, and started to head downstairs. "Where are you going?" Her needy voice stopped me in my tracks.

"I'm just heading to the gym. Go back to sleep." I took two steps toward her before changing direction and running down the stairs.

I sat in my car, turned the ignition, and powered on my wireless headset. As I drove away, I dialed Dean's number.

"Hey, bro, it's early." Dean's voice was raspy. Apparently I'd woken him up again.

"Shit. I always forget the time difference. Sorry."

"No big deal. What's up?" He yawned into the receiver.

"Chrystle lost the baby yesterday," I said as my emotions whooshed out from me.

"Oh God, really? I'm so sorry." I heard him shifting around in his bed. "Are you okay?"

"I will be."

"So what now?" he asked, the same way he always did when we were kids.

"What do you mean?"

"I mean, you'll get a divorce, right? You're not going to stay with her now that there's no baby?" He practically shouted in the phone, causing me to pull mine away from my ear a little.

"I can't leave her right now, Dean. She's devastated. She can't stop crying."

"So what? She's a bitch. I'll fly out today and help you pack." His voice was serious.

"Even I'm not *that* heartless," I commented with a snicker.

"Does Cassie know?" I heard his question and my mind drifted as the trees in the neighborhood rushed past my window.

"No."

"Are you going to tell her?"

"Not right now," I admitted.

"Why not? What is going on with you? Leave Chrystle and come make things right with Cassie!"

"Not yet."

"What are you waiting for?" He sucked in a gulp of air. "You're not in love with Chrystle, are you?"

My hands gripped the steering wheel, my knuckles turning white with the force. "Are you fucking crazy? I don't even know how to love anyone other than Cassie."

"Just making sure."

"I'm gonna go. I just wanted to tell you. Can you tell Gran and Gramps, please, and tell Gran I'll call her soon. Don't tell Cassie. She shouldn't hear it from you," I demanded.

"Fine. But you better tell her soon."

I arrived at the clubhouse gym to find three of

my teammates already working out. Coach sat in his office, the phone in one hand and a cup of coffee in the other. I smiled when he placed down his coffee and reached for a donut, shoving part of it in his mouth while he tilted the phone back behind his shoulder. His eyes darted out the window and met mine before his head nodded in time with his moving mouth. He put the phone down, stood up, and wagged his finger. "Carter."

Anxiety shot through me as I walked into Coach's office, my stomach dropping.

"I just got off the phone with the head of the organization. You got the call, kid. They're moving you up for the playoffs. Pack your stuff, grab that wife of yours, and get ready to leave tonight. You start playing with the team tomorrow."

My feet wouldn't move and my ass felt like it was super-glued to the chair I was sitting in. "What?" I asked like an idiot and he laughed.

"Get outta here, Carter. Your flight leaves at ten tonight. We'll messenger the tickets to your house. Congratulations, kid, you're a hell of a pitcher."

"Thank you, Coach. Thank you so much." I stood, my hand shaking as I reached for his.

I throttled the gas, a million thoughts racing through my head, the most prominent one being how badly I wanted to share this moment with Cass. After everything we'd been through, she was still the first person who came to mind when I had news to share. It made me fucking sick to think I wouldn't be moving her to Arizona with me. When I dreamed of the future, this had always been part of it. Getting to The Show was the foremost thing on my mind. But Cass at my side went hand in hand with that vision.

When I got home, I searched through the house. "Chrys? Chrystle?" I shouted.

"In here." Her voice drifted in from the kitchen.

I walked into the kitchen and caught her eye. "Start packing. We leave for Arizona tonight." I smiled.

"What? Really?" Her voice radiated with excitement as she threw her tiny arms around me.

Since she was no longer carrying my child, I didn't move to hug her back.

*I'm an asshole.*

"A messenger will drop off the tickets and a car will pick us up at eight thirty."

"What do we do with all our stuff? Just leave it?"

"We'll come back here when the season ends and pack everything up. But for now, just bring the necessities. I'm not sure how long we'll be there."

"This is so exciting! I'm married to a big leaguer." Her voice rang out in song as she reached for her cell. "I'm going to call my mama."

"Alright. I'm gonna hop in the shower," I said as she hummed to herself.

313

I ran upstairs and turned the shower on, closing the bathroom door behind me as I wished for a moment of solitude. Wished for a moment that Cass was here. Wished I hadn't fucked things up. Realizing I'd left my cell phone in my gym bag downstairs, I opened the door to ask Chrystle to get it for me. "Chrys?" I scanned the bedroom, but she wasn't there.

I wrapped a towel around my waist and headed downstairs when I overheard Chrystle say, "Oh please, Tressa, I've got him wrapped around my finger. I'll have him so guilt-ridden by the time the night is through, he'll never leave."

I paused on the stairs, listening with intent as she continued. "I know, right? No, he's in the shower. Tressa! He doesn't suspect a thing. And plus, I'll make him sleep with me until I actually do get pregnant…for real this time."

My jaw worked as I saw red and my ears started to burn. "He has no idea I made the whole thing up. How could he? What does a guy know about being pregnant? Nothing."

She laughed and my temper flared. I stormed down the rest of the stairs and into the kitchen, my eyes burning a hole right through her. "Hang up the phone," I demanded as her face twisted with surprise. "Hang up the goddammed phone. NOW!" I lunged for the device in her hand, but she pulled it away.

"Tressa, I have to go. I'll call you later. 'Bye."

"Tell me you didn't, Chrystle. Tell me you didn't fucking lie to me about being pregnant." I vibrated with emotion, my hands balling in and out of fists, and she moved away from me.

She didn't answer. Instead, she stared at me with her stupid face, and I wished for a brief second that it was socially acceptable to punch a chick. "Who else knows?" She didn't move. "WHO…ELSE…KNOWS?" I shouted through my rage.

"J…j…ust Tressa and Vanessa," she stuttered.

"You're lying!"

"I'm not lying, Jack. I swear. They're the only ones I told." Her voice shook with her admission.

I glared at her, my adrenaline pumping like wildfire through my already heated veins. "Why would you do that to me? You ruined my fucking life! You made me lose the only person I've ever loved for a *lie*?!! Why, Chrystle? TELL ME WHY?" I screamed from the other side of the granite island in the kitchen, pounding my fist against the top.

"Because!" she shouted back.

"Because why?"

"Because I just wanted a major league baseball player for a husband! Okay? I wanted to marry a professional athlete. I wanted a rich and famous husband," she screamed.

"And it didn't matter that you ruined my life, as long as you got what you wanted?"

"Oh, save it. I didn't ruin your life, Jack. It's not like I killed your career or anything." She rolled her eyes with a huff, any guilt she felt dissipating.

"Get your stuff and get the fuck out. I don't care where you go, but you can't stay here." I pointed toward the front door.

"But you leave for Arizona tonight. At least let me stay while you're gone." Her whiny voice sent irritation through me like the sound of nails on a chalkboard.

"No. If you step foot in this house while I'm away, I'll have you arrested for breaking and entering, right after I file the restraining order against you and annul this sham of a marriage for false pretenses and lying."

"Whatever, Jack. Good luck getting Cassie back after all this. No one will ever *really* love you. Your own mom didn't even stick around." She hurled the insult and I took it like a ninety-mile-an-hour fastball to the gut.

"I changed my mind. Get out of my house now. I'll set your things on fire and mail you the ashes." I grabbed her by the arm, forcefully removing her from the premises before engaging the dead bolt on the door behind her.

"Jaaaaaaaaaaaaaaack!!!!" she screamed as she pounded her fists against the door. For a bitty thing, she could sure make a lot of noise.

"You're dead to me," I shouted through the door before turning around and heading upstairs to pack.

# TWENTY
## CASSIE

*We need to talk.*

I stared at the text message from Jack for nearly twenty minutes before putting the phone down on my dresser and walking out of my room.

"Melis?" I asked, poking my head through her doorway.

She was sprawled out across her bed reading. "Yeeessssss?" she responded, dropping her electronic reader to her side.

"Jack just sent me a text."

She adjusted her body to an upright position before crossing her legs Indian style. "Say what? What'd he say? Did you text him back?"

"It just said we need to talk. What do we need to talk about? And why now? Do you think he knows I'm leaving?" My eyes darted around the room, pausing at the various photos of us on the walls.

"It's possible. I'm sure Dean told him. But why would he need to talk to you about that?" she asked, patting the spot next to her for me to sit down.

"I have no idea."

"Are you gonna text him back?"

"Should I?"

"Hell yeah, you should. You should be like, 'What do we need to talk about? I'm all talked out from spilling the entire contents of my heart to you the night before your wedding. I think we're done

318

talking,'" she finished with a sassy head gyration and my jaw dropped.

"I'm not saying that!" I leaned back into her mountain of fluffy pillows.

"I know. I'm just kidding. Just be super casual and ask him what's up. Give me your phone, I'll do it for you." She reached for me and I fell backward onto the other side of the bed, typing quickly.

*What's up?*

"There. Sent." I pretended like my insides weren't doing somersaults.

"Now we'll just wait for his—" Melissa's voice was drowned out by the sound of Jack's ringtone. I'd forgotten to change it. I shot her a horrified look before she whispered, "Answer it! Just answer it."

"Why are you whispering?"

"I don't know! Answer it!" she screamed.

"Hello?" I answered, scooting my body from her mattress.

"Hey, Kitten." His familiar voice sent chills racing up and down my spine.

"Hi." I didn't protest at the nickname. I was too busy being caught up in the sound of his voice. I never realized how much I'd missed it until it was beaming into my eardrums, the comfortable familiarity forcing nervous energy to ping throughout my insides.

"I have to tell you some stuff," he started to say and my legs immediately gave out, the words a reminder of the heartache I'd experienced not that long ago.

"What do you possibly have to tell me now, Jack?" I snapped at him, hoping to mask the pain I still carried, as Melissa gave me a thumbs-up of support.

"Chrystle lost the baby." His voice relayed the unfathomable information and I fell to the floor, my back sliding against the wall in Melissa's room.

"What?" My breath hitched and a lone tear rolled down my cheek.

"I mean, she didn't lose the baby. Well, that's what she told me, but she was really never pregnant. She lied." He paused to take a breath, then let out a sigh. "About everything."

"Oh my God, Jack, I'm so sorry. That's…insane. How'd you find out?"

"I overheard her on the phone telling her best friend how stupid and gullible I was. And that she'd try to get pregnant for real." His voice lowered.

"That little bitch." The words escaped my lips as my mind drifted back to the night in the parking lot.

"Cass, I left her. I'm annulling the marriage and I got called up tonight. I leave for Arizona in an hour." His tone changed and I recognized the joy in his voice.

"Jack." I smiled, my eyes meeting Melissa's. "That's incredible! Congratulations."

"Thank you. But, Cassie?" He paused. "I'm really sorry. I should have listened to you. I never should have married her."

"You didn't know she was lying, Jack. And you were just trying to do the right thing…no matter how misguided. Your heart was in the right place. I was just devastated that it wasn't with me."

His breath whooshed over the phone line. "My heart has always been with you. Since the day you first rolled your gorgeous green eyes at me. You've always had my heart. I'm the one whose been lost without it."

His words were everything I wanted to hear and didn't. We'd come so far from where we once were. So much damage had been done and while I still loved him, I was scared to give my heart to him again…at least not easily. "I've had to learn how to live without you."

"And how's that working out for you?" he asked with a slight laugh.

"Not that great," I reluctantly admitted.

"Yeah, it didn't really work out for me either."

"It sure seemed to." I wondered if his words meant what I thought they did.

"I never stopped loving you. I know I hurt you…shit." He stopped as a loudspeaker echoed in the background. "I have to go. I really want to finish this conversation, okay?"

"Sure," I answered, knowing that eventually I'd

need to tell him I was leaving.

*****

*Left tickets for you and Melissa at Will Call.*
*Please come. I really want to see you.*

"Are you still staring at that text?" Melissa
teased.

I rushed to look away from the screen and into
Melissa's eyes. "Not anymore." I smiled.

"I feel like I'm having déjà vu," she announced
with a sigh.

"Why's that?" I rolled my eyes.

"Because I'm begging you to come to Jack's
baseball game and you won't. Cassie, it's his major
league debut! At Dodger Stadium! You have to
come to that!" She pleaded with me, her eyes wide.

"No, Melissa, I *can't* go to that." I answered
quieter than I intended.

"Postpone your flight! How will you forgive
yourself if you miss this?"

"If I go to that game and see him, it will change
everything. I'll want to wait after the game for him,
and then we'll go to dinner, and then I'll spend the
night…and it will never end!" I shouted.

"Our cycle will start back up and before you
know it, I'll have not only missed my flight to New
York, but I'll be turning down a job so I can follow
him to Arizona! And then eventually I'll hate him
because I gave up the one opportunity I was given
to follow *his* dreams, which have nothing to do with

mine. I'll leave him and it will be ugly and messy and then I'll become some old crazy lady with twenty dogs who talks about the days she used to be a good photographer and dated a professional baseball player!!!!!!"

"Holy shit, over-think things much?" Melissa's laugh echoed throughout the apartment.

I started laughing too and when I couldn't stop, I started crying. "Going to watch Jack play just reminds me of everything we used to have, the couple we used to be. I can't watch him and pretend like I don't want to be with him."

"Then don't pretend, Cassie. Be. With. Him."

"I can't, Melissa. I have to *be with me*," I said, mimicking her tone. "This job is an incredible opportunity and I need to do something for myself. If I go to that game tonight, I won't want to ever leave him again. And I have to be able to leave him. For me."

Her eyebrows pinched together as she nodded. "That actually makes a lot of sense. Which sorta pisses me off because I really want you to come."

"I know. Trust me, I want to be there. I really do. I just know I can't handle it. That boy could talk me out of buying an umbrella during a hailstorm."

"I know what you mean. He's gonna freak out, though. You know this."

"You don't always get what you want," I said matter-of-factly.

"At least Dean will be there so I won't have to sit alone."

# TWENTY-ONE
## JACK

I made the public relations girl at the field show me exactly where the seats were that I'd left for Cassie. When she pointed them out, I shook my head. "Those aren't gonna work. They're fine for my family, but I need two seats right here."

I pointed to the row of seats directly in line with the dugout. "I don't care if I have to buy them, I'll buy them. Just get me two seats right here."

I wanted to be able to see Cassie. I needed to see her.

"I can do that for you. I'll just check and make sure the seats are available. I'll be right back." She flipped her hair with a smile before walking away.

I looked around at the stadium I'd been to so many times as a kid, my pride swelling. I hopped over the short wall and onto the field, turning around to view the seats I'd chosen. I walked to the mound, glancing at the seat choice, before settling into the dugout. The seats were perfect.

"Jack? Jack?" The PR girl's voice reverberated.

"I'm here," I said, climbing out of the dugout and onto the field.

"You're in luck. The seats are available. What name should I put them under?"

"Please put them under Cassie Andrews and Melissa Williams. Thanks for the help, I appreciate it."

"No problem. That's what I'm here for." She batted her lashes before spinning on her heel and walking off.

*****

Ever since my coach in high school reinforced the message of "Keep your head in the game and your eyes outta the stands if you want to get drafted," I've never looked. But tonight, I couldn't help myself. I glanced at the empty seats to my left at least a hundred times, waiting for her to be there.

*Focus, Carter. You're being ridiculous.*

I breathed deeply, looking up at the bright lights of the major league stadium before releasing the breath slowly. I glanced to the left again.

Feet! Black tall girly-shoes!

Noticing the pair of heels, I hustled to the side of the dugout nearest the seats. I glanced to my left, spotted Melissa, and smiled as she turned toward me and waved. I gave her a quick wave back before pointing to the seat next to her with a shrug. She shook her head and my smile dropped, along with my heart. I tried to mouth, "She's not coming?" Apparently she couldn't read my lips.

"Carter! Get over here," the manager yelled and I jerked my head behind me. "Go get warmed up."

I grabbed a pen and a program, and scribbled out *Where is she?* before walking up to our teenaged bat boy. "Hey, Cody, do me a favor. See that girl over there with the curly brown hair and the giant pink purse?"

Cody craned his neck. "The one in the Diamondbacks shirt?"

"Yeah. Can you give her this?"

"Sure, Jack." His face lit up and I only imagined what he thought I was trying to do.

"Make sure you wait for her response and then hold on to it for me, okay?"

"Okay."

"Thanks, Cody," I said, before grabbing my glove and running toward the outfield.

I failed to realize that I'd be spending the majority of the game in the bullpen, which couldn't be further away from the seats I'd reserved if I tried.

I sprinted into the dugout, looking around for Cody like a madman. "Cody?" I yelled.

"Here, Jack." He held out the folded program.

*She couldn't come. She said it's too hard. Jack, she's leaving to\*night for New York! She's moving there!!*

I ran to the far end of the dugout, my face frantic as I caught sight of Dean sitting in the seat I'd bought for Cassie. I whisper-shouted his name and he turned, his eyes wide at the sight of me.

"What time's her flight?" I shouted, not caring who heard.

Dean turned his head toward Melissa before turning back to mine. "She's leaving the apartment at ten thirty."

I glanced around frantically looking for a fucking clock, knowing full well there wasn't one in the visitor dugout. I leaned over the cold railing and craned my neck toward the scoreboard. The numbers 9:03 splashed across the black board in yellow lights. I released a breath. I still had time.

*****

The sound of my tires squealing into the parking lot caused Cassie to turn in my direction. A cab driver tossed the last of her suitcases into the trunk before slamming it shut.

I hopped out of my car and rushed toward her. "Cassie!" I shouted, not stopping as my hat flew off.

"Jack, what are you doing here? Don't you have a game?" Her eyes widened.

"It's done and I drove straight here." I reached her and grabbed her shoulders with both hands, as if my touch alone would stop her. "So it's true? You're really leaving?"

"It's an incredible opportunity, Jack," she responded, her voice cold.

"But you're not even finished with school yet." I could hear a little whine in my own voice, but hell, I was desperate.

"You weren't either when you left to pursue your dreams. If it doesn't work out, I'll come back and finish. But I don't have to get my bachelor's degree to do what I want to do." Cassie looked so resolute, her arms crossed over her chest.

"Don't go."

"What?"

"Don't go, Kitten. Don't move across the country," I pleaded, this scene all too familiar in my head. "I know things are different and maybe I fucked them up so badly that they're beyond repair. But I want to try. I need to try. I can't let you walk out of my life without knowing that I did everything in my power to keep you in it."

"What are you saying, Jack?" Her eyes welled up as she blinked back tears.

"I'm saying that I love you. Nothing in my life is right if you're not with me. You're a part of me. And I can't let that part go. I want to be with you. I know I messed up, and I know you don't trust me, but I'll prove to you that you can. I promise I'll spend the rest of my life making it up to you if you'll let me."

I held my breath as I waited for her to respond.

Her brows drew together as she looked away from me. "I can't stay here. I already accepted the job. And I *want* to go."

"Then say we'll work it out. Say we're back together while we figure things out," I begged, willing to say anything to not lose her again.

"Long distance doesn't really work for us," she admitted, and I cringed.

"It will be different this time. I've learned my

lesson. I know what's at stake. I know how much I have to lose. I promise you I'll never fuck up again." I reached for her hands, squeezing them as I pleaded. "I know my promises mean nothing to you right now, but I'll make them mean something again. I'll give the words meaning."

I caressed her hands with mine, not wanting to let go.

"Prove it," she said with a shrug, before sliding into the cab and locking the door.

My heart thumped as it battered against my chest. The cab sped away and Cassie's image in the rear window faded from view.

# TWENTY-TWO
## CASSIE

I'd spent the last four months falling in love with New York City. I hadn't heard from Jack at all since the night I left, which not only surprised me, but broke my heart all over again. No matter how many times Dean tried to assure me that Jack was still in love with me and to give him time, his silence proved otherwise to my doubtful heart.

I wasn't sure what I'd hoped for, exactly. I guess a part of me wanted some sort of grand gesture. I wanted to walk outside one morning and find him waiting there for me, like he'd done that one time when I got out of class. And when I told him to "prove it" the night I left, I honestly thought he would. I just wanted something from Jack. Anything but silence. And when nothing came, I tried my best to move on.

I shuffled out of the jam-packed subway car and moved along with the crowd up the stairs and into the chilled air outdoors. I was still awestruck daily by the sights and the sounds of New York and constantly forced myself to keep walking, when I was dying to drop to my knee to shoot the scenes around me.

The building I worked in was thirty stories tall with rectangular windows spaced three feet apart in all directions. I opened the oversized gold door before shaking off the chill.

"Morning, Craig." I squeezed the shoulder of our salt-and-pepper-haired security guard.

"Morning, Miss Andrews," he said with a nod, before pressing the elevator button for me and holding the door open once it arrived.

"Thank you." I smiled, repeating the same routine we acted out each morning.

I hopped in, pressing the button for the twenty-seventh floor before I heard, "Wait! Hold the doors!"

I threw my arm between the closing doors, forcing them to stop abruptly and stutter back apart. Joey, an adorable brown-haired, blue-eyed copy editor from Boston, hopped inside, his arms full of papers.

"Thanks! Oh...morning, Cassie." He glanced over his shoulder at me, and I looked away, embarrassed. He'd asked me out a few times since I moved here, but the truth was, I wasn't ready to date. After everything I'd been through with Jack, I wasn't sure I'd ever be ready again.

"Morning, Joey. Can I help?" I asked, reaching for the papers that threatened to fall.

"Thank you." Half his mouth twisted upward into a smirk. "So, what you'd do last night?" he asked with his cute Boston accent.

"Uh, I worked until a little after eight. Then I grabbed some amazing Italian food on the way home from this tiny café, and that's about it."

"Where do you live again?" He asks me this every time we talk. I haven't figured out why, but he does.

"Lower East Side, not far from here."

"What street?"

"Clinton," I responded as the elevator announced our arrival.

The doors opened and the sounds of rushed voices filled the air. The floor was packed with wall-to-wall cubicles spilling over with the previous day's work. Privacy was not something one could find in this office. I secretly loved the chaos and the constant rushing around.

"So, do you like it?" he asked, watching my eyes. "Living in the lower east?"

"Oh, I do. Most of my neighbors are young and super artsy so it's kind of inspiring and annoying all at the same time." I laughed as I followed him to his cubicle.

"We should grab dinner sometime." I started to turn him down as he held up a hand in the air to stop me. "It doesn't have to be a date. Just friends sharing a meal together. I don't think you get out of your Clinton Street apartment enough."

He smiled and I shook my head. "I don't know."

"Think it over. Just friends, no pressure." He leaned in close and I could smell his cologne as he grabbed the papers from my arms. "Thanks."

"I'll see you later, Joey," I answered, feeling a

little flustered as I rushed across the hardwood floor.

"Think it over!" he shouted, although no one else seemed to notice in all the chaos.

I quickened my pace, my cheeks burning as I scurried past the wall-mounted antique mirror. I slid into my cubicle, pushing the button on my computer as the screen flickered to life. I scrolled past the spam that always seem to get through the e-mail filters and landed on Melissa's name. She'd gotten into the habit of sending e-mails to my work address so that I would have something to read from her first thing in the morning. And in return, I had to write back, *no matter what*, so that she'd have something from me when she woke up.

*Hooker,*

*Do you think your IT guy reads my e-mails? Because if I was an IT guy, I would totally read my e-mails. Maybe he would if he knew how hot I was. I should probably attach a picture. LOL*

*So, tell me more about this Joey kid. Is he hot? Where's he from? What's his deal? Are you gonna go out with him, or what? What is it with you and making guys beg? You're really sort of a bitch, Cassie Andrews. JK, LOL, smiley face (say it super fast like this.) JKLOLSMILEYFACE*

*Ooooh, I think Dean has a crush on this really cute freshman, so make sure you give him shit the next time you talk to him, K? K. I'm not going to ask about "him" this time, so don't freak out. But hey, if he does call or text or anything, I'd better be the first person to hear about it! Just sayin'! :)*

*I'd better go. I know this was like the most boring e-mail ever, but what can I say? Life is sorta boring without you. I miss you.*

*Melis <3*

I hit the Reply button and watched as her message scrolled to the bottom half of the page.

*Dork,*

*I'm pretty sure our IT guy (Hi Shawn!!!!!) is far too busy to sift through my e-mails and read them. But if you want to attach some super-hot photo of yourself, I'm pretty sure he wouldn't be opposed. LOL*

*You're crazy, just so you know. Joey is really cute, with an accent that kills me every time he talks. He's from Boston and is "wicked" smart, as he would say. LOL He seems like he totally has his shit together, which is kind of intimidating, to be honest. He asked me out today, just as friends. I don't know, I don't want to lead him on...*

*Tell me about this girl Dean likes. Is she nice? She's not in a sorority, is she? Make sure she isn't a bitch, Meli. Dean's too nice.*

*I'm pretty sure "he's" done with me. Although to be honest, I have no idea why. If I ever hear from him again, which I highly doubt, you'll be my first call.*

*I love you and miss you so much. Move in with me after you graduate. Just kidding. Not really. When are you coming to visit?*

*xoxox C.*

Even talking about Jack in an e-mail forced my stomach to spin. I tortured myself constantly, thinking up scenarios as to why he stopped liking me. I'd pushed him too far this last time. I'm never happy. His words never mean enough. I'm always asking him to jump through hoops for me.

Ugh. I hated this feeling of self-blame and discontent.

*****

The next two months flew by in a blur. The snow finally melted and spring filled the air with its warmer temperatures, its colors, and its smells as flowers bloomed and trees budded. The dull, colorless winter that was so often gray and dreary quickly gave way to full green trees, white flowers, and bright blue skies. In a word, New York in the spring is amazing.

"Hey, girl," I answered after seeing Melissa's name flash across my screen.

"How's New York today?" she asked happily on the other end.

"So beautiful! Seriously, when are you coming to visit me?" I was so dying to show her the sights of the city.

"Soon, I think! Maybe over break, is the

weather nice then?"

"I don't know. Probably not, to be honest. I think that's when everyone goes to Florida."

"Wait, what? They go to Florida willingly?"

"Melissa!" I giggled. "It's a quick flight and the weather is way better! It's no different than everyone in So Cal heading to Hawaii."

"Uh, yes it is. It's *H a w a i i* and really, who goes to Florida on purpose?" Her voice sounded so exasperated, it made me smile. "So, have you heard from Jack?"

I should have known that was why she called. The Diamondbacks were coming into town, and she and Dean wouldn't stop blowing up my phone.

"Nope."

"Really?" she said, her voice laced with disappointment.

"Really. We have to stop talking about him, Melis. I mean, when will we stop talking about him?" I hated that we had to go over this again; it really didn't help.

"You're right. You're totally right. I'm sorry, Cassie, I really just don't get it."

"Yeah, tell me about it." I sighed. The sadness still got to me sometimes.

"So tell me, how's Joey from Bahhston?"

"He's good." I laughed at her attempt at his accent.

"Still making him beg?"

My lack of an answer was all the answer she needed. "Cassie, you can't stay closed off forever. You need to open up your heart again."

"I know, it's just...I'm scarred."

"We're all scarred. That's how we know we've lived a life worth fighting for. Love is a battlefield! Thank you, Pat Benatar." She belted out an off-key rendition of the chorus that made me giggle before continuing. "Our scars don't point us in the direction we're headed, Cass, they simply remind us of where we've been."

I remained silent, taking in the very truth of her words. "Cass?"

"I'm here."

"I think it's time to let him go," she suggested, her voice tinged with pain.

My breath whooshed in and out of the phone before she spoke again. "I'm just saying that sometimes letting go is the only way to find out who you're meant to hold on to."

"Oh, I like that. Did you make it up?"

"I think I read it online somewhere before." She laughed. "But let's pretend it came from this gorgeous head of mine."

*****

I rested my camera on top of my messy desk and watched as Joey waltzed into the building, his business attire looking more than good on him. He flashed a smile in my direction before walking into the kitchen. I followed him, pretending I needed to fill my already half-filled coffee mug.

"Are you ever going to go out with me?" he asked, his confidence reminding me of Jack.

"Are you ever going to stop asking?"

"Not until you agree." He stirred his coffee before taking a sip.

"Fine. This is me...*agreeing*," I responded, an eerie, all-too-familiar feeling creeping over me.

"It only took me six months. I think that's a new record." He leaned in and planted a peck on my cheek. "We'll leave at six. No overtime for you tonight."

"Tonight?" I repeated, horrified.

"Tonight. No backing out."

"I'll make it work." I pressed my lips together to stop them from smiling.

*****

"So where are you taking me?" I leaned my head back in the passenger seat of Joey's car and watched as the city whizzed by us in a blur.

"It's a surprise." Joey glanced over at me and smiled.

I really hated surprises. But this guy didn't know that. He didn't know anything about me.

He turned onto Grand Central Parkway and I almost started hyperventilating. "Where are we going? Are we going to the game?" I choked out, noticing the stadium on the horizon.

"I overheard you one day talking about baseball and how you went to college with one of the guys on the Diamondbacks. So I got us tickets. Maybe you can see your friend."

"Oh God. Joey, that's really sweet and thoughtful and romantic, but I...can't go to this game with you."

"Of course you can. Don't be silly. We don't have to stay for the whole thing. Have you even seen a game yet? Or been to either stadium?"

I shook my head, unable to come up with a reasonable explanation to stop this train wreck from happening.

"It will be fun. New Yorkers are pretty cool fans. I mean, as long as they aren't playing the Sox. But you have to experience it." Joey sounded so excited as he tried to sell me on it while he parked the car.

*I've already experienced pretty cool fans. Back in college. You have no idea, buddy.*

"Promise me that if I want to leave, we will. No questions asked. Okay?"

He stared at me as if I'd asked something completely foreign of him. "Joey, you have to promise me or I'm not stepping one foot out of this car."

"Fine, I promise."

"Promise what?" I tested.

"I promise that if you want to leave, we will.

Even though you won't want to leave at all because these seats are choice. You can probably high-five your friend if you want to."

My legs shook as Joey took my hand, leading me toward the blue and orange gate. Security checked my bag before ushering me through in a slightly less friendly way than I was used to. New Yorkers are a little more brash.

We walked down the stairs toward the field. I could tell by Joey's pace that we weren't stopping anytime soon. My stomach knotted up while my heart struggled to remain consistently beating. I refused to look around for Jack, terrified at how my body would react.

When he stopped at the very front row, he turned around and threw out his arms. "Well? What do you think? Pretty great, right?" he asked, clearly proud of his seat-purchasing ability.

"Uh-huh. They're really close to the field," I said between laboring breaths, my gaze desperately pinned to his face.

"Are you okay?" He put his hand on my shoulder and I winced.

"I need to get a drink."

"I'll get it for you," he offered, his face creased with worry.

"No, that's okay. I need to use the restroom too. I'll be right back." I tried to force a smile, but my lips felt broken as I rushed back up the stairs and out of view.

I sprinted to the closest bathroom, locking the stall door behind me as my upper body crumpled. With my head between my knees, I began rocking back and forth.

*Stop it. You're acting like an idiot. Jack won't see you. He never looks up in the stands. He doesn't even like you anymore, so stop freaking out. It's time you moved on with your life and got over Jack Carter once and for all. You have got to stop thinking about him because he is clearly not thinking about you.*

I nodded as my own thoughts struck a chord within me. I could do this. I could be strong. I could watch Jack play baseball and not want to die from it.

*I think.*

A few more calming breaths and I unlocked the latch, walking out to face my reflection in the mirror. I wiped at the smears of mascara under my eyes and washed my hands under the running cold water.

I stopped at a concession stand to buy a bottle of water before heading back down to our dugout level seats. Joey smiled as he caught sight of me, his bright white teeth a welcome sign to anyone.

"You okay?" He stood up and took my elbow in concern before sitting down again as I plopped into my seat.

"Much better, thanks," I answered, taking a drink of water.

"So which one's your friend from school? Can you tell?"

If seeing Jack didn't kill me tonight, this guy's questions were sure going to. I couldn't really get mad at Joey, he didn't know any better. It's not like I'd told him Jack was my ex-boyfriend whom I'd given my entire heart to and he'd given it back to me in pieces. Want a sliver?

I squinted my eyes and pretended to look around the field for Jack. "I can't tell, sorry. They all look alike in their uniforms." I bit my bottom lip.

"Do you know if he starts? Or what position he plays?"

"I have no idea, honestly."

"Well, what did he play in college?" He kept pushing questions at me and I wanted to scream.

"He was a pitcher," I replied, forcing back the burning in my chest with another gulp of water.

"Ahhhh, I see." Joey nodded. "Then he might not even play tonight. I'm sorry if he doesn't."

"That's okay. I wasn't planning on watching him anyway. You forced me here, remember?" I attempted to smile and he tossed an arm around my shoulder.

"You haven't even told me your friend's name. What is it?"

*Jesus. This guy was relentless.*

"Jack Carter." I almost stumbled on his name. I hadn't said it out loud to anyone in almost six months, not counting Dean or Melissa.

"You know Jack Carter?" His jaw dropped before he continued. "He's an incredible player! And he's starting tonight."

"Really? He's starting?" I braced myself.

"Yeah! Pretty cool, huh?" He leaned his head back before tossing some peanuts in his mouth.

By the time the game started, my body was filled with so much anxiety that I kept shifting in my seat. I grinned as Jack walked onto the field, pleased to see that he still sported the number twenty-three on the back of his jersey.

"That's your boy, right?" Joey said, pointing at Jack as he made his way to the mound for pre-game warm-ups.

*Was.*

"That's him." My eyes followed the lines of Jack's new uniform, noting the muscle he'd gained in his legs and chest. He took my breath away.

Jack stood on the mound, every motion and move he made careening through me with familiarity. The fluid movements of his body—the way it bent, curved, kicked, and then released the ball—destroyed me emotionally.

Tears started to burn my eyes. "I can't be here. I have to go." I bolted from my seat, shooting up the cement stairs.

"Cassie! Cassie, wait!" Horrified at the volume at which Joey shouted my name, I stopped dead in my tracks and turned slowly to face him. Then I made the mistake of glancing at the field.

Jack's eyes were focused on me, the look on his face unlike any expression I'd ever seen on him before. My hand flew to my mouth as Joey reached me, placing his arm protectively around me. I noticed Jack's jaw working as he dropped his head and refocused his attention toward the batter's box.

"What's going on, Cassie?" Joey asked, his arm still circled around my waist.

"Jack and I used to date." I pursed my lips together and squeezed my eyes shut.

"Was it serious?" His voice sounded confused but curious.

"It was." I took a quick breath and opened my eyes, and looked squarely into his. "But it didn't end well. I'm sorry, Joey, I should have told you."

"You're not obligated to tell me anything you're not comfortable with. You basically told me earlier that you didn't want to come, but I didn't listen."

"I don't know what to say." I tilted my head to one side and he rubbed my neck.

"Look, Cassie, I like you. I'd still like to take you out. But I promise, no more baseball games." He threw up his hands in a surrender pose.

I snickered. "That sounds nice. But right now I really want to go home. Would you mind dropping me off?"

"Of course not. Come on." Joey reached for my hand, interlocking his fingers with mine as he guided me away from the stadium and Jack. I climbed the stairs behind him grimly, the look I'd seen on Jack's face running circles in my already fragile mind.

## TWENTY-THREE

After Joey dropped me off, I ran upstairs and slammed my apartment door, tossing my body like a rag doll onto the gently-used couch I'd purchased as soon as I arrived in New York. I cried into the velvet-like cushion, my tears soaking in as I reached for my cell phone.

"Yo," Melissa answered, rowdy cheers screaming in the background.

"Melis?" I choked out.

"Cass? What's wrong? Shit, I can't hear anything. Hold on a sec, 'K?" She didn't really ask. "Excuse me. I said excuse me, move please. Ugh. Cass? Cassie, can you hear me?"

The noise faded into the background with each word she said. "Oh my God, Melissa. I saw Jack tonight. He saw me. It was horrible." The words tumbled from my lips.

"What do you mean? Slow down and tell me everything."

"I finally agreed to go out with Joey from work. He's super nice, by the way, but anyway. I guess he overheard me talking to someone about how I was good friends with a baseball player in college and how that player was on the Diamondbacks. Well, Joey thought it would be sweet to surprise me—"

"Oh no, he didn't. This guy needs a Cassie 101 lesson," she interrupted.

"Anyway, so he won't tell me where we're

going and then we pull up at the baseball stadium because they're playing Jack's team and Jack was warming up and I lost it, Melissa. I fucking lost it." I covered my eyes with one hand.

"Go on."

"So I practically ran from my seat and Joey screamed my name. I mean, he shouted it so loud I think the people in space heard!"

"Oh my God." Melissa sounded horrified.

"I turned around and Jack was just staring at me with this look on his face."

"Oh. My. God."

"I've never seen that look on his face before. I think he hates me." I sobbed into the phone, wishing she was next to me.

"He doesn't hate you. Stop saying that," she chastised, her voice irritated.

"You didn't see his face or his eyes. What do I do? Should I text him? Should I do nothing?"

"What do you want to do?"

"I'm so tired of doing nothing when it comes to him. For the last six months, I've just accepted that he hasn't tried to talk to me. But the whole time I'm sitting here going insane trying to figure out why. I know I could end all my suffering by picking up the phone and talking to him. But do I do that? No, because that's what a normal, sane person would do. And clearly, I'm neither."

"I think you should text him. Or call. But you're

right. You should say something. This has got to stop between you two. Either work it out, or give each other closure and move the hell on."

The word *closure* caused my insides to twist again. "I don't want closure. I don't want to move on."

"I know you don't," she agreed calmly, "but this thing between the two of you…whatever it is…I know it's not good for you. I don't give a fuck if it's good for him."

"Okay, well, I think I'll call him while he's still playing and leave him a voice mail."

"Wimp."

"I know, but that way the ball's in his court."

"Let me know what happens. Love you." She made a kissy sound into the phone before hanging up, and I dialed Jack's number.

Straight to voice mail. "Hey, Jack, it's me…Cassie. I just wanted to apologize for the craziness at the game tonight. It's sort of a long story, but I…" I paused, my chest deflating. "I just miss you."

He didn't call back.

*****

Two weeks passed since the game which Melissa and I now referred to as "the incident" whenever it was discussed.

My doorman's kind and raspy voice blared through the speaker box in my apartment. "Miss

Andrews, there's a package down here for you. Do you want me to bring it up, or would you like to come get it?"

"Can you bring it up, Fred? I'd really appreciate it." I released the button before quickly pressing it again. "Unless you're busy, then I can come down. Whatever is more convenient for you, Fred. Thanks."

"Okay, Miss Andrews. I'll be up soon."

I plopped back onto my couch and continued to watch TV until the doorbell rang. I opened it to see Fred, dressed in his dark gray work suit and black bow tie. He was all smiles as he warned, "Careful, Miss Andrews, it's really heavy." He heaved the package into my arms.

"Holy crap, Fred, what the heck is this? Someone sending me weights? I'm sorry you had to carry this all the way up. Thank you."

"Not a problem, Miss Andrews. It's my job," he said with a warm smile that made me want to wrap my arms around him and squeeze.

I closed the door as he left, lugging the incredibly heavy package back onto the couch with me. I tore through the brown paper wrapping to reveal an old shoebox with a note on top.

*I can't live without your Touch. You'll see that I've provided enough money to pay for at least twenty years or so.*

I lifted the lid to reveal the entire contents of the

box filled with quarters. My heart raced as my mind tried to figure out if this meant what I thought it did. I glanced toward the corner of my living room where the original mason jar filled with *Cassie's Quarters* sat on a shelf. Confused, I reached for my cell to call Melissa when my doorbell rang again.

I tossed my cell on top of the quarters and shoved off the couch to answer the door. I cocked my head when I noticed Fred standing there, holding another box in his arms. "Fred?"

"Sorry I didn't call. I just figured I'd bring this one up too." He held the package out and I grabbed it, relieved that it didn't weigh three hundred pounds like the first one.

Confusion sprinted marathons through my head. "Was this with the original package?"

"No, miss, it arrived separately." Fred gave me a big smile.

"Okay. Thanks again," I said before closing the door and returning to my seat on the couch.

I tore through the same brown paper wrapping to reveal another box with a note on top.

*Your Passion is inspiring. I can't live without the way you use it to see the world.*

I opened the lid to reveal four individually framed photos that I had taken for the magazine's website over the last few months. One of them was from when I'd first gotten here. He'd chosen some of my favorites of the scenes I'd shot of the city, the

351

people I'd captured, and the way a building caught the light of the sunset. He'd been following my work the whole time.

The bell ringing caused me to jump from my current revelation. I peered from around the door to see Fred standing there yet again, another package in tow. "Fred, what's going on?"

"I'm not really sure, Miss Andrews. They just keep arriving." He shrugged.

"Okay. I'm sorry about that."

"Oh, don't be. It's kind of fun!" He laughed.

"Who keeps bringing them?" I asked, wondering if Jack was here before I realized that his team played in Houston this week.

"Some young kid," he offered.

"Weird."

"Weird indeed." He nodded before turning away.

I took two steps toward the table closest to the door and sat, peeling the wrapping back.

*Your Mind is filled with tests and goals and reasons why you should always say no. But I can't live without you and here are reasons why you should say yes.*

I removed a framed eight-by-ten photo of my rules typed in a girlish font that I wondered who helped him pick out.

*Cassie's Rules for a Happy Life:*
*#1 - Don't Lie*

## #2 - Don't Cheat

## #3 - Don't Make Promises You Can't Keep

## #4 - Don't Say Things You Don't Mean

Attached underneath rule number four was a handwritten note taped to the glass.

*I know I've broken your rules and I don't deserve a second chance, but I promise you that I'll never break them again. I think it was Ghandi who said, "Forgiveness is the attribute of the strong." I hope you have the strength to forgive me.*

*#1 – I lied because I was terrified of losing you. I know that's not an excuse, but it's the only reason I have for being untruthful. I'll never lie to you again.*

*#2 – This one kills me more than I can put into words. I have no excuse for my behavior that night but I can only tell you that I'll never even look at another girl again if that's what it takes. I'll never drink another drop. Just tell me what I have to do to get you to forgive me. I'm not asking you to forget, just forgive.*

*#3 – I promise to spend the rest of my life making you happy if you'll let me.*

*#4 – I told you once that you were my game changer. I meant it then and it still holds true*

*now. There's no getting over you.*

Tears dropped from my eyes as my heart caught in my throat. All my emotions jumbled together as I tried to sort them out but failed.

Another quick ring of the bell and I didn't even attempt to wipe my eyes before I answered it. "Hi, Fred," I said, the tears still rolling down.

"Good tears or bad tears?" His tired eyes widened at the sight of me.

"Good tears." I snickered.

"Whew!" he exclaimed as he playfully wiped the non-existent sweat from his brow. "Here's the latest." He handed me a large manila envelope.

"Thanks again." I reached for it before closing the door, already undoing the small fastener on the back.

*Eye-rolling is bad for you, Kitten, and here are the reasons why.*

I laughed out loud as I turned through the pages filled with ridiculous pictures of people and pets rolling their eyes. He attached a few completely made-up articles about "The Unknown Dangers of Eye-Rolling!"

I rolled my eyes as the doorbell rang for the last time. "Fred. I feel like I should just leave my door open for the rest of the night," I teased.

"This is the last one, Miss Andrews," he said, handing me the last brown paper-wrapped box.

I breathed in deeply before giving Fred a quick

hug. "Thank you for not getting irritated by all of this, Fred."

"It's been fun. Have a good night." He closed the door for me as I settled into the couch next to the box of quarters.

I unwrapped the box more slowly, knowing that it would be the last. There was an envelope taped to the top of the box that said READ ME FIRST. With my emotions in overdrive, I ripped open the envelope, reaching for the paper inside.

*Kitten,*

*Letting go of someone who owns your heart is hard. Sometimes holding on to that person is even harder. I know I'm not the easiest person to love, but you are.*

*It's not that I can't live without you; it's that I don't want to. There's a difference. We all make choices in life and I choose you.*

*My heart belongs to you. And I'm not asking for it back, even if you don't want it anymore. I'm just asking for the chance to have yours again. I promise I'll be more careful with it this time.*

*Love Always,*

*Jack*

I opened the box, the tears blurring my vision almost completely as I looked inside. The box was empty, except for a lone envelope that sat taped to the bottom with the words READ ME LAST written in black Sharpie marker.

My finger tore through the thick sealed paper before pulling out the small note folded over once.

*Kitten,*

*Open your front door.*

My head spun around and my mouth opened as I eyed my front door, unsure of what would be behind it. I hopped off the couch, turned the knob, and pulled it open.

"Oh my God."

Jack stood outside my door carrying a dozen red roses. It was only once he lowered his arms that I could see the uniform he was wearing. The word METS was written across an all-white jersey with dark blue and orange lettering. It reminded me of his old uniform from college and my mind instantly flashed back to seeing him on the mound. "Why are you wearing a Mets jersey?"

"I got traded." The sound of his voice melted through my every pore like butter, instantly sending me back in time.

"They traded you?" I managed to ask through my surprise.

"Well, technically," he said, his trademark dimples flashing, "I asked."

"You asked what?"

"I asked to be traded to the Mets." He looked down at his feet.

*****

*I rapped my knuckles against the manager's glass door. He looked up from his computer. "Come in." He motioned with his hand before glaring at me. "What's up, Carter?"*

*"Well, um, I know this is really unorthodox but I was wondering if I could get traded, sir," I asked him nervously. My agents were going to kill me when they heard what I was attempting to do.*

*"Why the hell do you want to go and do that?" he snapped as the irritation spread across his face.*

*"It's just that I love this sport and I want to play. But there's a girl I love too. And the only way I can have both is if I move."*

I sound like a total pussy.

He is going to ream me for this.

*He dug out a pencil from the mess on his desk and twirled it around in his fingers while he thought a moment, before he used it to point at me. "So you're telling me that you want me to put you up for the eligible trade options because you need to be closer to some girl?"*

*"She's not just some girl, sir. And I know it sounds bad, but I need this. If it's possible, I need this. And if it's not, just tell me. I won't ask you again. But I couldn't live with myself if I didn't at least ask."*

*"Son, you realize that you can live with this girl during the off-season, right? That's three, sometimes four months."*

*"That's not enough time," I responded respectfully.*

*"Where's this special girl live?" He tapped the pencil against his desk in an irritated* rat-a-tat.

*"New York."*

*"Hell! We're in New York a couple times a season. And Florida and Boston aren't far!" He stopped and glared at me. "And you're telling me you'd like me to trade you to New York? You know after your contract expires, they won't have the budget to pay you like we have?" He threw the pencil down on his desk before he stood up to face me with his hands on his hips.*

*"With all due respect, sir, it's not about the money."*

\*\*\*\*\*

"So you live here now?" My eyes widened.

"Just got in. Can I come in?"

"Of course. Yes." I stumbled as I moved aside, and gestured for him to come in.

"These are for you." He pushed the roses toward me.

"Thank you. They're beautiful," I replied, sniffing at them before moving to put them on the counter in the kitchen.

He looked around my apartment, taking in the details, then focused on the pile of things he had sent.

"I see you got my gifts." He motioned toward

the couch.

"Mm-hmmm," I mumbled, still in shock that he was actually here.

"Cassie." He moved his body close to mine and ran his fingers through my hair, tucking pieces behind my ear. I scanned the scruff on his face, the black of his hair, the chocolate color of his eyes, before reaching out to touch him.

"Do you still love me?" he asked, his eyes unsure.

"I never stopped," I admitted breathlessly.

"Me either." He grabbed the back of my neck and pulled his mouth to mine. His tongue caressed mine with slow, deliberate movements, and if I could have turned to liquid and dissolved into his arms, I would have.

He pulled away, his hand still caressing my neck. "I'm sorry for lying to you that morning. I'm sorry for cheating on you that night. I'm sorry for not being the person you knew I could be." He leaned in, his mouth sucking lightly on my bottom lip before kissing me again. "And I don't know if you can ever forgive me, but I'd never forgive myself if I didn't at least ask you to try.

"And I'm sorry it took me so long to get here. *She* was fighting the annulment and it took months to get it processed and finalized. I refused to come fight for you while I was still carrying that baggage. But it took a lot longer than I had expected. I should

359

have called you. And I'm sorry I didn't."

"I thought you hated me," I whispered. Unable to look at him, I dropped my gaze to his chest.

He reached for my chin before tilting my head up, forcing me to meet his eyes. "I could never hate you. I thought I was going to have to come before the annulment was complete when I'd heard about you and the guy from your work."

"How'd you know who he was?"

"Dean. I kept tabs on you, Kitten. Not in a creepy way, I swear. Just in a making-sure-I-wasn't-going-to-lose-you-all-over-again way. See, you've always been able to see past the front I put up. I never thought I'd be able to find someone who would know the real me and still want to stick around. And then I saw you at that frat party and my life was never the same."

A tear ran slowly down my cheek as he continued. "I know I don't deserve you, but I need you." He finished talking and wiped the tear from my cheek with his thumb, his touch reminding me how much I've missed it.

"I need you too. I hate feeling vulnerable and I want to pretend like I don't, but it would be a lie," I said with a half smile.

"Then don't pretend. Tell me you'll try to forgive me so we can move on from our past."

"I already have," I admitted, and felt the weight of trying to be strong for so long drop away from me. I felt lighter and freer than I had in a very long time.

Jack leaned his forehead against mine. "I'll earn your trust again. I *promise*."

I leaned into him, burying my head into his shoulders as I wrapped my arms around him. I smiled into his neck, and snuggled closer as I closed my eyes with happiness. Then I lifted my mouth to his ear and breathed two little words.

"Prove it."

# EPILOGUE
## -One Year Later-

Jack settled into our apartment while I cooked dinner. He'd just gotten back from an away game, and his stuff was scattered in every direction, making the living room look like a bomb had gone off. "You're such a slob. At least throw your crap in the bedroom where it belongs," I teased from behind the stove.

"I'll throw you in the bedroom where you belong," he sassed, his dimples appearing on his tanned cheeks.

He'd moved in that night when he first arrived in New York last year, refusing to leave me ever again and I didn't object, even though his presence made my already cramped apartment even smaller. With two incomes, we were soon able to afford to move into a nicer apartment in Sutton Place, not far from Central Park on the east side of the city. My commute to work became longer, but it was worth it to live in this gorgeous place with him. Our view consisted of the Upper East Side and we spent our evenings on the balcony as often as we could.

Jack took it as a sign when they offered us a two-bedroom apartment on the twenty-third floor. "*It's my number, babe. We've gotta take it!*" And after we toured the place, admiring its granite countertops, stainless steel appliances, and marble bathrooms, I couldn't agree more. The fact that it had a fitness center and a pool was just an added perk. I also felt safe living here, what with the twenty-four-hour doorman and the front lobby concierge.

Jack traveled frequently with the team and I was often away on assignment for work, so the security of our apartment while we were out of town or if I was home alone gave us both much-needed peace of mind. Not to mention the fact that Jack was a Mets player now, which made him a local celebrity in New York. Fans had tried to sneak into our place on more than one occasion. We found it necessary to give our doormen extra bonuses last Christmas for their efforts.

We loved living in Manhattan, the hustle and craziness unlike anything we'd ever known in Southern California. The people were also completely different. For us, it was a welcome change of pace that suited us for now.

As I stirred the pasta, the sparkle of the diamond shining from my left hand caught my eye. I glanced down at it with a smile. The three-carat round diamond mounted on a diamond-encrusted band practically took up my entire finger, but I didn't mind. It was the most beautiful ring I'd ever seen and more than I'd ever dreamed of.

We hadn't set a date yet, what with Jack's limited time off between the season ending and spring training, plus my assignments that seemed to pop up without warning. I didn't mind, though. For now, it was simply enough just to be together and know where our future was headed. Especially after living through the time when I thought our relationship was dead and buried, with no chance for resuscitation. If we could get through that, we were certain we could get through anything.

"I picked up my mess. Happy?" Jack walked up behind me and wrapped his arms around my waist, then dropped a kiss on my neck.

"Yes. Thank you." I turned, his lips moving to mine with a passionate fire we'd yet to put out.

"I'm tired of waiting to make you Mrs. Carter." He grabbed my left hand and kissed the top of my ring finger. "Marry me tomorrow."

"You're crazy." I laughed, pulling my hand from his lips.

"I'm serious." His brown eyes narrowed with his smile.

"If I can wait for a real wedding with all of our friends and family, then you can too." I kissed his nose before turning back to the bubbling water.

"Fine. But I'm just going to tell everyone you're my wife, whether it's official or not." He pressed his body against my back.

"You're so weird."

"You're the weird one. What kind of girl can just wait patiently to get married?" he whispered into my ear, nibbling on my lobe before chills raced through me and I shoved him away.

"The kind of girl who doesn't need to a piece of paper to tell her how to feel. The kind who knows that being married won't change anything between us." I turned again, wrapping my arms around his neck and pulling him close. "I'm the kind of girl who wants to share our special day with everyone who's important to us. They deserve it. It's not like we've made it on easy on them."

He exhaled through his nose. "You're right. Plus, Gran and Gramps would kill us if we eloped."

"That's what I'm talking about!" I chuckled.

"Let's set a date though, okay?"

"Okay," I conceded, pouring the boiling water and pasta into a strainer in the sink, the steam rising around my face.

"Tonight." His voice echoed as he walked toward the calendar on the wall.

"So pick a date."

"And you'll make sure you're not on assignment?" He raised an eyebrow.

"Jack." I grabbed a jar, pouring the contents into a bowl and stirring before I continued. "Pick a date and I'll tell the office on Monday." His expression softened with my words.

He flipped the calendar to November before muttering to himself, "November has Thanksgiving, and then December is Christmas. No one wants to have to go to a wedding during the holidays. I think we should wait until after New Year's. What do you think about a January wedding?"

He glanced over, his hand still holding the calendar. "January sounds cold." I shivered over-dramatically to make my point.

"Not if we get married back home," he suggested, as if it was the most obvious plan in the world.

"Yay!" I squealed, delighted at the thought. "January sounds totally doable then! I love January."

"Alright, woman, you become a Carter on January twelfth." His dimples deepened as his smile widened.

I glanced down at my ring, its brilliance losing focus as my eyes blurred with an unexpected tear. "Cassie Carter. I like the sound of that."

"Kitten Carter. I like the sound of that better," he said, as I placed two plates on our table.

"January twelfth," I repeated, watching as his eyes relaxed with the permanence of our decision. I smiled as I scooped out a heaping serving of pasta and placed it on Jack's plate.

Jack twirled the pasta against his spoon before looking up and smiling at me. "I love you."

"I love you too."

"I can't wait to knock you up and have a whole team of little baseball players running around this place!" He reached under the table and rested his hand on my thigh, then slid it upwards teasingly.

"Slow down, Mr. Carter!" I swatted his shoulder.

"Aw, come on, Kitten. Let's start now." He badgered me good-naturedly, sensing my discomfort.

"That's a discussion for another time. Like *after* we're married," I insisted as warmth coursed through my cheeks.

"Alright. On January thirteenth, we'll start making babies."

## Thank You's

This book could not exist in any form had I not lived the life I lived... experienced the things I experienced... and loved the people I loved. This story (per usual) is influenced by a lot of real events and people from my past.

To the *real Jack Carter*, thank you for being such a cocky asshole in college and screwing it all up so that I had good material to work with for this story. Lol I'm so happy we're still friends. xo

Meli, what would I do without my soul sister and all of our college memories? I don't know and I don't ever wanna. I love you. xo

I have to give a very special thank you to all the girls and authors in BA- especially the one's who let me "*borrow*" their names and use them in this book. You guys have changed my life for the better with your support, excitement and word of mouth. I sincerely cannot thank you enough for all your awesomeness. Please know how much I appreciate it- and you. How awesome was Chicago?! :)

A few bloggers deserve an extra special thanks- Gitte & Jenny from Totally Booked, Maryse from Maryse.net, Lori from Lori's Book Blog, Ana from Ana's Sexy Attic, Lisa from Lisa's Reads, and Mollie Harper from Tough Critic

Reviews- these women have influenced thousands of readers to look beyond the books you can only find on the shelves of stores, and read Indie/Self Published authors instead. Ladies, you change the lives of readers and authors every.single.day. The publishing landscape is shifting and you're a big part of the reason why. Thank you so much for that. <3

Rebecca Donovan (my beautiful and graceful fairy friend in human form- where do you hide your wings?), Michelle Warren (aka the longest, best and most beautiful eyes/eyelashes known to mankind), Shannon Stephens (one of the most kind and strongest people I know), Colleen Hoover (my author soulmate), Jillian Dodd (my mother f'n partner in crime. Who needs sleep in Chicago? NOT.US.), Tarryn Fisher (my angsty little nymph)... Thank you ladies for reminding me why I love my fellow Indie (and ex-indie) authors so.damned.much. I feel lucky to be in this brave new world with you all.

Jenny Aspinall, thank you for your opinions, your help, your suggestions, your genius, talent, love and friendship. I appreciate your support and belief in my writing more than I can express with mere words. Thank you for existing. xo

Lori, Sam & Sali- Thanks for always having this bitch's back. I love you.

Melissa Mosloski- you are a freaking rockstar! Thank you for all your little catches and pointing out some obvious things I'd forgotten. You helped me make the book better and I appreciate it so much. :)

Thank you to my family and friends for your continued support and belief in me. You know who you are.

Thank you to my editor Pam, who takes me awesome story and literally makes it AWESOMER! I would have crappy books without you.

And to Ryan S., Dom P., & Chris B.- thank you for all the feedback and help with baseball related questions when I needed you (you know, when you weren't busy giving me crappy advice). Ha!

A baseball player and a baseball team is a dynamic unlike anything or anyone else. I truly hope I've done it justice. Lord knows I tried.

## About the Author

Jenn Sterling is a Southern California native who grew up watching Dodger baseball and playing softball. She has her Bachelor's Degree in Radio/TV/Film and has worked in the entertainment industry the majority of her life. This is her third novel. She loves hearing from her readers and can be found online at:

Blog & Website- https://www.j-sterling.com
Twitter- http://www.twitter.com/RealJSterling
Facebook-  http://www.facebook.com/TheRealJSterling

18681220R00201

Made in the USA
Charleston, SC
15 April 2013